Cedarwood Pride

# TOGETHER IN CEDARWOOD

MEGAN SLAYER

Together in Cedarwood
ISBN # 978-1-83943-881-3
©Copyright Megan Slayer 2020
Cover Art by Cherith Vaughan ©Copyright April 2020
Interior text design by Claire Siemaszkiewicz
Pride Publishing

# TOGETHER IN CEDARWOOD

# Dedication

For my editor because you rock.
For JPZ. You know why.

# Chapter One

"Hi. My name is Robert, but everyone calls me Bobby. I'm a single father to two great kids—er, young people. My son says he's not a kid. Chris is fifteen and my daughter, Darcy, is twelve. I've got a teen and an almost teen." Christ, he felt old.

"My daughter swims and my son's a runner." Bobby stuffed his hands into his pockets. Talking in public didn't bother him, but talking about himself did. He had to press on, though. If he didn't talk, he'd never get this out. "I didn't plan on being a single parent, but I also couldn't deny who I am. I tried the traditional route and got married to a woman. Helene and I had some good times. Darcy was our best creation, and when we adopted Chris as an older child, I thought things were great. They were happy and I thought I was, but I was miserable. I knew I was gay, but there was no amount of therapy that my folks could find to fix me before I got married. It took me a long time to understand I wasn't the one who needed fixing.

Anyway, I came out to my wife, and she left me. It turned out all of the happy feelings were a joke. A sham. She had a guy on the side and didn't want the kids. She'd had Darcy to please me and went through with the adoption because she thought I wanted it. She never wanted either. She turned over parental rights, so for the last five years it's just been the three of us. I've had boyfriends, but nothing worth much. The kids come first."

He sat down and exhaled. *Holy shit.* He'd babbled his head off. It felt oddly good to talk, though. He had so much bottled up since the divorce. He hadn't even mentioned that he was the son of the police chief or that he'd grown up in Cedarwood and left because his parents couldn't handle him being gay.

Another man stood and told his story, then a woman talked about being newly single. The group had been called the Single Father Society, but they'd changed it to the generic 'LGBTQ Support Group'. Two lesbians and a straight woman whose best gay friend had just died and she needed someone to talk to were now members. He appreciated the mix of people and not being the only person with problems.

He barely paid attention to the other speakers. His mind kept returning to his schedule for the next day. With the kids out of school, he'd spend the morning at the metro park. Darcy had to get to swim practice by eight, and Chris had conditioning for cross-country starting at half-past eight. He toyed with the fitness band on his wrist. He'd probably end up running the ten-mile course while he waited. He needed to get stuff done at work. *Shit.* He'd have to call his mother to see if she'd keep an eye on the kids.

"Bobby?"

*Fuck.* Someone had called his name. He snapped his attention back to the group. "Sorry." He wasn't — not really. He'd never been able to focus.

"We're done." Colin Baker grinned. "You were a million miles away." He flipped his hair off his brow and shook his head. "A hundred million miles."

Bobby had been back in town for a month and had only spent time with his kids, the parents at the various practices and his clients. Besides work situations, tonight's meeting was his first venture out without his children.

"Yeah. Sorry. I've got too much on my mind." And on his plate. He appraised his friend from high school. "You've changed," Bobby said. But so had he. "You're taller? New glasses? Dyed your hair?"

"Nope, nope and nope." Colin twiddled with his phone. "I'm busy at the bookstore and I lost some weight, but that's it. I'm in charge of the group here, but I'm not single so I guess I should step down. Remember Jordan?" He turned his phone around. A photo of Colin, a kid and a guy in a police uniform graced the home page. "That's him and my son, Gage. We're getting married. Me and Jordan — not Gage. That would be silly. He's a kid."

"I knew what you meant." The longer he looked at the photo, the more memories from high school came back to him. He did remember Jordan Hargrove. He hadn't been in Jordan's social circle, but he'd been good friends with Colin. He wouldn't have put Colin and Jordan together. "He used to be a real dick."

"Funny. My brother says that exact same thing." Colin tucked the phone into his back pocket.

Farin, Colin's younger brother, strolled over to where they stood. "What am I guilty of that I might or might not have done?"

"You call Jordan 'Officer Dick,'" Colin replied.

"I used to." Farin smiled. "He's grown on me." He slid his gaze over Bobby. "I'm glad you're back, Bobby. This town is becoming a strange version of a high school reunion. If you're not from school, then we've got kids in common." He held up his cell phone and pointed to a photo on the screen. "My partner is one of the swim instructors over at the metro park. I've probably seen you there, and if I haven't, I'm sure we'll cross paths there."

"Partner?" He was coupled up too? *Christ.* Everyone in the damn support group already had someone. No, he was wrong. Two of them did, but still.

"Steve." Farin pointed to another photo. "He's my boy toy and I'm the elder statesman." He smiled, then wandered over to another group of men who were deep in conversation about what sounded like comic books—Bobby wasn't sure.

Colin rolled his eyes and folded his arms. "They're getting married too."

"So this is a dating pool?" Bobby snorted. The last thing he needed was a date. Actually, he could use a good fuck, but he wasn't high on bringing random guys home.

"Kind of." Colin collected the papers from one of the tables. "Jordan and I met because I got a speeding ticket."

"He nabbed you with his radar, eh?" Bobby asked and gathered up some of the other papers.

"I earned the violation, sadly. I sped through a school zone. Not my best hour, but I learned." Colin shrugged. "Farin met Steve at the metro park. They've bonded over comics and art." He paused. "I don't see Colt or Ashley, but they're together. Colt owns the diner. Best fries around. Ash teaches at the elementary school. His son, Wyatt, is a trip. We had a new pair of members join. Dr. Adrien Ellet and his boyfriend-slash-manny, Nathan, are part of the group. Adrien's son, Kyle, goes to school with Wyatt and Gage. Oh, and our friend Niall is now with Michael, who happens to be in a band and goes by the name of Bandit. Got all that?" He grinned. "Niall and Michael don't have kids, but they're part of our group, so other than them, yeah, this has become a dating pool."

"I'm not interested in getting a date." He'd told himself that lie so many times he almost believed it. Almost.

"None of us were either. Jordan and I sort of happened, and I might have had a hand in getting Farin to notice Steve."

"You set me up," Farin called but didn't leave the other group.

"Something like that. Ash and Colt were their own organic thing. They met on their own, and Michael and Niall met at the school." Colin paused again. "How old did you say Darcy was? Twelve? She'll be too old for their classes. They're both at the elementary school."

Bobby rocked on his feet. He'd forgotten how much Colin could talk. "Middle school and high school for us. I got them registered two weeks ago, and Chris has already joined the cross-country team. He ran for his old school in Chagrin and had a couple of records."

"That's awesome." Colin beamed, then sobered. He put one hand up. "I have to say this. If you're contacted by the Coalition for Order in Cedarwood, tread lightly."

"The anti-gay group?" Bobby asked. He'd had run-ins with them a couple of times and hated it. "I had one approach me at the diving finals at the beginning of the month. The school superintendent talked to me."

"Yes. Just… They're trying to rid the town of anyone they don't like. Doesn't matter if you're gay, lesbian, have purple hair, or a pet giraffe. They want to clean up the town." He hooked his fingers in the air like quotes. "It's garbage, but we're working to change it."

"There are lots of sports parents who don't care. They know about me and haven't treated me any differently. It's been refreshing, actually." Bobby widened his stance. "They've been very inclusive."

"That's great, but it only takes one or two die-hards to cause serious trouble." Colin handed Bobby a flyer. "The big festival is this weekend. Anyone is welcome. There'll be rides, games, fireworks and a concert. Please come. Bring the kids."

"Sounds good, but my folks are taking Darce and Chris to the lake this weekend," Bobby replied. "However, that doesn't mean I can't support the cause." God knew he could use a night out. "I've still got tons of shit in boxes at the house, and I won't get done unpacking this weekend, so yeah, count me in."

"You'll have fun." Colin clapped Bobby on the shoulder. "I'm glad you're back. I missed you."

"Thanks. I missed home. Yeah, I had that falling out with Dad, but it's getting better." He winked. "See you this weekend or at the next meeting."

"It's a deal. You can meet Jordan and the rest of the guys." Colin waved and headed across the room to his brother.

"Re-meet him," Bobby mumbled. He waved then made his way out to the parking lot. The sun had already set, but the heat hadn't dissipated. Before he reached his car, he shrugged into his T-shirt. He hated sleeping in humid evening air — unless he had a hot guy to share his bed. He sighed and climbed behind the wheel of his car. *Who am I kidding? I'm not going to find anyone in Cedarwood.*

He turned the key and the engine roared to life. He rolled the windows down, then headed out of the lot. He'd thought coming back to Cedarwood would be a smart idea. The notion had ended up being a mixed-bag result. Things were good because the schools were top-notch with great academic and athletic programs for the kids. The move was also beneficial because he was closer to his parents, which gave his children a better chance to get to know them. *But, man, there are some big negatives.* He hadn't expected to run into so many former classmates or to have to deal with so much of his past. He hated running from things, but his high school years hadn't been the greatest. He liked change and being free.

He turned onto the main drag. The streetlights threw odd shadows on the pavement as he passed the buildings. He remembered zipping up and down the road a hundred times during his senior year. He smiled and scrubbed his forehead with the back of his hand. He'd driven to clear his mind and to forget the way he'd felt about Damon Barnes. The soccer jock hadn't noticed him, and he'd been too embarrassed to admit he was gay back then.

He sighed and headed north of town to his development. He'd had so many missed opportunities in life — missed connections with guys he'd liked, jobs he'd wanted and situations he'd have liked to experience. After Helene had left, he'd sworn he wasn't going to have any more regrets.

Right now he regretted not having a hot fuck in his bed. He needed someone to share his life with, even for just a couple of days, but his self-imposed rule kept most potential partners away. He refused to bring random guys home for sex. He scrubbed his face again, then pulled into his driveway. He'd seen a man around town but hadn't made a move. What if the guy said no? Or what if he was turned off by a man with kids? What if he wasn't even gay? He groaned. *Time to stop thinking about sex and hot men.* He was a dad and had to think about his children—not his dick.

He eased the car into the garage and shut off the engine. He hit the button to close the door, then left the vehicle. He thought about the guy he'd seen running at the metro park. If he was meant to find a lover in Cedarwood, then it would happen, but he doubted it. Fate had a certain way of kicking him in the teeth when it came to relationships.

He stopped in the middle of the dark garage. His thoughts turned to Helene. He'd believed they were all happy when he was with her. Well, no. They'd been fine. Not happy, just fine. He shook his head. He wasn't fine, and they hadn't been back then either. Sure, he was glad he had Darcy and Christopher, but he wished he'd been honest with himself from the start. As much as he'd come to dislike Helene, he knew down in his heart that she'd deserved better. She'd left him in a tough spot, but she hadn't been the one for him and he hadn't been himself with her.

He made his way over to the main door leading into the house. It was time to stop thinking about the past.

He needed to be Dad now. He strode into the house and stepped around the boxes in the dining room. One day he'd have everything put where it belonged, but not tonight.

Chris sat on the couch and Darcy was stretched out beside him, but under a blanket. A bowl of half-eaten popcorn remained on the coffee table and sitcoms that were almost as old as Bobby played on the television.

"Watching educational television?" Bobby asked, sarcasm dripping from his words. "I remember this show." He didn't, not really, but sometimes getting Chris to talk was harder than complex taxes.

"I like their style," Chris replied. "She's asleep if you want to carry her upstairs."

*Crap.* He'd planned on getting home before she conked out. "Sorry I was late." He tossed his keys onto the table, then rounded the couch. He scooped Darcy into his arms. Although she was twelve and strong from hundreds of thousands of laps in the pool, the girl was tiny. He carried her up to her bedroom and left her under the covers.

"Thanks, Dad," she murmured, then rolled over.

Bobby kissed her head. "Night, Peanut." He left her door open a crack, then went back downstairs.

"She wanted to swim. I know you said no, but it helped her blow off steam." Chris turned off the television. "She's angry about the move."

"I know." He'd expected this. He'd waited until after school let out before he'd had them transferred. Both kids would be starting in new buildings — Chris as a sophomore and Darcy in the seventh grade. He felt for Chris, but the kid could make friends anywhere and had a knack for getting his sister to open up about almost everything. Bobby sat opposite his son on the couch. "What upset her?"

Chris grabbed a handful of popcorn from the bowl. "There's a kid on the swim team who said she didn't belong. She made fun of Darcy's suit, then her cap because it wasn't the same as the other kids'." He rolled his eyes. "She wants her old friends and her old room back."

For being fifteen, the kid could be incredibly mature. Bobby picked up the bowl of popcorn. "We can't go back to the old house. It sold within hours of putting it on the market. I've told her however she wants to decorate her room, we'll do it." As for the young man on the team, he'd have to pay attention at practice in the morning. He wouldn't involve the parents, but he'd listen in and see if he could give his daughter better advice in dealing with the little shit.

"She's worried you'll replace Mom." Chris shrugged. "I'm not." The muscle in his jaw twitched and, if Bobby wasn't mistaken, the kid had a thin growth of hair on his cheeks.

"Still mad at Mom?" He didn't blame Chris. Helene's leaving had been difficult all the way around. "Part of that was my fault."

"Dad, you're gay. So what? Mom didn't have to abandon us because she hated you." Chris shook his head and stuffed the popcorn into his mouth.

Bobby admired his son's ability to be frank but still act his age. He grabbed a handful of popcorn but didn't say anything. If Chris wanted to talk, then he'd listen.

"She acts like she hates us. She won't come to the swim meets or my meets. I don't understand." Chris flipped his hair out of his eyes. Normally, he had his tresses back in a ponytail. When he wore his hair loose, most of the strands ended up in front of his face. "We're not bad kids."

"No, you're not."

"It fucking sucks." Chris' voice cracked and he averted his gaze when he swore. "Sorry, Dad, but it does. She's our mom and doesn't want us, but she's pregnant with Glenn's baby."

Bobby bristled. He knew Helene had moved on, but he'd thought she was with a guy named Trent, not Glenn. He'd also never expected her to get pregnant — not after the way she'd pitched a fit post-pregnancy with Darcy.

"Yeah, she's gonna marry Glenn and have a perfect life." Chris hopped up from the couch. "She sent me an email." He retrieved his phone from the table, then handed the device over to Bobby. "Congratulations. We're expanding."

Bobby sighed as he read the words. Sure enough, his ex had announced via email she was going to change her last name again and have a baby. "Good for her." He only half meant it. "If this makes her happy, then we should be happy." *Kind of.* "You've got me and we're a team. If Mom doesn't want to be around, then don't force it."

"You're taking it well," Chris said. He plopped onto the couch. "When are you going to get a boyfriend? No one cares if you do. Darce would love it."

He paused and measured his words carefully. "I'm waiting for the right one to come along. Nothing drastic or quick. I've got you two to worry about, and that's what's important."

"Couldn't find a hookup at the support group?" Chris crooked his eyebrows. "Maybe next week?"

"You want me married off, huh?" He hugged his son and laughed. The last thing he needed to worry about was a relationship, yet his kids wanted him to be happy and thought that was what he wanted. *Fuck.* He had no idea what he needed.

"Dad, you're depressed. Darcy might not understand, but I see it." Chris shrugged. "You and Terry were pretty happy."

"I guess." He clapped Chris on the shoulder. "You'd better get to bed and stop worrying about my love life. Worry about your own and that cute girl at practice. She seemed nice. Nicole? Or was her name Nichelle?"

From his hairline to the neckline of his shirt, Chris blushed. "Her name is Carrie."

"She's cute." He grabbed the popcorn bowl and carried it to the kitchen. "Get some rest so you're fresh for practice."

"Got it." Chris dipped his head and scrambled up the stairs.

Bobby returned to the kitchen and scrubbed both hands over his face. *Well, fuck.* His kids were worried about his relationship status. It wasn't their problem, and besides, he'd thought he'd been doing a decent job raising them alone. He groaned. He should call his parents, if for no other reason than to find out what they knew. He loved his mother and father, but with the problems they'd had in the past, he wasn't sure he wanted them to know his kids were upset about him being alone. He grabbed another handful of popcorn. Being a single parent wasn't his idea of fun.

He'd never dated a man who could understand him. He'd thought he found the right man in Terry, but Terry never could accept the kids — not totally. Neil had never been a good choice and couldn't care emotionally for anyone but himself.

He finished the popcorn, then ruffled through the stack of mail. He recognized the names on the envelopes. Two were bills, one was a check, and the fourth... He wished he had his glasses. He held the envelope closer and reread the return address.

*The Coalition for Order in Cedarwood*

*Good God.* He checked the name on the front once more. "Dear occupant," he mumbled. They hadn't necessarily zeroed in on him. No, they were blanketing the community. He shook his head and opened the envelope.

He scanned the letter and bit back a gag. The Coalition made it sound like they welcomed everyone to town and looked forward to the festival. They wanted unity within the community. *Sure, they do.* He tossed the letter into the garbage. He didn't want his kids seeing that crap.

He locked the back and front doors and turned the lights off along the way upstairs. A dull ache started behind his eyes. He glanced over at the clock. *Shit. Almost eleven already?* He stripped out of his clothes and put on sleep shorts, then collapsed onto his bed. Maybe things would work out in the morning.

* * * *

The next morning, Bobby drove the kids to the metro park. He parked by the wooden fence. If he came back to the car, he could see the cross-country team and the pools.

"Thanks, Dad." Chris climbed out of the vehicle first. "Meet you here at noon?"

"Practice is that long?" he asked.

"The high school practice lasts longer than the junior high, but they're having a meeting too." Chris pointed to the pond. "You'll be able to see us when you're done with your run. If we get done early, I'll come over to the pools."

"Good deal." He waited for Chris to join the knot of runners before he turned his attention to Darcy. "I hear there's a kid giving you trouble."

"I knew Chris would tell." She folded her arms. "It's not a big deal."

"No?" He turned around as best he could in the seat and met her gaze. "Peanut, no one has the right to make fun of you, but what have I told you?"

"If they make fun, they're doing it because they're not feeling good about themselves," she answered, her tone flat.

At least she'd heard him. "Okay, then don't let her get to you."

"Dad, you don't understand." Darcy grabbed the back of the seat and scooted forward. "I want to go home. I hate it here. We were good in Chagrin. My room is there and so are my friends. We can visit Grandma and Grandpa without being in the same town."

"Sweetheart, I can't change what happened." But now he felt helpless.

"You said not to let people make fun of me, but when Neil made fun of you, we moved."

"He didn't make fun of me." There was so much more to the change than just Neil's attitude and he knew damn well she'd never understand. How should he put some of this into a way to explain? "We moved from Chagrin because I wanted to have my own accounting business. I could get the building and our new house for the best deal. If I'd opened the same business in Chagrin, I still would've had to sell the house. Yes, Neil acted like a jerk, but that's his problem."

"Oh." She toyed with her swim cap. "Sorry, Dad."

"I know this is tough. Moving isn't fun for any of us."

"Chris isn't having a bad time," she replied.

"He handles things differently than you do. I'm sure he's having some problems, but he found friends." He pointed over his shoulder at the pool. "Other than the girl who is jealous of your suit, aren't there other kids who are nice?"

"Yes." She half-smiled. "Some of them."

"Be yourself, Peanut. Until you do that, you won't be happy." He turned and climbed out of the car. He opened the door for his daughter. He knew all too well now about being honest with himself. Things were different for Darcy, but it all boiled down to her being happy with who she was.

Darcy flung her arms around his waist. "Thanks, Dad." She held on another moment. "At least you bought the house with the pool."

"For a certain swimmer. Grab your bag and get moving so you're not late. I'll be on the trails, then I'll meet you when you're done. I might even watch during practice." He winked as she slung her duffel bag onto her shoulder. "Okay?"

"Thanks." She nodded and her smile widened. "Have fun on your run."

He sagged against the side of the car and watched her join the other kids at the pool. Things weren't settled with her and she'd have more questions, but he'd bought himself some time.

Bobby clipped the lanyard onto his keys, then draped the lanyard around his neck. He picked up his water bottle and downed half the cool liquid. He ran through his battery of stretches while he also mentally worked through his schedule for the day. Once the kids were done with practice, he had to drop them off with his parents so he could get a solid six hours in at the office. Thank God tax season was over and he'd waited until after April to move the family. He'd never have been able to finish taxes for his various clients and box up his belongings at the same time.

"Dad." Darcy bounded back up to him, without her bag. "They're moving practice to the indoor pool so they can open the outside pool up to everyone else."

"Okay. I'll catch you there." He waited once again until she disappeared into the building with the other kids on her swim team before he set out on his run. He glanced over at the cross-country team. Christopher, plus two boys and three girls, were off to the side going through their stretches.

At least he knew where his kids were. He adjusted his fitness band and rolled his shoulders. He hadn't done enough pre-run stretching, but he needed to get moving. The stress of the day—which hadn't even really started yet—washed over him. He had too much on his plate. He checked his laces and finished loosening up.

Bobby headed off in the direction of the trails. He liked to start at the north end and work his way back around the serpentine track. The sound of the crushed limestone under his shoes lulled him. He could get lost in his thoughts during his runs and preferred things that way. As he rounded through the woods, he noticed a pair of runners coming toward him.

A woman and a man. He didn't mind sharing the track with others, but liked the solitary qualities. He wasn't one for talking while he worked out.

The pair hustled up to him, and he made eye contact with the guy. A shiver ran the length of his spine and he could've sworn he'd been hit by lightning. He'd never felt so off balance in his life.

The man smiled and nodded but didn't stop running. The woman seemed to look right through him.

He kept going and tried to shake the prickly feeling. He had no idea if the handsome shirtless man was even gay. This was his problem. The men he was attracted to weren't attracted to him. He flexed his fingers and kept running. He wasn't an ugly man—was he? He kept himself in shape and wasn't covered in body hair. He wasn't tattooed up or pierced in strange places.

Maybe that was his problem. He wasn't original enough. He blended in everywhere he went. He'd been told he was handsome but distant. He had kids! He had to make sure things were on the level before he introduced the new person into his family equation. He and Terry hadn't been able to make the distance thing work, and he was okay with that. He hated not having his lover there to hold at night. *Better to be without than with and not getting any.* He chuckled. Only he could come to that conclusion.

Then there was the second long-term boyfriend, Neil. The guy had sworn he loved Bobby, but when the truth came out, that hadn't been the case. Neil hadn't wanted to be a father. He'd wanted someone in his life who could take care of him, but God forbid he'd have to care for other human beings. He should've known the moment he and Neil got together that they weren't going to work. He'd pushed his better judgment aside in favor of a hot man. That was his problem. He'd lowered his standards.

He was crazy. He glanced over his shoulder, but the man and woman weren't on the track. *Probably good.* He needed to get his head out of his ass and stop thinking about sex and hot men.

He kept going down the trail. Sooner or later he'd run his problems out of his mind or he'd simply work off his breakfast. Something like that. Running helped him clear his brain. He noticed the cross-country team through the trees. He'd pass them soon. He'd promised Chris he wouldn't embarrass him. He picked up the pace and smiled at the runners as he went by. He waved at Chris, but didn't say a word.

"That's Dad," Chris said. He turned his attention to Bobby. "Hi, Dad."

"Hey, kid." He focused on the path ahead, but could've sworn he heard one of the girls speak.

"That's your dad? He looks so…not like a dad."

Bobby smothered a smile behind his hand and continued running. He wasn't invisible to everyone, and now he didn't look like a dad. Maybe next he could look like a hot guy and get a date. *Maybe.*

# Chapter Two

Remy stopped at the end of the trail and gasped for breath. The run hadn't worn him out, but looking at the guy on the path sure had. He bent over and rested his hands on his knees. He couldn't believe what he'd seen. He knew the men in town. Hell, he knew pretty much everyone in Cedarwood. This guy was new. *Different.* Goddamn, he made Remy feel alive and with nothing more than a look.

"You're not going to keel over, are you?" Julia, his best friend, collapsed on the nearby picnic table. "I said we ran that too hard."

"It wasn't the run." He managed to stagger over to the table and sat beside her. "Did you see that guy?"

"Everyone saw him." She gulped her water. "He's handsome."

"Handsome? He's a freaking god. Where has he been all my life?" Remy threaded his fingers into his hair. He needed to get a grip.

"Okay, so he's hot. I've got a wild idea...talk to him. Introduce yourself." She stood and stretched her back out. She rested her hands on her hips. "Or are you too chicken?"

"I'm not…" He was. He'd lied to himself plenty of times. He could be forward when he wanted to, but not in front of good-looking men.

"You are too." She kept her back to him. "What's the deal? When Leonard came around, you were all chatty and couldn't wait to jump the guy. I barely got out of the room before you were fucking. The running god might be the same way." She glanced over her shoulder at him. "But now you're all shy and shit. Rem, I can't introduce you to everyone. People already think I'm married to you or I'm the one who is scared to get into bed with a guy. For Christ's sake, if you like him, say hi. See if he'd like a running buddy. I don't want to run with you any longer. My knees can't take it, and I can't keep up with you and your crazy long legs."

"I'll give it a shot." *Tomorrow. Or at the festival. Maybe at the coffee shop.* "Come on. I'll take you home."

Remy walked Julia to the car and stopped on the passenger side as she plopped onto the seat. The handsome runner was over at the pool with a kid who had to be high school age. Remy's heart sank. He wanted a boyfriend, not someone's dad. The thought of kids or being with a father churned his stomach. He hated the idea of cleaning the kid's snotty nose or having grabby, dirty hands on him. He'd been told he talked down to children. His own childhood hadn't been terribly eventful or fun, and he didn't know how to associate with children. Growing up, he'd been expected to act like a miniature adult. The kids at school had made fun of his maturity, then of him being gay. He wasn't sure he wanted to accept the responsibility of kids. They were too much work.

"Hey, it looks like your guy." Julia closed the car door. "Talk to him."

"Nah. If he's got kids, that's a deal-breaker." He rounded the hood and opened the driver's side door. "You know me and anyone under eighteen. I steer clear."

"No one said you have to date the kid. If that guy is the father, he's a DILF for sure."

"Dad-I'd-like-to-fuck. *Jesus*." He stole another glance at the DILF's ass, then backed out of the parking spot. "He's probably not gay."

"Here we go again." She rolled her eyes. "You'd find any reason to get out of talking to him."

"Don't start." He knew better. Julia was his voice of reason and wing woman. She'd been his best friend from the moment they'd met at *The Courier* in Cleveland. She'd stuck by him after the paper downsized and he lost his job. Without her support, he wouldn't have gone for the job in Cedarwood. He loved her with his entire heart, but he wasn't in love with her any more than she was with him. He drove across town to her townhouse and parked in her miniscule driveway.

"I'm going to say this once, then I'm not going back to it." She faced him and remained in her seat. "You can drool all over every man you see for all I care. You can dream about them, masturbate to their images in your head, and I wouldn't bat an eyelash. You can fuck whomever you want, too."

He stared at her. He'd heard this speech so many times, but there was something new in her voice. Something stronger.

"Stop selling yourself short." She patted his cheek. "If you could see yourself the way I see you, the way your ex-boyfriends saw you, then you'd stop this bullshit. You'd have confidence. You're so handsome. I know lots of people who would kill for not only your head of thick hair, but those cheekbones and your eyes."

"Ju." She'd never understand.

"You've got the clearest, palest blue eyes I've ever seen. I'm jealous. Look at me. I'm stuck with mud-brown eyes." She snorted. "Jesus. You don't get it. You could have any man you wanted. Hell, any woman you wanted if you were bi, but you're not. Stop cutting on yourself and believing you're still that chubby kid I met at the paper ten years ago."

"I can't." He'd tried. *Dear God.* No matter what he did, he still saw himself at eighteen when he looked into the mirror. No amount of running, weight lifting or dieting seemed to change his reflection.

"I know you can't." She recoiled from him and averted her gaze. "Look at us. I can't get a date if I try because everyone thinks I'm with you. Guys don't approach me, but they do you, and you're scared. I haven't had sex with a human being in a year."

He didn't want to know that, but he appreciated her honesty. "Ju. I'm sorry." She was right. He hid his sexuality unless they were in the clubs — all far away from Cedarwood. He dragged her along and expected her to have fun looking at the pretty bodies but knowing full well she couldn't touch.

"Look, whether he's a dad or not, if you're attracted to him, you should at least introduce yourself. What's the worst that could happen? You fall for him?" She sighed and left the car. "I need a shower and a fat cock. Unfortunately, all I'm going to get is the shower." She grasped the door frame. "Call me if you want to talk."

"I will, sweets." He'd fucked everything up. Remy drove back across town to his closet-sized apartment. He couldn't get the image of the runner from the park or Julia's words out of his mind.

He pulled his cell phone from his pocket. The little green light was blinking. Someone must've called or texted. He swiped his thumb across the screen. A text. Not from Julia. She used her phone for calls. Texting, she claimed, was against her religion. He knew better. She hated the poor grammar everyone used when they texted. She always used proper punctuation and spelling.

He checked the screen.

*Saw U @ the pk*
*Run w/me 2moro*

His heart skipped a beat, but the good feeling disappeared instantly. This wasn't a text from the hunky runner. That guy wouldn't have his number. He groaned and realized who'd texted him. Seth, his ex-boyfriend. *Fucking balls.* He and Seth had been a mistake from the start. Seth hadn't come through Julia. No, he'd met Seth at a club on a night he'd gone alone. After a blow job in the parking lot, he'd sworn he'd fallen in love. They'd tried to date, but that hadn't worked out. Well, no, they might have been decent for each other if they'd actually gone out on a 'date'. Instead, they got together for sex and called it something else. All Seth ever wanted was sex.

'*Love between men doesn't exist,*' Seth used to say. '*It's all fucking sex, and I want it all.*'

Sometimes he wished he had Seth's outlook on life. He liked sex too, but he needed more than just fucking for a relationship.

He should reply to Seth. If he didn't, Seth would keep sending texts, and eventually he'd break down. He refused to give in this time.

*Can't. Mtgs all day.*

It wasn't a total lie. He'd be up to his eyeballs at the paper tomorrow. He wished there were more people working for *The Cedarwood Tribune*. Maybe then he wouldn't be writing sports articles instead of the pop culture stories he loved. He knew almost nothing about sports, but he'd ended up in that department during the last downsizing. It was either write about softball and wrestling or give up his job.

He abandoned his phone on the couch and stripped down. Sweaty clothes were fine in the club or during a run, but gross afterward. He turned the knob in the shower. While he waited for the water to heat, he strolled around the bedroom. Steam billowed from the stall.

Remy stepped under the spray. His muscles ached from the run and the stress in his life. He lathered the washcloth and turned his back on the water. These were the times he wished he had a partner. Showers were better when shared. He loved the feel of his man's hands on his body, stroking him, caressing him. Soap sliding down his belly to his cock. He curled his fingers around his shaft and closed his eyes.

Hunky runner should be there with him. He imagined the man sharing the stall. They wouldn't have to speak, just feel. He stroked his dick and pictured the handsome guy in front of him. Would the fantasy match up to reality? He wondered what it would be like to have the man's hands all over his body.

Would he and hunky runner kiss? Rough or soft? Would the guy take the lead or bottom for Remy? Was he the type to shove his partner against the wall and take what he wanted?

He increased the speed of his strokes. He hadn't needed much to reach orgasm. Hell, he'd been on a hair-trigger since the run. God, he was so close. He tipped his head back and rested his shoulders on the wall.

"Fuck," he growled. The heat in his belly spiraled through his body. His nerve endings tingled as the climax hit. He squeezed his eyes shut as he came. He shivered and sank to the floor of the stall. Cum slid down the drain along with the bubbles.

Remy panted and his thoughts returned to the runner. He could go back to the park and try to catch him, but he doubted the guy would still be there. He'd probably finished his run and left too.

Julia had been right. He should've said something when he had the chance, or better yet, made a chance. For all he knew, he could've been in the shower with hunky runner, not jerking off alone. Still, the memory of the guy and the way his eyes flashed when they met played on a loop in Remy's brain. He liked the man way too much for only making eye contact with him.

He staggered to his feet and dipped his head under the spray to clear his thoughts. Whether the guy had actually noticed him or was just being nice was still up for debate. Not that hooking up with him would matter. Life went on despite Remy being alone.

He switched off the water and grabbed the towel. The mirror was steamed over, and that pleased him. He hated looking at his reflection. Every time he looked in a mirror, he swore he saw the chubby kid he'd been at eighteen staring back at him. He ducked into the bedroom and toweled the rest of the way off. He wasn't going to think about his ex, his past or the guy from the park. He had a novel to work on and it wouldn't get written unless he put in the wordage.

Remy draped the towel over the laundry basket to dry, then stepped into a pair of boxers. He wished he didn't have to work at the paper and could focus on his book, but someone had to pay the bills. He needed a fairy godfather to come along and take care of everything. *How about a boyfriend to encourage me and give me moral support? Oh, and hot sex?* Unfortunately, none of them had shown. He plopped down at his desk and sighed. Being grown up and single could really suck.

* * * *

Remy managed a little more than six thousand words before he crashed for the night. The next morning, he completed write-ups for two swim meets and a wrestling tournament. He still had to attend a gigantic softball tourney, but it wouldn't be too awful. He drove over to the softball complex and parked by a light pole. The festival would take place that afternoon too. If he remembered right, it was over at the community park. He locked up and tucked his notebook into his back pocket. At least he'd be in between the events if he decided to attend the festival.

He snorted. Technically, he was supposed to write an article about the festival too. Somehow being there on official business was not as much fun as attending because he wanted to be there.

*Oh well.* He'd take the required notes and come up with something good. He owed Colin and Farin that much. But once the sun went down, he was on his own time.

He sat through the first two games of the tournament in the announcers' booth and scribbled notes for later. He couldn't wait until he could get back to his novel. There was something off about his characters, but he wasn't sure what. If he had a boyfriend or someone not Julia, he'd run through the problems. Julia hated his book but never told him to quit. She'd been his rock. Too bad he wanted cock instead.

Once the games concluded and the winners were given the trophy, he walked around the softball complex to the park. Music played, but he couldn't make out if it was singing or just a band. Bubbles floated on the wind and the scent of food frying caught his attention. People milled around the various booths and trailers. A line of food trucks ringed the east end of the park. Across from them were a string of games, including a fishing one and a ring toss. His belly gurgled.

Remy headed in the direction of the food trucks. He wanted something fried. A gyro, barbecue or even one of those massive cups of French fries, but his diet wouldn't allow for it. He scratched his stomach. *Fuck my diet.* He deserved a cheat day anyway. Everything smelled too good to pass up. He queued up to the line for the gyros and pulled his notepad from his pocket. He scribbled notes as he waited for the food. With all the hen scratch, he just might have the makings of a few good articles for Monday.

He ordered a smoothie to go along with his gyro, then waited by the pick-up window. He noticed a crowd gathering in front of the band shelter. A group of musicians strode onto the stage. Rock music blared from speakers on either end of the tiny band shell. Those kinds of music weren't his thing. He preferred hip hop and techno, but at least the band made the tunes sound good. He picked up his food and ventured to the edge of the crowd.

His nerve endings tingled, and when he glanced across the hill, he noticed the hunky runner. *Holy hell.* The guy was just as good-looking in jeans and a button-down as he was in his joggers and the tight T-shirt.

Blood rushed to Remy's dick. *Damn.* He leaned on the closest tree and shifted his jeans to relieve the pressure on his cock. He'd been drawn to men before, but nothing like with this guy. He wanted to run across the lawn and throw himself into the man's arms. He didn't even know the guy's name! *God.* He was either undersexed and starved for attention, or he was losing his mind.

Remy finished the gyro, then worked on the smoothie. He studied the runner. The guy didn't seem to have kids—or at least none were hanging around him this time—so that was a plus. He worked the tight jeans look well and filled out the shirt like a model.

He could hear Julia's voice in his head. *'Talk to him.'* Oh sure. *Just waltz right over there and say something intelligent.* Like he could do that. He'd probably trip or, worse, open his mouth and come across like a fool.

He gathered his courage. If he wanted to get to know the man, he'd have to take the first step. Besides, if he stopped walking, he'd lose his nerve. *Damn it.* He wasn't going to wuss out this time. He navigated through the crowd to where the hunk stood. Two guys joined him—Colin and his partner, Jordan.

*Well, shit.* Remy ducked behind another tree. He liked Colin, but Officer Hargrove was another story. He and Jordan would never be friends. He hated the way the cop tended to act as though he was better than everyone. Remy would never forget the summers he'd spent just outside Cedarwood at his grandparents' house. Like clockwork over those three weeks, he'd run into Jordan, and every time they were out of earshot from the adults, Jordan had made a big deal about Remy's weight. He growled under his breath. He'd used to be fat, and he knew Jordan would bring the matter up.

Remy held back and waited for Colin and Jordan to leave. He wasn't about to make a move with them around.

As the sunlight faded, so did his spirits. Colin and Jordan weren't leaving. *Hell.* They'd spread out a blanket near the man. He didn't want to interrupt, but damn it. He'd lose his courage.

He stole another glance at the man. Remy wanted to feel the guy's hands on his body and his cock deep in Remy's ass. He longed to have hunky runner's teeth grazing his dick. He bit back a moan.

*Jesus, I need sex.*

He spotted Seth over by the speakers. *What in the name of God is Seth doing here?* He hated anything that wasn't a club. The desire to go to someone who he knew was a bad deal overwhelmed him. Seth would definitely sleep with him, but was that worth it?

*Probably not.* He'd been down that road, and it had taken him a year to get over the devastation of Seth leaving. He'd been more devoted to Seth than Seth had been to him, but still. He'd fallen hard for the guy. He blew out a long breath and turned his attention back to the hunky runner.

He spied Colin and Jordan on the blanket, but the hunk was nowhere near. *What the hell?* He finished the rest of his smoothie and chucked the cup in the closest garbage can, then rested his hands on his hips. The sunlight was gone and the stars were out. If he wasn't alone, it might have been a romantic evening. He wished he could be like Colin and Jordan—with a partner and happy as hell.

The music resumed and lights flashed on the stage. Remy crossed over to where he'd seen the guy last and pretended not to see Colin or Jordan. He wasn't in the mood for one of Jordan's comments. He turned on his heel and headed back toward the parking lot. He should've known he wouldn't find the guy.

"Hi." Hunky runner stepped between Remy and the path to the lot. "Leaving already?"

A shiver raced the length of his spine and he stopped in his tracks. "Uh...no." He wasn't going anywhere now.

"Are you enjoying the festival?" he asked. He stuck out his hand. "I'm Bobby."

"Remy." The moment he touched Bobby's hand, sparks shot along his arm. His nerve endings tingled again. "The...festival is getting better." *So much better.* He nodded to the softball fields. "Thought I'd head over here to watch the fireworks. Want to join me?" He'd stepped way out of his comfort zone by asking that question, but he'd never know if Bobby was interested if he didn't try.

"Sounds like a plan." Bobby fell into step beside him. "You were at the trails yesterday, weren't you?"

"I was. I run with Julia." *Well, no.* He ran, she jogged, then walked, but who was keeping score?

"What's your best time?" Bobby's hand brushed Remy's.

Remy waited a moment before answering. He wanted to grab Bobby's fingers, but damn, that would be too forward. Besides, his running times depended on who was at the track that day. "I don't clock my times." *Liar.* "I just run to clear my head." He wasn't totally lying there. He used the quiet time when Julia didn't come along to think and sort out his issues.

"Yeah?" Bobby nodded. "I do the same thing, but I have to keep a record of my time. It's my being anal." He bumped shoulders with Remy. "Next time you're ready to run, call me. I'd love to have someone to run with."

"Sure." Remy stopped by the wooden fence separating the softball fields from the rest of the park. "I wasn't sure if I'd like the festival." But then Bobby had arrived and knocked him for one hell of a loop.

"Oh? I wasn't sure, either. I'm not a crowd kind of guy." Bobby glanced over his shoulder. "Colin and Jordan are nice to talk to, but they're not you. I was kind of hoping you'd be here." He draped his arm around Remy's shoulders. "I'm also seriously hoping you're gay."

"I am." He snuggled up to Bobby. *Thank you, God.* Bobby was interested. He breathed in the scent of Bobby's cologne and sighed. Bobby smelled like pine and sex, and he loved the way Bobby took control. He was a natural bottom and needed a top to keep him in line.

The fireworks exploded overhead. Splashes of blue, pink and green light illuminated Bobby's face for a moment here and there. He noticed the flecks of amber in Bobby's dark eyes and the curve of his lips when he smiled.

"You're studying me, aren't you?" Bobby murmured.

"Kind of. It's nice to see you close up, rather than running past you at full blast." He brushed his nose along Bobby's cheek. "I've been dying to talk to you since I first saw you."

"I don't bite." Bobby turned Remy around until he faced the fence, then eased behind him. He wrapped both arms around Remy's waist and rested his chin on Remy's shoulder. His breath tickled Remy's ear. "No, I do bite, but only if you want me to."

Remy groaned. When Bobby spoke, he rubbed the bulge in his jeans along Remy's ass. The man was packing the goods, and Remy wanted to unwrap his present. He threaded his fingers around Bobby's and ground his butt into Bobby's groin. Hell, yes, he wanted that dick in his hole tonight.

"You don't hold back, do you?" Bobby asked. He nipped Remy's earlobe. "Want me that much?"

"Uh-huh." He'd rather skip out on the fireworks and make some of their own. "My car's not too far away."

"Neither is mine." He scraped his teeth along the side of Remy's neck. "You taste as good as you look."

He paused. *I look good?* "Nah." He knew better. "I'm no one special."

"Right." Bobby groaned. "Don't want to fuck in the car."

"Me neither." He managed to turn around in Bobby's embrace. "Then let's go to my apartment."

"I'll follow you." Bobby let go of Remy long enough to grasp his hand, then made his way across the lot to the cars. "Where am I going?"

"The Deer Crossing apartments. I'm in the strip of apartments facing away from the road." He stopped at his car. "This is mine."

"Nice." Fire lit in Bobby's eyes. He pinned Remy to the back bumper of the vehicle and mashed his mouth down on Remy's. When Remy gasped, Bobby swallowed the sound.

Remy draped his arms around Bobby's neck. Things had moved rather fast, but he didn't regret a moment. He preferred men with the in-charge look like Bobby wore, and he couldn't wait to get to the apartment. Hell, he couldn't believe a handsome man like Bobby was even there with him, much less kissing him in public.

Bobby broke the kiss and rested his forehead against Remy's. "You're deep in thought. Either I'm a shitty kisser or I'm not keeping your attention."

"You're all I'm thinking about," he confessed. "I'm not sure why you picked me, but I love it."

"You're hard on yourself." Bobby released his grasp on Remy. "You should stop. You're creasing your brow too much."

He rubbed the patch of skin between his eyebrows. Sure enough, he'd etched worry lines there. "Sorry."

"Take me home, handsome." Bobby swatted Remy's hip, then started away. "I'm following you."

"Good deal." He managed to climb behind the wheel of his car but didn't turn on the engine right away. He needed another moment to think. Bobby, the man he'd fantasized about, was following him home. *Fucking hell yeah.* He backed out of the parking spot and headed out. He glanced in his mirror. Sure enough, Bobby, in a black sedan, was behind him. His hands shook as he drove the eight blocks to his apartment complex. He stopped in his space, then waited for Bobby to park.

"I looked at these apartments, but there wasn't one available." Bobby joined Remy by his car. "Nice, though." He slipped his hand into Remy's pocket. "What's this?" He pulled out the notebook.

"I'm a journalist." He reached for the notebook but didn't fight Bobby. "I write for *The Cedarwood Tribune*. I'm supposed to do a piece on the festival, along with a few softball games and other sports."

"You're into sports?" Bobby handed over the notebook.

"Not really, but it meant keeping my job, so I'm sucking it up."

"I like suck-ups." Bobby dropped his voice an octave. "Do you?"

"Uh-huh." He nodded to the path. "I'm up here." He started away from the lot, but Bobby grabbed his hand.

"I like to walk with my date." Bobby threw his arm around Remy's shoulders again. "I'm a touchy kind of guy."

His date...*wowza*. Remy unlocked the door and allowed Bobby entry. He flipped on the lights. "It's not much, but it's home."

Bobby closed the door, then pinned Remy against the chilly metal. "I need this. Need you."

"Yeah." He mashed his mouth down on Bobby's and groaned. He couldn't get his hands beneath Bobby's shirt fast enough. He tugged the button-down free of Bobby's jeans, then caressed the smooth skin. Holy fuck, Bobby was ripped. All muscle, as advertised in the tight T-shirt.

Bobby broke the kiss first and growled. "Like that?" He shrugged out of his shirt and popped the button on

Remy's jeans. "I'm loving this." He freed Remy's dick from his underwear. "Take them off."

Remy couldn't reply. The words weren't there, no matter how hard he tried, but he did yank his shirt up over his head. He braced his shoulders against the door and focused on breathing. Each time Bobby kissed him or tugged on his cock, Remy's brain misfired. Fire licked him from within. He smoothed his hands over Bobby's chest. He liked hairless men, and Bobby didn't disappoint. He plucked Bobby's nipple.

"Fuck, yeah." Bobby yanked at his belt and unbuckled, then shoved his jeans down around his thighs. He took his dick and Remy's in his hand.

Remy stared into Bobby's eyes. For a split second, the world seemed to fade away around them. The only thing that mattered was what Bobby did to his cock.

Bobby stroked both shafts and rested his forehead on Remy's. He brushed his lips across Remy's mouth.

Heat sailed through Remy's body. He rocked his hips, thrusting his cock into Bobby's hand. He loved the way Bobby's dick felt against his own. His breath wrenched from his body and his nerve endings tingled. He stared at the amber and mocha flecks in Bobby's eyes. *A man could get lost in those.*

Bobby bit Remy's bottom lip. "Fuck, I'm close." He kissed Remy again and bumped noses with him. Their teeth clashed a couple of times, and Bobby swallowed Remy's groan.

The taste of Bobby's kiss—cola and mint—along with the scent of him curled around Remy. He liked the scrape of Bobby's five o'clock shadow on his cheeks and the feel of his strong hand around his dick. Even Bobby's moans pleased him. He wanted to drop to his knees and suck Bobby clean.

He broke away from Bobby long enough to grunt. The orgasm washed over him faster than he'd expected. He sagged against the door as a ribbon of cum streaked onto his lower belly.

"Came ahead of me." Bobby smiled and gripped their dicks tight. "I like it."

He likes a lot of things, doesn't he? Remy fought to catch his breath. His knees were weak.

"Fucking balls." Bobby closed his eyes and gritted his teeth. He shivered and shoved his hips forward. His cum splattered onto Remy's belly as well as his own. He bridged the gap between them and smeared the sticky mess. He pinned Remy to the door again and panted.

"You sure know how to break the ice," Remy said. He winced. *God.* He wasn't good at post-sex conversation. He paused. This wasn't exactly sex, but 'post-masturbation discussion' sounded silly.

"I've been dying to do that since I saw you in those shorts." Bobby nipped Remy's bottom lip. "Either you're thinking really hard and I suck at jerking you off, or I've completely blown your mind. Which is it?"

"Me overthinking." He couldn't lie. "I never know what to say. Not after…this."

Bobby smiled and braced his hand on the door. "Do you have a roommate?"

"No."

"Are you expecting someone to come by?" Bobby asked.

"No. My best friend is probably asleep by now." But if Julia knew he'd brought Bobby home, she'd be cheering. "There won't be any interruptions."

Bobby rubbed his nose along Remy's. "Then how about you ask me to stay tonight?"

Yeah, he should do that…once he found his voice. Remy blew out a long breath and summoned his courage. He could do this. If Bobby wanted to sleep over, then he wasn't about to tell him to go home. "Would you like to stay over?"

# Chapter Three

Bobby kissed the corner of Remy's mouth. He admired the shy man and liked how he'd been able to reduce him to speechlessness. He had nowhere to go and wanted to be with Remy instead of just playing with Remy's dick.

"I'd love to stay," Bobby said. "Could use a towel too." He pulled away from Remy. He'd smeared their cum all over his stomach. Having a lover's jizz on his body wasn't awful, but he hated the stickiness as it started to dry.

"Let me get..." Remy managed to stand and pushed off the door. He kept his jeans low on his hips.

Bobby admired Remy's body and the way he worked the low-slung denim. *Damn.* He followed Remy to the bathroom and waited in the doorway. He'd expected Remy to be a neat freak and wasn't disappointed. The bathroom looked lived-in, but everything had a place and nothing was out of order. Remy wetted a washcloth.

"Want to watch a movie or something?" Remy asked. "I'll need some recovery time before we can have round two."

He needed a few minutes as well. "Sure. I'm game."

Remy wiped the cooling jizz from Bobby's stomach. "I don't have many movies. There's one with a hot tub." He shrugged. "It's a porno and there's no plot."

"So?" He didn't care if they watched something or cuddled together and talked. This was one of the few chances he allowed himself for nights like this and he didn't want it to end.

"My television is in the bedroom." Remy cleaned his belly. "Through there."

Bobby leaned against the sink and took the cloth from Remy. "Strip."

Remy's eyes flashed, but he did as he was told. He shoved the jeans down to his ankles and kicked out of his shoes. He hopped twice as he untangled the denim from his legs.

"Nice." Bobby grabbed Remy's hand and swept his gaze over Remy's nude body. He'd expected Remy to be tatted somewhere or pierced. He wasn't sure why — maybe because Remy gave off an *I've-got-a-secret* vibe. He had nothing but sexy smooth skin and muscle. He nudged Remy into the bedroom.

Without saying a word, Remy crawled onto the mattress. He wagged his ass at Bobby and dug through something on the other side of the bed. "Give me a minute and I'll find the movie."

"Don't worry about it." He moved the blankets. "Stretch out with me."

"Huh?" Remy faced him. His eyes widened, but he didn't speak.

"I want to get to know you." He settled under the covers and patted the mattress. "How have I not met you until tonight?"

Remy shrugged and scooted under the blankets. "I'm shy?"

"Are you?" He tangled his legs with Remy's and draped his arm across Remy's stomach. He preferred to take charge during sex, but his dominant streak receded afterward.

"Yeah." Remy rolled onto his side to face Bobby. "You have no idea how much courage it took just to go across the lawn to say hi. I saw you with Colin and Jordan and lost my nerve."

"They're harmless." He grinned and moved his hand to Remy's chest. Remy's pulse thrummed under his fingertips. He liked the closeness they'd created already. He wasn't sure he was ready to disclose his entire life story to Remy, but he wanted to go on an actual date with him.

"Maybe, but I'm leery around Jordan." Remy tensed. "We don't get along and haven't as long as I can remember." His eyes widened again and he sighed. "Sorry. We didn't grow up together, but I spent summers at my grandparents' house. His grandparents lived next door, and they liked to get us kids together in order to stay out of their collective hair."

"What's there to be sorry about? I get it. Jordan can be hard to take. He's not my favorite person, but then I'm not dating him, so it doesn't matter." He remembered plenty of incidents with Jordan before they'd left school. He hadn't been the most athletic young man, and Jordan had always seemed to be close by when he tripped or fumbled. The only reason he talked to Jordan was because he'd hooked up with Colin.

"It's not cool to insult someone's friends." Remy half-smiled, but the light didn't reach his eyes.

"Don't worry about it."

"I will. I've had my fair share of crap in this town. It's best to be careful." Remy laced his fingers with Bobby's. "That Coalition. They want to run everyone out of town."

"Oh, I don't know." He'd received the letter, but otherwise the group hadn't bothered him. "Have they done something to you?"

Remy paused. "I write for the paper. I cover entertainment and sports. When some of the parents see me coming, they avoid me. I'm there to write a story about the game, match or whatever, but all they see is a gay man who used to go around town with his boyfriend."

"Well, you are." But he understood. He'd dealt with people disliking his sexual orientation. "Not everyone in Cedarwood hates gay people. I've got friends who don't care what we do."

"Huh." Remy snuggled up to Bobby. He laughed and finally offered a real smile. "I thought I was bad at post-sex conversation. This is the strangest discussion I've ever had in the nude."

Remy might not have a good handle on conversation, but damn, he was cute. Bobby had shoved aside his normal reservations about potential lovers when he'd first clapped eyes on Remy. He wanted him so much.

"You haven't mentioned an ex or called me by his name, so it's fine." He snorted. The last time he'd slept with Terry, the man had shouted out his other boyfriend's name. The pain of knowing Terry cheated and was ready to move on had damn near killed him.

"I won't." Remy kissed Bobby. "I don't understand why you came home with me, though. You're so handsome. I'm boring compared to you."

Bobby bit back a sigh. He'd have to work with Remy if they were going to have a relationship beyond tonight. "What happened? Who fucked with your head instead of your ass?"

Remy stared at him. "It's that obvious?"

"Uh-huh." He curled his fingers under Remy's chin. "Someone fucked with your confidence." He wasn't wild about playing the role of therapist for Remy, but the guy had to get whatever he'd bottled up out of his system. "Tell me. You'll burst if you don't."

"You'll laugh." Remy flattened his palm on Bobby's chest. "I was fat. Sounds silly when I say it out loud, but that's what I can't quite get past."

"We've all got issues with ourselves. I'm only thirty-four and going gray." He'd considered coloring his hair plenty of times but had never committed. He rubbed his semi-hard dick against Remy's hip. "Don't let it bother you."

"Easy for you to say." Remy curled his fingers around Bobby's dick. "It's funny. I don't tell many people about my hang-ups. You make talking easy."

"I like listening." He patted Remy's ass. "I like fucking too."

Remy closed his eyes and moaned. "I do too." He draped his arm around Bobby's neck and brought him close for a kiss. "I'm scared this will all be a dream."

So was he. Bobby feathered his mouth over Remy's and savored Remy's taste. He wasn't sure how long things would go on with him. For all he knew, this night was it.

"Fuck me." Remy opened his eyes. "Hard. Fast."

"Wow. I didn't think you had a dominant bone in your body." Bobby ground his cock into Remy's groin. He knew how to take control, even if Remy didn't. "Roll over."

"Yes." Remy flopped onto his belly and dug through the nightstand. He offered up a bottle of lube and a condom. "Ready?"

"You sound so sure of yourself." Bobby draped his leg over Remy's. "Do you want me?"

"More than I've ever wanted anything."

"Then relax." He held the lube and condom in one hand, then situated his knee between Remy's legs. He kissed his way along Remy's spine and slid his fingers over Remy's hole.

"Oh fuck." Remy balled his fist. "I just came and I'm ready to go again."

"Bet you are." Bobby grinned. He licked and nipped Remy's shoulder blades. The man tasted as good as he looked. He squirted lube onto his fingers, then teased Remy's hole.

"God. Put it in." Remy arched his back, offering up his ass. "Please?"

"Relax. If I go too fast, I'll hurt you, and I'm not into that shit." He eased his middle finger into Remy's ass and twisted. When Remy groaned, he pulled out then pushed back in again.

Remy bore down on him and sighed. "Damn."

"You've got a nice ass." He kissed Remy's back and raked his teeth over Remy's skin. "Hot and tight." *Holy fuck, the man's snug.* "Relax."

"Can't. I want you in me." Remy arched his back even more. "Need you."

"I will." He couldn't hold back much longer. The way Remy pleaded got to him. He liked the need tinging Remy's voice. He ripped the condom wrapper with his teeth. Not great for his smile, but he wasn't worried about his dental health. He smoothed the rubber down his erection, then dumped lube onto his hand. He eased his finger from Remy's body and stroked himself. He straddled Remy's legs and rubbed the head of his cock along the seam of Remy's ass.

"Do it." Remy groaned. He grabbed his butt cheeks. "Please?"

The man knew what he wanted. Bobby moved with care, despite every cell in his body urging him to rush. He couldn't wait to be balls-deep in Remy, but he needed to go slow. Inch by inch, he slid into Remy's body.

"Jesus," Bobby growled. "You're so tense."

"I'm on the edge."

Bobby grasped Remy's hips and built a steady rhythm. As Remy relaxed, Bobby thrust harder into him. He let go of Remy's hips and threaded his fingers into Remy's hair. He palmed the back of Remy's head.

"Fuck." Remy bucked against Bobby, shoving him deeper into Remy's hole. "Faster."

The man was demanding, too. Bobby braced his knees. He slid in and out of Remy, loving the feel of him surrounding him. He gasped and shook his head. A bead of sweat slid down his temple. He gritted his teeth as the orgasm welled within him. His restraint held by a tiny thread, and one more moan from Remy would be all he needed for it to break.

"Bobby," Remy panted. "God, yeah." He bucked into Bobby, meeting him thrust for thrust. A rumble escaped his chest.

Bobby tipped his head back and growled again. He couldn't hold back the climax. Not any longer. He slammed his cock deep into Remy and shuddered. He filled the condom as Remy shivered beneath him.

"Jesus God." Remy opened his eyes and sagged on the bed. "You know how to wear a guy out too."

Bobby added a couple of extra, slower pushes into Remy as the orgasm flowed over him. He doubted his knees would hold him up much longer. But Remy had been good. He'd been worth the second look at the park.

Bobby eased out of Remy's ass and left the bed long enough to ditch the condom. When he returned to the bedroom, Remy hadn't moved, but he did smile.

"Don't go. I don't want the night to end, even though I know it will." He patted the mattress. "Just stick around a little while."

"I don't fuck and go." Although he wasn't much of a cuddler after sex, either. Well, no. He liked to hold his lover, but this was a one-night thing. Still, he settled beside Remy again. Why blow the good night to hell by leaving already?

Remy rested his back against Bobby's chest. He grasped Bobby's hand and kissed his knuckles. "Stay the weekend."

He should've known this was coming. "I can't." Not when the kids would be coming home in the morning. He suppressed a snort. He hadn't thought about his children since seeing Remy. He shouldn't have been unnerved by that thought, but he was. Normally they were his first priority.

"Why? Got another boyfriend? A hot date?" Remy asked. "A better offer?"

"You're so down on yourself." He kissed Remy's shoulder. "I've got work in the morning." It being the end of the month, he had payroll for two small businesses to complete and finances to balance for a mowing company, all while keeping an eye on his kids.

"On Sunday?" Remy held his hand tight. "I like it. At least you're driven."

"An accountant's job is never done." *Boy, don't I know that…but enough about work.* He was with a hot man, still in the post-sex glow, and sleepy as hell. His brain wouldn't shut off, but he was tuckered out.

"Just tell me before you leave in the morning…or whenever you go." Remy's voice softened and his breathing evened out.

*So much for the movie.* Bobby bit back a chuckle. He appreciated knowing he'd worn Remy out. He closed his eyes, but thoughts pummeled his brain. This had been one of the oddest one-night stands in his life, but that worked for him. Remy was original, and even if he was rather hard on himself, Bobby liked him. There was a sexiness about him that Remy didn't understand. He wanted to see Remy again and go on a date. He needed to feel the guy out more. Sex and masturbation were fun, but he didn't know Remy all that well. What he did know, he enjoyed.

He sighed and cuddled up to Remy. Sleep overcame him. They didn't have forever together, and he accepted that. He'd take their one night of heat.

\* \* \* \*

Bobby rolled onto his back and yawned. When he opened his eyes, he froze. *Where in the hell am I?* He didn't recognize the cream-colored walls or the furnishings. As he surfaced from sleep, he remembered his surroundings. He'd slept over at Remy's.

He scrubbed both hands over his face and sighed again. He needed to get home. Would Remy care if he left? Remy had said he wanted to know before Bobby walked out. He glanced over at Remy. He looked so sexy asleep.

He nudged Remy. "Hey. Rem?" He kissed Remy's neck. "Remy?"

"Yeah." Remy didn't roll over and didn't appear to be all that awake.

"I have to go." He kissed Remy again. "Want to walk me out?" *Or at least wake up enough to see me out of the door?*

Remy snuggled deeper into the blankets. "Uh-huh."

He wasn't going to get too far with Remy right now. Bobby ignored his better judgment and slipped out of bed. He gathered his clothes from the floor and strode into the bathroom to dress. He wasn't worried about Remy seeing him naked, but it was still dark out, and he didn't want to blast light on Remy while he dressed.

He stepped into his wadded-up underwear and jeans, then balled up his socks on the sink. He'd worry about those when he got home. He shrugged into his shirt and buttoned it halfway up. Instead of fastening his belt, he yanked it from the loops on his jeans. He'd carry that with his socks.

Bobby left the bathroom and found his shoes in the living room. He patted his pockets. He had his keys, but where was his phone? *Shit.* He scrambled, scanning the floor for the device. He spotted the Cincinnati football logo and breathed a sigh of relief. His phone. He picked it up and checked the messages. None. No texts, missed calls, or emails. *Huh.* Usually he had something waiting for him.

He paused at the small table and glanced back at the bedroom. He wanted Remy to call him, so he put his number into Remy's phone. He could've sent a message from Remy's to his own phone but thought better of it. He'd breached enough privacy by adding his number. He abandoned Remy's phone on the table and headed to the door.

He felt like he should've said something more to Remy but didn't. He left the apartment and strode out to his car. He settled behind the wheel and checked his appearance in the rearview mirror. The creases around his eyes weren't so deep for a change. He grinned and averted his gaze. *Time to get back to the real world.*

Bobby drove across town to his street. The leaves rustled in the early morning breeze. He turned into his driveway. The grass needed to be mowed, and the flower boxes on the porch could use watering. He'd worry about that later.

He parked in the garage and closed the door before he headed into the house. He needed a shower and shave before the kids came back.

He made his way upstairs to his bedroom and stripped down. He kicked out of his shoes and vowed he'd never go sock-less in loafers again. He waggled his toes. Bone-deep weariness settled over him as he stepped into the shower. He rested his forehead against the tile wall as the water sluiced down his body.

What did he have to complete that day? Work, as always, the yardwork, and his parents would probably want to spend time there. Since he'd moved back to Cedarwood, the relationship with his folks had improved. He wasn't sure what had changed their mind but he wasn't questioning his good fortune. He appreciated the help with the kids and not having that void in his life.

So many years had gone by with his parents hating him for being gay. He could still hear the insults, although time had mellowed the entire situation. He wasn't as flamboyant about his sexuality, and they didn't seem to be as flustered, either.

He dipped his head under the hot water and groaned. He had so much to do. He wanted the myriad boxes out of his room, in addition to getting the other work done.

*God.* He couldn't shut his brain off again. He lathered and washed. That was his problem — not the washing, but the overactive thinking. He didn't settle down well.

Terry hadn't minded his frantic qualities, but then Terry was just as driven and work-minded. Neil hated it. He wanted to party, eat out and not grow up. Having kids made maturing inescapable.

Bobby sighed and switched off the water. If he didn't get going, he'd never leave his own head. He dried off and dressed in a pair of jeans and a T-shirt. Although he had the air conditioning on, the heat of the late June day already permeated the house. He decided against socks and padded downstairs to his office. He settled behind his computer and opened the spreadsheets.

Two hours later, he had both sets of payroll complete as well as having sorted out the finances for the mowing company. He drummed his fingers on the desk. His parents wouldn't be there for another forty-five minutes — unless they were running early. *Always possible.*

He could start the yardwork, but he hesitated. Remy came to mind. He opened his web browser and searched for the Cedarwood newspaper. Once he'd located the main page, he clicked on the staff tab. Sure enough, Remy's name was under the sports and entertainment banners. The photo used for the site wasn't great. Remy looked tired and old. A thought occurred to Bobby. How old was Remy? Legal, yes, but he hadn't asked. Just like he hadn't asked about his last name or a lot of other info.

God, he was slipping. Still, he was impressed with Remy. He read through Remy's bio twice, then closed the browser window. He liked a man with accomplishments, and Remy seemed to have a few. He leaned back in his seat and crossed his ankles. Coming back to Cedarwood looked good on paper but had some negatives. The kids still needed to adjust to the new surroundings and get into the swing of things. He hadn't been bothered by the Coalition, but there was still time.

There were positives. Christopher and Darcy were getting to know their grandparents. Each had bigger rooms, and he had an office in his home. They'd made friends and had sports teams to occupy their time. He had the support group and some of his old friends from school too. He could call Colin and get the scoop on Remy.

He spotted his mother as she pulled her sedan into the driveway. The kids were back. Relief washed over him. As much fun as he'd had the night before, he preferred the family atmosphere.

Darcy bounded into the house first. "Dad!" She raced into his office. "The movie was awesome."

He hugged her. "Which one?" He'd remembered one of them mentioning something about going to the drive-in, but he wasn't sure which movie was playing.

"The comic book one. So much fighting." Her eyes lit up. "Dave Klein was in it." She sighed. "He could save me."

"You're twelve." Besides, he wasn't ready for his daughter to have a crush on anyone, even if the guy was an actor and not at all within her reach. Darcy wasn't supposed to be growing up so fast.

Chris strolled into the office and plunked his iPod on the desk. "This died."

"Hello to you too." He picked up the device. "It's waterlogged. What'd you do?"

Chris winced. "They tossed me into the pond during the last practice, and I forgot I had that in my pocket. My earbuds are ruined too." He met his father's gaze. "Sorry, Dad."

"Things happen. Where are your grandparents? Or did you abandon them?" He hugged his son, then headed into the main portion of the house. He found his mother on the back deck. "Thanks for watching the kids, Ma."

Esther smiled and shielded her eyes, despite wearing sunglasses. "I forgot this house had a pool."

"That's why Darcy wanted it." He hadn't been thrilled about the price tag, but he wanted to encourage Darcy's love for the water.

"They were good. We saw some movie with fighting and men in tight pants." She folded her arms. "Both of them loved it. I still don't get it. Must be the next generation's thing."

"Kind of." He was a sucker for those movies too. He'd never admit it in front of his children, but he liked looking at the myriad hot asses in tight leather.

"I'll make lunch if you want to stick around. I can grill something." He had burgers and hot dogs in the fridge.

"I'd like that. Your dad had to work. The Coalition's been giving him fits." She shook her head. "I don't understand."

"You should. You hated me for the longest time for being gay." He turned on his heel and went back into the house. He'd known the topic would come up sooner or later. He retrieved the pack of burgers, a spatula and the bottle of seasoning. He left the food on the deck table and switched on the grill.

"I did, and we were wrong." She dragged a chair from the table. "You're our son, no matter who you love, and you have two wonderful children."

"Speaking of." He glanced over his shoulder.

Darcy hurried onto the deck. "Can we swim?"

"I'm watching. Sure," he replied. He widened his stance and folded his arms. Sure enough, Chris strolled onto the deck too. He'd already donned his swim trunks.

"Told you," Chris snapped. "She doesn't listen to me, Dad."

"With that tone, I wouldn't either." He sighed as the kids jumped into the pool. He turned his attention to his mother. "You fed them nothing but sugar, right? As payback for me being a hellion as a kid?"

Esther shook her head. "They were good. We had sundaes last night, but that was it." She left the chair and joined him by the grill. "You weren't a bad kid. Energetic, but not bad."

"Funny. That's not what you'd say when I got into trouble." He checked the heat on the grill, then opened the pack of burgers. "For the longest time I thought my name was Oh-For-The-Love-Of-God." He spaced the hamburgers on the grate, then shut the lid.

"When Dad wasn't around, it was tough." She stood beside him. "I hear you met someone."

He froze. *She knows already?* Yes, the park was a public place and he had no idea who all saw him with Remy, but how'd she find out so fast? He sighed. He'd better play this cool and not get her hopes up. "Kinda, but I'd rather not discuss it."

"I heard he's cute, has a job and is single." She smiled. "Sounds like a catch."

"Ma." Sometimes he wished his parents were still in the dark about his sexuality. "Just because he's got good qualities doesn't mean we're going to be together forever. I met him. That's enough."

"Please." She snorted. "If he's cute, single and not an axe murderer, then go on a date."

"Eventually. I just met him." *Jerked him off, slept with him and looked him up on the Internet.* She didn't need to know all of that. "I thought I saw his last name, but I don't remember it."

"Remy Nicholas."

"Ma." She'd gotten pushier with age.

"I've met him. He's nice." She turned her back on the pool. "My friend Maureen works with him at the paper. She's been trying to fix him up with her daughter and couldn't understand why it wasn't working. Now I know. I won't say anything." She put both hands up. "I didn't want to say anything in front of the kids, but I'm glad you met him. You need help around here and to not be lonely."

Smoke from the grill wafted around them. He stared at her. Would she give him the lecture? "I'm not twelve, Ma. I know how to conduct myself, if that's what you're going to say. I'm lonely, but after Neil, things were rough. I'm not ready to jump into something. The kids are still adjusting to Cedarwood, and I'd like to get over that wrinkle before I do anything else."

She frowned. "I know you know how to conduct yourself, as you put it. You wouldn't have kids if you didn't." She lowered her voice. "I meant, I want you to be happy. Don't forget about you."

"I won't." He hadn't expected that from his mother. She'd never been good at subtlety or interested in fixing him up with other men.

She kept her voice low. "I wanted to tell you. A bunch of ladies and I are forming a group. I'm tired of the Coalition giving your father hell. It's too much."

"Another group of well-meaning, well-intended citizens is just what Dad needs." He tried not to sound like a shit, but he didn't see a good outcome to this.

"I agree he needs some help." She shrugged. "The people who aren't part of the Coalition or don't agree with it need a voice. I've had plenty of folks tell me they're tired of the fighting. It's getting old. This used to be a nice place to live for whomever wanted to live here, but with them trying to run people out of town…it's not good any longer."

She'd stunned him to silence. He hadn't expected her to say that, either.

"I'm tired of my son and his friends being targeted for doing nothing more than living their lives. It's not like you're dancing down the street in high-heeled shoes and feathers."

"Gee, Ma, I didn't know you cared." He chuckled and flipped the burgers. "But if given the chance, I'm sure some people in the gay community would love to have a pride parade complete with drag queens, feathers and anything else they can think of."

"It could be fun." She shrugged again. "Bobby, I want to see you happy, no matter who you're with. The kids deserve to grow up in a community filled with love and diversity, not whatever we've got going on in Cedarwood."

"If you need my help, say the word." He wasn't sure what he could do, but he'd try. "Is it going to be an organized group, or are you just rounding people up to visit businesses friendly to everyone?"

"I thought we'd start there. Colin Baker's doing such a great job with the bookstore. He'd probably like the business. So would Colton over at the diner. This past spring, the group picketed the diner, then someone beat him up. Why would they do that?"

He wasn't entirely sure. "Some folks aren't ready for change, even if we're not ramming it down their throats."

"We're losing good teachers because the head of the schools doesn't like gay people." She folded her arms and turned back to the pool. "You're really willing to help?"

"I said I would." He turned the heat off and left the lid open on the grill. "I need to get a plate. Keep an eye on them, please?" He meant the kids, not the food, but didn't bother to clarify. He figured she knew. He hurried into the kitchen and retrieved a paper plate, then returned to the grill.

"Date Remy."

"Ma." He moved the burgers to the plate. "What if he doesn't want to?"

"Oh please. It's a date, not marriage." She held up both hands. "But if you decided to marry him, I wouldn't object. I'd like another son."

"You've got me and Chris." He carried the plate and spatula over to the table, then turned his attention to the kids. "Food's ready."

"Be happy. Have a boyfriend and raise those kids." Esther grabbed his arm. "Let us deal with the Coalition. Not everyone is against having gay people in town. Have a life." She smiled. "And if you're willing to be a financial officer at some point for us, we could use you."

He wasn't sure how they'd need him, but he was game. "Sure."

"Great. Now where are the buns? I'll help."

He shook his head. He'd settled a few parts of his life, but others were in chaos. Trust his mother to help him upheave more of it, and all because she wanted him to have a date. Wouldn't she flip if she found out he'd gotten a whole lot closer to Remy besides learning his name? He sighed. Coming home had been a blessing and a curse.

# Chapter Four

On Monday morning, Remy sat at his desk at the paper and flipped through his notes. He'd written the majority of the articles at home on Sunday afternoon. He wished he'd written down Bobby's number. Bobby had mentioned having to work, but still. Maybe they could've had dinner together.

He sighed. He couldn't get Bobby out of his brain. His nerve endings sizzled at the thought of Bobby jerking him off. When he flexed his asshole, he remembered Bobby being there. The tips of his ears burned. He'd never let a guy get to him the way he had with Bobby.

Saturday night had been one for the books. A whole lot of good and a little not so good. Not getting Bobby's number and having Bobby leave before he fully woke up kind of sucked. He could've sworn he heard Bobby get up and even remembered Bobby speaking to him, but he had no idea what Bobby had said.

He should've called Julia on Sunday afternoon, but he'd been so wrapped up in writing and not thinking about his sort-of date that he'd forgotten about her.

He picked up his cell phone. He didn't smoke, but he could use a jaunt outside to the former smoker's den in order to have some privacy. Before he could dial her number, one of his co-workers, Maureen, strode up to his desk.

She plunked a pamphlet and a short stack of papers beside his laptop.

He tucked his phone into his front pocket. "How are you today?"

"Can we talk?" she asked.

"As long as it's not about me getting fired, I'm all yours." He rolled his chair back and rested his ankle on his knee. "What's up?"

"Couple of things." She scratched her forehead, then dragged one of the other chairs over to his desk. She sat and faced him. "First, I brought over your schedule for the different sports events this week. Some Hot Stove league games, a traveling softball team game and a swim meet over at the metro park today."

"All of those are today?" he blurted, then reread the schedule. He needed to stop speaking before thinking and reading. "Sorry. All week. Okay, I knew about the swim meet. It starts at four." He checked his watch. He had about five hours until he was due at that event.

"That's why I said all week." She shook her head. "You'll be fine. You'll have to interview a couple of the athletes, but I wrote those down for you." She lowered her voice. "You've heard of the Coalition, right?"

He groaned. "Who hasn't? Don't tell me you're part of it."

"No." She held up both hands. "Wouldn't touch them with a ten-foot pole."

"Good." He'd tried to ignore the group as much as possible since the last incident. He could still hear the woman shouting at him to leave the softball game because she didn't want the youngsters, as she'd called the players, to see that being gay was a positive thing.

"No, I brought these papers and the brochure over because I think you should do a story about them. I'm sure there are quite a few people in Cedarwood who don't agree with their tactics and/or have been victimized by them. Those people need a say. You can do it." She tapped the stack of papers. "I bet that guy you were with at the park would appreciate it."

"You know him?" He sat up a little straighter. "Maureen, you've been holding out on me."

"I'm friends with his mother." She grinned and adjusted the scarf around her throat. "I finally got the hint that you weren't interested in my daughter, but it took talking to Esther about it for things to make sense."

"Do they live around here?" He suddenly wanted to know everything about Bobby. "Do I know his mom?"

"You've seen Esther. I went to lunch with her last week. The tall blonde woman with the huge black sedan."

He nodded. How could he forget the boat of a car pulling into the lot? She'd taken up two parking spaces.

"Bobby's dad is the chief of police. I thought you knew that." Maureen frowned, drawing her dark eyebrows tight together. "Well, you do now."

He sat back in his chair and fought to hide his shock. *Talk about a small world.* No wonder Bobby was so low-key about everything concerning their getting together.

With his dad in the public eye, he probably didn't want anyone knowing his business.

"Anyway, check into that group. I got you some of their info. There's got to be a way we can all get along in this town." She patted his shoulder. "I need to get back to the front desk. I left the new girl in charge, and while she's decent at answering the phones, she's more concerned about her social media status than her employment status."

"Thanks, Maureen." He waited for her to leave before he flipped through the documents. The more he read, the more his stomach churned. The Coalition for Order in Cedarwood wanted to 'keep the sanctity of marriage in the town. Marriage should be between a man and woman. Children grow up better and more mature in a heterosexual marriage household.' *Who comes up with this stuff?* His parents weren't thrilled he was gay and let him know their thoughts, but that hadn't convinced him not to be gay. He snorted. He'd be willing to bet somewhere in the Coalition rhetoric was the notion that homosexual people could flip a switch and not be gay. He scanned the page and found the sentiment.

"Christ," he mumbled. How in the hell was he supposed to write a decent story about this? He wanted to fling the papers across the room and never look at them again. Unfortunately for him, he was there to do a job. He shoved away from his desk and picked up the stack of papers. If he wanted to make it to the swim meet on time and digest the information on the Coalition, he needed a working lunch—not at his desk.

Remy stuffed the papers and his computer tablet into his messenger bag. He turned off the laptop. He moved his phone from his pocket to his bag and twirled his keys. He ducked out of the side door leading to the parking lot. The sun beat down on the sticky blacktop and birds chirped in the apple trees. He gripped his keys and strode away from his car. It was too nice a day to drive. He'd stroll down to the city square and hit up one of the food trucks, then eat at the little memorial park. He doubted anyone would bother him there.

As he walked the two blocks to the center of town, he called Julia. After three rings, she picked up.

"Hey," he said. "I thought I'd get your voicemail."

"Normally, you would've, but my lit teacher canceled class. She came down with a case of Las Vegas," Julia replied.

He stopped in his tracks. "A case of Vegas? What's that?"

"She ran off to get married." Julia chuckled. "Seems like every available woman in the county is either engaged, married or at least dating — except me."

"You've got me." He doubted she wanted to hear that. "I'm loyal to you and think you're adorable."

"But you suck when it comes to sex. You're not interested in me."

"Sorry." He understood her situation. They'd bonded over the end of their respective relationships. She'd helped him get over Al, his second lover, and he'd helped her prove her then-boyfriend, Dillon, had cheated on her.

"So? Dish. I know you went home with Bobby."

"Guess everyone noticed, huh?"

"I saw you at the festival, so yes, I noticed. I was at the concert and happened to see you leave with him. I'm glad. He's cute, funny and sweet," Julia said. "He's stable too."

"I guess so." He plunked his bag on his lap and folded his arm across his chest. "We slept together."

"Good."

He couldn't tell if she was happy, proud or being sarcastic. "We watched the fireworks together, cuddled and I invited him back to my place."

"And? Was he good? He looks like he'd be the take-charge type who's awesome in bed."

"He was." He couldn't lie. He'd replayed their time together in his head a hundred times, including that morning in the shower. "I really like him."

"Wonderful."

"I invited him to run with me."

"There is a God. I can't keep up with you." Julia paused. "I feel a 'but' coming on. A big one. Spill. What's wrong? You're usually so bubbly with info after a hook-up."

He pinched the bridge of his nose and sighed. This was another reason he loved Julia — she cut to the chase and knew him so well. She didn't put up with his bullshit either. "The thing is, I'm scared. I blurted out a bunch of crap in front of him. I swear I was practically incoherent."

"Were you drunk? You don't drink to excess."

"I was completely sober, just nervous and saying everything that came into my head." He groaned. "I told him I was a fat kid and it still messed with me. We had sex, yeah, but he left in the morning without so much as a note."

"Really? Are you sure? He's a stand-up kind of guy. I've known him since he was a little boy."

"Okay, he spoke to me. I think he said something about it being great, but I can't be sure. He wore me out and I dozed off after he left." His confidence dipped. "I messed up, didn't I? I find a guy I like, one who is normal and decent, but I can't seal the deal."

"You sealed something if he stayed over."

"I can't call him to sort things out or set up a time to run. It's crazy." He'd been hungry when he'd left the newspaper offices, but the longer he talked to Julia, the more he was glad he hadn't eaten yet.

"It's a miscommunication," she said. "Maybe he thought he left a note or that you understood him when he said bye. Did you check your phone? Maybe he put his info in? I don't know. I'm not him, but I've done that. I've asked the guy for his phone and input my info. Usually the guy doesn't call, but that's my problem. We're talking about you."

"I'll look when I hang up with you." He dropped his hand onto his lap. "You don't think I fucked it up with him?"

"I think you're worried and overthinking. Once you see him again, you'll be sure. Don't freak out."

*Easy for her to say.* He sighed. "I've got to do some reading on the Coalition here in town, then head over to the metro park for a swim meet. I'll call you later tonight."

"Why are you reading up on the Coalition? If you tell me you're considering joining or going along with their ideas, I'll come over there and smack you."

"Because I'm going to write a counter piece." He hadn't really planned on doing such a thing, but as he thought about the language in the flyer, anger bubbled in him. He wasn't a freak or a problem in the community, and if someone didn't start standing up, then nothing would change.

"Go you," she replied. "Keep your head on and write that piece."

She hung up, leaving him in silence.

Remy tucked his phone back into his pocket and watched people mill about the square. Reading about the Coalition angered him, but so did skipping lunch. He kept the papers in his bag. *No reading on an empty stomach.* He headed back to the food trucks and ordered a falafel sandwich and a green tea. As he waited for his lunch, he surveyed the traffic in the square. Only a couple of the benches were open, and none of the picnic tables were free. At this rate, he'd need a table…

Once the food was ready, he headed back to the bench in the little park. The shade helped, and so did the lack of others in the general vicinity. He tucked the strap of his messenger bag under his thigh, then opened his sandwich. As he ate, he flipped through the info on the Coalition.

He frowned. 'The mission of the Coalition is to keep the sanctity of family and marriage alive in Cedarwood.' Who the hell said they weren't alive? He kept reading.

*While gay people aren't inherently bad, they pose a problem to the community – religion dictates they're full of sin.*

*Jesus. Where are these people getting this stuff?* He turned the papers over and finished his sandwich. He thought about a conversation he'd had in college with a buddy who'd come out and expected every other gay to be as open as he was. Jack swore up and down that the closeted gays were the reason the LGBT community was screwed. Remy had argued otherwise. There were so many things fucked up about the world. After reading the crap from the Coalition, he understood why some gay folks chose to stay in the closet. If they heard the Coalition bullshit all of the time, they wouldn't want to be themselves for fear they'd be ostracized.

"They don't understand because they don't want to understand," he murmured. He'd told Jack the same thing, only to get crickets in return.

He wondered what Bobby would say. Unlike Bobby, he never knew when to shut up. He'd blabbered on about so many things. He sighed. Still, he had good memories of their night together. He wished he had Bobby's number, but he'd get it sooner or later. The conversations with Maureen and Julia encouraged him to hold on to hope. If they liked Bobby, then good.

He balled up the paper from his sandwich and polished off the rest of his tea. He should probably get back to his reading. He tucked the paper into the cup, then set it between his feet. Just thinking about the Coalition irritated him.

He scanned through the member interviews and more literature from the group. The testimonials churned his stomach. He'd never read so much hate in his life. He frowned while re-reading the words of the members. There was no way all of the different run-ins with gay people had occurred — not in the manner these people described. He'd never seen anyone picket anything in Cedarwood until the Coalition had picketed the diner. None of the teachers had been fired because of their sexuality until recently, and those who were fired or laid off didn't speak publicly about the layoffs. The only assault had come at the hands of suspected Coalition members. Something wasn't right about the situation.

Anger, hurt and frustration battled within Remy. He might be respected as a man if he hadn't come out, but because he'd admitted he was gay and carried on with another man in public, he'd become lesser to those in the Coalition. That wasn't right. The damn fools feared what they didn't understand.

He dug through his bag for a pen and scrawled notes in the margins of the Coalition rhetoric. The festival had been a good start, but it wasn't enough. The people in Cedarwood who believed in freedom for everyone needed to come together. They needed to prove to those who hadn't come out or were afraid to do so that there wasn't any shame in admitting who they were.

Remy switched to a fresh notebook. He wasn't going to marginalize the gay community. He grinned as he outlined his first piece about the Coalition. Once he got the article written, he'd head to the swim meet and hopefully run into Bobby. Boy, did he have one hell of a story to tell his crush.

* * * *

Two hours and almost half a notebook later, Remy stretched on the bench. He'd taken one hell of a long lunch, but at least his hours at the paper were fluid. They didn't expect a written account of where he'd been as long as he had the stories to fill the pages of *The Tribune*.

He stood and tucked his work back into his bag, then tossed his cup into the trash. He hurried back to the parking lot. If he kept moving, he'd get to the swim meet on time. He drove across town to the metro park. As soon as he turned into the lot, he groaned. He should've known there wouldn't be any spots open.

Instead of cruising the aisles for a spot, he continued around the corner to the gravel lot by the running trails.

He grabbed his bag and locked the car, then headed to the building. Once inside, he took his place at the edge of the room. He was supposed to interview a girl from Lakeside after the one-hundred-meter breaststroke. As he surveyed the crowd, he noticed Bobby. *Fuck yeah.* Remy left his usual spot by the doors. Hopefully Bobby wanted to see him as much as he wanted to see Bobby.

"Bobby? Hey. Hi." He bit back a groan. He'd already started babbling. "How are you?"

"Remy." Bobby smiled and stepped aside. "Are you covering the meet?"

"Yeah. I'm doing an interview at the end. It'll be the athlete of the week feature." He folded his arms. "I didn't expect to see you here." *But I'm glad as hell you are.*

"I like swimming." He tapped the kid next to him. "Chris, this is my friend Remy." He turned his attention back to Remy. "I'd like to introduce you to my son, Chris. He runs cross-country. My daughter, Darcy, is in the one-hundred-meter backstroke."

"Hi." Remy shook hands with Chris. "Nice to meet you."

"Nice to meet you as well," Chris replied. "Maybe this fall you'll do a feature on me. I'm all ready to shatter the competition."

"Christopher ran cross-country for his former school and managed three school records." Bobby's smile widened. "I'm proud of my boy."

"You should be." Remy tried not to stare, but wow. He hadn't expected Bobby to say he was a parent, much less the parent of a teenager. *Jesus.* He'd seen him with the kids, but for all he knew, they were his niece and nephew or something. Chris didn't look a thing like him, either. He tamped down his irritation as much as possible, but *damn*. Why did the hot guys all have kids? Was he at that age where he'd have to settle for someone with children because the single, childless men weren't available?

He focused on the swimmers shooting across the pool. He didn't want Bobby's status as a parent to be a big thing. It shouldn't be a deal-breaker, he reasoned. But it was. He wasn't a kid person. He didn't know how to relate to kids. He treated them the same way he'd been treated—like a miniature adult. Kids yelled, screamed and were messy. Kids required attention all of the time, and maybe he was a jerk, but he liked to focus on his partner. If the partner couldn't give him adequate attention, he might as well move on. But that was part of his problem. He'd been ignored by his family until he got old enough to take care of himself. Maybe he expected too much from his partners and kids. He wasn't sure.

"You look like you're going to jump in the pool," Bobby said. His breath tickled Remy's ear.

"No. I'm okay." He'd get over his issues in a moment. He jotted down the names and times for the swimmers. He had to focus on his job. He wasn't at the meet to get a date.

"Think we could talk later? Or do you have plans?" Bobby asked. "I'm taking Darce and Chris to the Italian place over by the freeway once we're done. She's always starving after a meet and the prices are decent. My treat."

*How can I say no?* Remy didn't answer right away. As much as he wanted to spend time with Bobby, he wasn't sure he could do it without sounding like a dick.

"I'll assume you're busy." Bobby stuffed his hands into his pockets. "I pushed, didn't I? Too much, too soon?"

He ground his teeth together. This wasn't Bobby's issue, even if he was part of it. "No, you're fine."

"But you're not." Bobby bumped shoulders with Remy. "We can consider the other night a freak occurrence and not talk about it again. I understand."

"I doubt you do." He closed his notebook. He needed the list of the specific winners and overall highest finishers.

"No problem." Bobby stood tall. "We're good."

Remy left the stands and headed back to the doors. As the other events took place, he took notes and glanced over at Bobby. He'd been a dick. A hundred percent, qualified dick. Bobby had been a gentleman, really, and invited Remy to dinner. Why in the fuck had he walked away?

Remy groaned. In the last few months, a ton of things had changed in his life. He was now single, he'd switched jobs, taken an apartment in a town that seemed to be full of strange people bent on running him out of Cedarwood and met a man who had the power to change his thinking. He hated being single. Hated it. He was the relationship type. Switching jobs was tolerable but not great. He'd rather be back in Cleveland, covering major news, but at least he had a job. As for the Coalition, they hadn't bothered him all that much. Once he started his series of articles and opinion pieces, the problems would probably ratchet up, but he'd deal with the fallout once it occurred.

As for the situation with Bobby... They hadn't exactly said they were dating. One night of sex and conversation didn't have to amount to the start of a relationship. He needed to keep an open mind and stop assuming things.

The announcer read off the names of the swimmers in the current heat. "Darcy Gagnon, lane three."

Remy snapped to attention. Darcy was Bobby's girl. He scooted over by the bleachers and focused on her. She wasn't very tall and didn't seem to have much to her. His heart leaped as the heat started. She sailed into the water and kept up with the girl on her left. He tucked his notebook into his bag and clapped. He wanted to see her win. He barely knew her, but so what?

As she touched the wall at the end of the heat, he blew out the breath he hadn't realized he'd held in. He didn't tend to get emotionally involved in the sporting events, but since he knew someone swimming...the circumstances had changed. His heart sank a little. Darcy finished second, but set a team record.

*Holy shit.* For being a tiny thing, she could really move.

He raked his fingers through his hair and headed out to the foyer. He'd do his interview out there. Plus, the cooler air would give him a chance to clear his head. He stood in front of the bank of windows and stared at the clouds. He'd always believed he wasn't a kid person. Always thought he wanted a dog or a cat, but no children. He liked Darcy and Chris. They busted his preconceived notions of how kids should behave. Not all kids were horrible, awful beings. If he could change his mind about Chris and Darcy, then why couldn't he allow himself to consider dating a guy with kids?

He noticed Bobby's reflection in the glass. "Hi again. That was a crazy heat."

"She did great, didn't she?" Bobby strode up to Remy. "Darce doesn't look like it, but she's a fish." He grinned but didn't make a move. "I swim, but nothing like that. I don't know where she got it, but I'm glad she did."

"I'll probably be writing about both of your kids before the end of the year." He marveled at Bobby's pride in his children. For a split second, he almost wished he had someone like Bobby or the kids in his life. But if he had Bobby around, then he'd be part of the family. The same old knot formed in his belly like it did whenever he thought about kids. He didn't have patience, but he had a temper. He swore when he got angry. He'd been known to take out his frustrations on a punching bag from time to time. Children required someone who could stand up to them while giving them a chance to screw up. He wanted perfection the first time around. *Jesus.* He was a jerk.

"This is just a summer team. She's not old enough for the school swim team. They won't take anyone until freshman year. We checked." Bobby shrugged. "She can't wait for ninth grade. I, on the other hand, don't want it to come. Time goes fast enough as it is."

"I bet the school can't wait for her to be old enough. They're probably already scouting her." Bobby wasn't kidding about time going by at warp speed. It seemed like only yesterday he was in college and dating his first boyfriend. Now? God, things had changed so much.

"The coach makes a point to talk to me at every meet," Bobby said. "They're supervised, but she's been training with the swim team on the weekends and probably will during the school year." He shook his head. "Hey, if she wants to swim, I'll make it possible.

Her grades are good and she's happy. I can't see a reason for her not to be in the pool."

"Nice." The guy seemed to be a dedicated family man. But Remy kept considering pushing Bobby away. *What the hell is wrong with me?*

Bobby turned his back on the windows and faced the people leaving the facility. "Hey, about the dinner invite. I didn't mean to be so forward." He bowed his head. "I forget sometimes that not everyone wants what happened the other night to be more than what it was."

*Fucking hell.* He gripped his notebook tighter and sighed. He'd screwed Bobby over so much, and all because he had his own fears. He feared he'd let his anger get the best of him in front of Bobby's kids and make a horrible impression. Anxiety hit him hard. He'd make mistakes. God knew he excelled at screwing up, but how long would he have to jack things up before Bobby gave him the ax? Another pang of fear swirled in his belly. He expected so much from those around him but wanted a pass for himself. He wasn't a good family man. He had too many worries and too much anxiety over things he couldn't control. He'd freak himself out and get into a bad situation. That was just his luck.

Were those worries justified? Not necessarily, but that didn't keep him from overthinking. Bobby hadn't welcomed him into the family and asked him to move in. They'd fucked and talked. Now he wanted Remy to go along with him to supper. How could he say no?

"It's cool. Just forget about it." Bobby smiled but didn't look Remy in the eye. "We're good."

"I accept," Remy blurted. His heart hammered and the knot was still in his stomach, but he didn't regret what he'd said.

"You what?"

He met Bobby's gaze. "I accept." He stood tall and smoothed the wrinkles in Bobby's shirt. "I'd love to go with you and the kids to dinner." Just saying the words was scary, but it felt right. He wasn't ready to give up, despite the potential roadblocks.

Bobby stared at him. "If you don't want to or you think I pushed, please, just say so." He didn't pull away or swat at Remy. "I'm not good at the dating thing, and I get it wrong more than I get it right."

He was nervous? Had problems dating? *No way.* Bobby was a handsome man. Anyone—gay or straight—would want to be with him. Remy glanced down the corridor at the remaining people leaving the facility, then focused on Bobby. He'd been given another chance with Bobby and refused to let it go. "Let me get this interview done, and I'll meet you at the restaurant." He inched closer to Bobby and dropped his voice to a whisper. "As for the other night, I wouldn't trade it for the world."

"Sounds good. See you in a few." Bobby grinned and strolled away.

He'd thought Bobby would be a little more hesitant about being with Remy in public, but no—and that was kind of nice.

Remy waited for the girl he'd been tasked with interviewing. He hoped she wouldn't take forever. He finally had a reason to leave and didn't want to blow it. The blonde girl strolled up the corridor.

"Mr. Nicholas?" She waved. "I'm ready. You're not taking my photo today, are you?"

"No." He hadn't even thought about it. "I'll grab the team picture. We can focus on you." He ran through the questions he had and verified her stats. Talking to the athletes wasn't hard, but he still wasn't used to being a sports reporter. When he'd finished with the interview, he thanked her.

"That was so much easier than I thought." She laughed and bobbed her head. "I thought you'd be that ginormous guy with the white hair. He's like ancient or something."

"I'm probably old enough to be your father, so I'm not far off from ancient." He smiled to hide his discomfort. Harvey, the ginormous guy she referred to, wasn't scary or that bad. "Thank you, and look for the feature later this week."

She grinned and waved, then bounded off.

Remy sighed and leaned against the wall. He had to get his notes sorted out and back into his bag before he lost them. When he looked up from his messenger bag, a woman with blonde streaks and a tight shirt stood next to him. She'd folded her arms, bunching her breasts in her blouse. She didn't smile or speak. Instead, she stared at him.

"May I help you?" he asked. He smoothed the front down on his bag. "Ma'am?"

"You spoke to my daughter."

"I did. She'll be the feature this week in *The Tribune*. Probably on Thursday, if you want to grab extra copies for friends and family." He'd given this speech so many times. The families wanted a paper for pretty much everyone they knew, and why not? It wasn't every day that a student made the news.

"Is that all?" she snapped.

"I believe so." He wasn't sure where she was going with her question.

"I'll be nice about this since there are still people around, but listen good." She sneered. "Please don't come back to the swim complex."

"It's a public place, and I was here on behalf of the paper." She was not going where he knew she wanted to go...

"You're giving the young minds the wrong idea," she growled.

"I'm sorry. How?" She'd gone there. "I'm confused." Fury boiled within him. He wasn't sure how long he'd be able to keep his composure. Young minds needed all of the facts and to know it wasn't wrong to be themselves. They didn't deserve to feel bad for being homosexual.

"You're gay." She practically choked on the word 'gay'. "This is a good town."

*Oh Christ.*

"This is a family situation. Go be gay somewhere else." She balled her fists. "Please."

"You're serious?" He snorted and gripped the strap of his bag. She had to be joking.

"We're trying to keep this place decent, reporter. Have someone else cover anything related to children. You're not welcome here, and I will call the law if I see you back at this complex." She glared at him. "Now leave."

Remy rolled his eyes, but kept his head held high as he walked away. He wasn't in the mood for her preaching or argument. She hadn't won, because he wasn't going to stop doing his job due to her objections. That was crap. He scanned the parking lot for Bobby or Bobby's car. *Nothing.* He headed to his vehicle and collapsed behind the wheel. The gravity of what the woman had said settled on his shoulders. He wasn't sure if she was part of the Coalition, but her rhetoric sure sounded like their chatter.

He groaned. He'd done his own damage to the day, but he had a bright spot — Bobby. Sure, there wasn't much of a chance they'd get together for more than a couple of platonic dates. He still wasn't convinced he could be with a guy with kids.

*Why do the great guys always come along when I haven't rectified my fucked-up self?*

# Chapter Five

Bobby sat against the wall and watched for Remy. He'd sensed the tension between them, despite Remy accepting the dinner date. He grabbed a piece of bread and dipped it into the olive oil. He sort of understood Remy's hesitance. Remy had probably felt cornered at the metro park and wasn't there to get hit on.

He hadn't really hit on Remy, though. He'd asked him to dinner so they could spend time together. Asking a guy out, especially with his kids involved, wasn't his idea of fun. So much could go wrong. But he liked Remy and wanted to introduce him to both of his children. He wanted his friends to like Remy rather than giving him reasons not to give Remy a chance.

He glanced over at the door one more time. Remy strode into the foyer, then made his way into the restaurant. Bobby's spirits soared. Remy had looked great at the festival and handsome at the metro park, but with his hair windblown and his collar open, he was hot as hell.

Bobby stood and pulled a chair out for Remy. "Hey. Glad you made it."

Remy hesitated, then crossed over to where Bobby stood.

"What's wrong?" Bobby's stomach clenched. "Something happen?"

"Nothing." Remy draped his bag on the back of the chair. "I didn't expect quite so many people."

"Oh." Bobby waved his fingers. "Some of the swim parents get together after the meets. Let me introduce you." He turned his attention to his dinner companions. "This is Shae and Bret. Their son is on the high school team. Archie and Lynn have the twin girls who swam with Darce. At the end of the table is Kell and Jayce. Their daughter, Jenna, swims and runs cross-country."

"Nice to meet you." Remy reached across the table and shook hands with the various parents. "That was a crazy meet. So much competition." He sank onto the chair beside Bobby. Although the others at the table spoke and held conversation, Remy didn't say anything beyond ordering his dinner.

Bobby wanted to pry, but he wasn't sure how to ask what was wrong. He toyed with his bread. Normally, the post-meet dinners were fun. Not tonight. He didn't understand what had gone wrong with Remy. He'd thought Remy would enjoy the new group of friends and the positive atmosphere. He bided his time, but was happy when Remy added here and there to the general conversation.

Once the other couples had left and Christopher and Darcy were engrossed in the driving arcade game at the restaurant, Bobby made his move.

"So," Bobby said.

"So." Remy sat back in his chair and folded his hands on his lap. "You've got kids. I wasn't expecting that."

"Yeah." He glanced over at Chris and Darcy, then back to Remy. "I was married for a while." If the idea of him having children threw Remy for a loop, this would knock the man completely down.

"No shit?" Remy's jaw tensed and the muscle twitched. "Man or woman?"

"Helene. A woman. She wanted to get married." He rarely spoke about her or how they'd ended up married. For whatever reason, he wanted to tell Remy.

"Oh. A chick." He nodded. "Explains why Darcy looks like you."

"Yeah, poor kid. Her mother was beautiful." He chuckled. "That was a fucked-up situation. Helene thought she could fix me. She didn't, and it was a disaster, but I got Darcy and Chris out of the deal. We adopted Chris after he'd been a foster kid in our home for two years. He was already older than Darcy, but I couldn't give him up. I'm glad we went through with it. He's a great kid." Of all the things he wished he could change about his marriage, his children weren't among the regrets. He'd grown up and learned a lot along the way, so maybe it wasn't a total loss like he sometimes believed.

"That's cool. I never married anyone, and I haven't been with a chick. Not even Julia."

Bobby draped his arm across the back of Remy's chair and rubbed the tips of his fingers across Remy's shoulder blades. "You're not a kid person, are you?"

"I don't know how to relate to them." Remy averted his gaze. "No clue."

"Like people?" Bobby suppressed a snort. Neil had been the same. He couldn't relate to kids and didn't try. Chris and Darcy were inconvenient baggage, as Neil used to say.

"You're funny." Remy met Bobby's gaze. He smiled.

Was Remy nervous? Or was he coming around a bit? Bobby hoped he was warming up to the kids. "It's true. Don't talk down to them or try to be their buddy. Be real." He nodded to the other end of the restaurant. "The kids don't know you, but I don't have that sinking feeling in my belly. They encouraged me to get out into the dating scene, so consider yourself honored."

Remy's smile widened. "I do." The muscle in his jaw twitched again. "Fuck."

"What?" Bobby sat up straighter. "What's wrong?"

"Nothing."

Something was bothering Remy, and Bobby wanted to know what, damn it. "I'm done, and it looks like you are too. Why don't I round up the kids and we go back to the house? They'll want to swim or goof off in the pool. We can talk on the deck."

Remy met Bobby's gaze again and nodded. "I'd like that."

"Follow me. I'll get the kids." He gathered up his bill and placed some money on the table for a tip. He headed over to the racing game. "Ready?"

Chris slid off his chair first. Darcy swerved again, then joined her brother.

"Is that your boyfriend, Dad?" Darcy asked. She removed the elastic from her hair and fixed her ponytail, then put the elastic back. "Can I meet him?"

"Sure." He stepped aside and motioned to Remy. "Darcy, this is my friend Remy. Remy, this is my daughter Darcy."

She grinned. "Hi. I've seen you at the pool before. You're the sports guy. My friend Annabelle thinks you're hot." She shrugged. "She thinks everyone is hot."

Chris rolled his eyes. "Last week Annabelle said Dad was hot, for an old guy."

Remy smothered a grin behind his hand, then composed himself. "I'm glad I got to meet you."

"Okay, let's go. If you want pool time when we get home, we have to get moving." Bobby stopped at the cashier and paid the bill. He grabbed Remy's bill and added that to his own.

"You don't have to," Remy said.

"I invited you." Bobby collected his change, then made his way out to the parking lot. He stopped at his car. "I'm on Evergreen Road. Five-sixteen."

"I know whereabouts that is. I'll follow you, though." Remy mock saluted, then climbed behind the wheel of his car.

Bobby settled on the driver's seat in his vehicle. He expected a barrage of comments from Chris and Darcy. Instead, his daughter cuddled up to her sleeping bag and closed her eyes. Chris twiddled with his phone.

"I invited Remy over tonight." Bobby glanced back at them in the rearview mirror. "Is that okay?" *Kind of late to ask them now, but oh well.*

"I'm cool with it." Chris nodded to his sister. "She's out, so I doubt she cares."

"Thanks." He drove the rest of the way home in silence. He couldn't wait to hear from the swim parents what they thought of Remy. He'd been pleasant enough, yes, but Bobby could tell there was something bothering him.

He turned onto the driveway and parked in the garage. Unlike the rest of the time, he left the garage door open. "Go inside and change or whatever you want to do to go to the pool. I'll be there in a few minutes."

Darcy didn't say anything as she left the back seat. Chris grinned and headed into the house behind her.

Bobby waited on the trunk of his car until Remy pulled in. He waved.

Remy parked. "Holy shit. This is a nice house."

"I got a good deal." He shrugged. "Mom knew the people who were moving out, and it had a pool."

"Sweet." Remy clicked the lock on his car. "I guess I expected something smaller."

"Sometimes people and things aren't always how you think they should be." He waved his arm. "How about a tour?"

"Sounds good." Remy fell into step beside him. "Nice job, putting me in front of the firing squad."

"The other parents?" He hadn't thought about it like that. He pressed the fob to close the garage and unlocked the front door to the house. He held the door for Remy. "Sorry. They're nice people."

"And not like the Coalition."

*Fuck.* Bobby stepped into the living room. "Want a beer? We can hang out on the deck."

"I'd love one."

"As you can see, this is the formal living room and foyer. Nothing too exciting and mostly empty because we don't use them. The family room is through there. The kids watch movies and leave it a mess, but I can deal." He gestured to the short hallway. "Can't miss the kitchen. The deck's through the sliding doors."

"You need a dog." Remy stuffed both hands into his jeans pockets. "Just seems like it would fit in."

"I've thought about it." He grabbed two bottles of beer from the fridge. "I bet Chris and Darce would love one."

"Probably." Remy strode out to the deck and gasped. "Holy shit. This is really nice. I never would've thought this was back here."

"The former owners loved landscaping and made sure the stuff in the house was top notch." He handed Remy a beer. "Have a seat."

"Thanks." Remy sat beside him at the table. "I bet Darcy loves the pool."

"It's helped, yeah. She does laps with her brother." He leaned back in his seat. "If it weren't for those parents, I would've been so lost when I came back to Cedarwood. They've welcomed me in and don't hold judgment. It's nice, and they're real people."

Remy downed part of the beer, then sighed. "The mother of the girl I interviewed stopped me. She banned me from the swim complex." The emotion drained away from Remy's words, and the sparkle left his eyes. He picked at the label on his bottle. "She accused me of putting ideas into the heads of the children on the swim team."

Bobby nearly choked on his beer. "What?"

"Because I'm gay." He groaned. "She doesn't know me from Adam, but she was right there reminding me I'm not as good as the rest of the people there." Remy shook his head. "It wouldn't have been so bad if I'd been a little more prepared for her. But it's done now. I knew someone would say something, but I held on to hope nothing would happen."

"She had no right." *Jesus.* "Most of the parents there aren't like her, I promise. They know I'm out and haven't treated me any differently."

"She saw me touch you." Remy stared at him. "Whatever. She's probably part of that group." He scrubbed the back of his hand across his mouth. "You invited me to dinner tonight, but I'm not sure of your phone number."

"What?" Bobby gripped the arm of his chair. "I did say something. I told you I had to get to work, and I think I said something along the lines of I'd put my number in your phone. I could swear I asked you to call me. I tried to wake you, but you wouldn't budge."

"Wish I would've." Remy rested his head on the back of the chair and sprawled out. "Now I feel silly. I got ahead of myself and forgot to even look. You've got to think I'm horrible."

"You were tired, and it was a long night. Don't sweat it." He grasped Remy's hand. "We're together now and can exchange numbers properly."

"I've got so many hang-ups." Remy squeezed Bobby's fingers. "I'm a mess."

"And I've got kids. Makes us both human and fallible." He chuckled. He could see them together on the deck with grandchildren and being perfectly happy together. He should've been unnerved. He wasn't one to go from just meeting to thinking about the future together, but something about Remy called to him.

"Are you suggesting we give this a go and be whatever we are together?" Remy asked.

"I don't invite just anyone home to meet my kids." He smiled and met Remy's gaze. "How about we go on a few dates? Get to know each other? I've never gone slow with a relationship in my life." But something about Remy made him want to savor each moment.

"You're not afraid to go public with me?" Remy scooted his chair closer to Bobby's. "Even with the Coalition around?"

He shook his head. He'd considered the issues with the irritating group, but at some point the garbage had to stop. He wasn't doing anything wrong or conducting his life in a way that would bring negativity. *Screw the Coalition.*

"Cool." Remy palmed Bobby's thigh. "I feel better about the article already."

"What article?"

"Your mother's friend Maureen wants to create a group to counteract the Coalition. They aren't going to be organized, but still. They want to show the town that no matter who you are or who you love, we accept you. It's a good idea." Remy shrugged. "We had the festival and that was fine, but there's more that can be done."

"You're a revolutionary as well as handsome? I might have to keep you around." Bobby draped his arm around the back of Remy's chair. The more they talked, the more he liked Remy.

"You'd be one of the few." Remy sprawled out on his seat. He folded his hands on his belly and crossed his ankles. "I decided to major in journalism because I thought one of the guys in the class was hot." He chuckled. "Imagine that. I based my whole career on someone's looks. But once I was in the field, I loved it. My folks didn't understand. Not like I had them around." He gestured to the pool. "That's where the kids are lucky. You're involved. My dad paid no attention to me. For all I know, he wasn't even my biological father. I was a problem. Until I got older, they

had no use for me. My parents were really old-school —
kids are not to be seen or heard."

"I'm sorry to hear that." Bobby toyed with the hairs
at the base of Remy's skull. He loved guys with just
enough hair to pull but not enough to braid. Boy, was
Remy's hair soft.

"I'm not. The guy was an ass. He hated me and
swore I wasn't going to amount to anything other than
a fat kid who ate chocolate all day."

"Ouch." *Christ. How could anyone say that to a kid?*
Bobby couldn't imagine even thinking that about Chris
or Darcy. If his children realized they were gay or
wanted to paint for a living or pretty much anything
that wasn't illegal, he'd back them.

"I went to college to rebel. Get the fuck out of the
house and start my own life. Thank God I was smart
enough to get a scholarship. If it wasn't for that, I'd
have been screwed." Remy looked over at Bobby. "I
went to the gym on campus every day. I decided come
hell or high water, I wasn't going to be that fat kid, but
when I look in the mirror…I still see him staring back
at me."

Bobby's heart went out to Remy. "How many
boyfriends have you had?"

Remy sighed and laced his fingers together on his
stomach. "Five, and none lasted more than a couple of
months. Jaden said I was too hard to live with —
although we never lived together. Dominic couldn't be
faithful if his life depended on it, and my first boyfriend
lived to remind me I'd never be a club kid. I couldn't
do heroin chic or the makeup. Seth and Dale were just
plain mistakes."

"Nothing wrong with knowing who you really are
and accepting what you don't like." Or having

standards. "Terry and I didn't work out because he wanted to travel. All through the year, he had to be going somewhere. Most of it was for work, but there were times I think he took off because he had a guy on the side." Bobby caressed the back of Remy's neck. "Neil was another story. He hated my kids. Never took the time to get to know them. All he wanted was sex and a place to crash after clubbing. I thought I could get him to settle down."

"He was hot as hell, wasn't he?"

Bobby detected the note of disdain in Remy's voice. Bobby wasn't a saint by any means, but he also wasn't about to walk away from Remy. He reminded Bobby of a wounded puppy — the guy needed a confidence boost from someone he could trust. Bobby understood. He'd been there too. "Yeah, but looks aren't everything. You can be the sexiest man alive, but if you're not willing to accept my kids or all of the fucked-up parts of me, then sexy means nothing."

Remy nodded and gazed back over the pool. "I never told anyone about my old man. I guess no one wanted to listen." He smiled and the muscle in his jaw tensed. "Or you make talking easy. That might be it."

"Maybe." He saw Remy in a different light. Each time Remy spoke, he revealed a bit more about himself. Bobby respected him for giving Bobby the chance to get to know him instead of pushing Bobby away.

Bobby turned his attention to Chris and Darcy. The sun had dipped low on the horizon, and the lights ringing the pool came on. He didn't mind a little night swimming, but after the day they'd had, he wanted Darcy to rest. "Hey, guys? Why don't you pack it in for the night? It's past sunset."

Darcy splashed her brother, then climbed out of the pool. Chris left the water and wrapped his towel around his midsection. He headed into the house, but Darcy hesitated.

"Are you coming in?" she asked. She clutched the towel and dripped water on the deck.

"Once I turn on the security system back here and clean up, yeah, I'm coming in." He stood. She hadn't asked him anything like that in a long time. Was she upset that Remy was there? He'd have to ask later.

"Are you staying?" She grinned at Remy. "Maybe you can write about me. I'll show you my trophies."

Remy scrambled off the chair and stood. He stuffed his hands into his pockets. "Not tonight, but if you keep up swimming like you did today, I'm sure I'll write about you soon enough. You did a great job at the meet."

"Thanks." She beamed and stole a glance at her father before she strolled into the house.

Remy kept his head low and nudged an acorn across the deck. He waited until Darcy had disappeared into the house before he spoke. "They're good kids. I'm glad I met them." He straightened his shirt. "I should go. I took up a lot of your family time."

Bobby grasped Remy's hand. "You're fine." He tugged Remy to his chest. "I like you being here." Hell, he liked Remy and wanted to keep dating him.

"You might like it, but this is your time with your kids—not me. I'm sorry." Remy sighed. "God. One of these days I'll get better at relationships."

"You have nothing to be sorry about." He slid his palms along Remy's sides, then up his shoulders. He brushed a kiss over Remy's lips. "How about you go with us to Chris' 5k run on Thursday? It's short notice,

I know, and you'll probably have to work. But think about it." He'd stepped out of his comfort zone by asking Remy to stay over, but he didn't want to let the opportunity pass him by.

"The Ford Open in Windham? I'm covering it for the paper."

"Oh." His spirits sank. *Well, shit.*

"It doesn't matter what time I get there or who I'm with as long as I cover the event. You'll want to get to the course early, though." Remy slid his hands into Bobby's back pockets.

"Come over Wednesday night. The kids go to bed around ten, but Wednesday they'll hit the hay closer to nine. We'll go together in the morning." As he sorted out the details, he liked the plan. He wanted to move on with his life and have Remy there for the journey. *Fuck the past and my hang-ups with Neil. Fuck the Coalition and their ridiculous rules.* He and Remy deserved to be happy and find a path together.

"You're not worried?"

"Nah. I've always said I want my kids to feel free to be themselves. If I'm hiding who I am, then I'm not setting a good example." He cupped Remy's jaw. "There's no shame in being yourself."

"True." Remy kissed him and nipped Bobby's bottom lip. He rubbed his crotch against the bulge in Bobby's jeans, then held him tighter to Remy's body. When he broke the connection, Remy sighed. "I'll call you — since I know I've got your number."

"Call me whenever." He let go of Remy long enough to drape his arm around Remy's waist. With Remy at his side, they walked through the house to the front porch.

In front of the entire neighborhood — not that anyone was particularly watching — Remy kissed him again. Bobby's lips tingled and blood rushed to his cock. If they weren't in public, he'd have Remy against the side of the house and begging to come. Part of him wanted Remy to stay the night, but the rest of him wanted to slow things down. *Christ.* Once he got a hard-on, his brain disengaged. He tucked his fingers into Remy's front pockets.

"So this piece about the Coalition…what exactly are you going to write?" He bumped noses with Remy. "You did just kiss me in public."

"I did." His voice dropped an octave. "Gonna try to dissuade me from doing it?"

"Nope. You're being yourself, and it's sexy."

Remy blushed and smiled. He kissed him again and whimpered. "I've been thinking about the article — a lot. The easy thing would be to allow my emotions to take control and write an inflammatory piece. It'd be no sweat, since I'm still pissed about the incident at the metro park."

"Her comments were uncalled for." His protective streak kicked in. If the woman had said something to Chris or Darcy, he would've come unglued. Knowing Remy was dealing with shit like that pissed him off just as much.

"I agree." Remy threaded his arms around Bobby's waist and rested his head on Bobby's shoulder.

"But killing them with kindness is better than pissing everyone off. I know you'd like to. Trust me, I'd like to give her a piece of my mind."

"How so?" Remy stood tall and met Bobby's gaze. "I don't disagree, but I'm dying to hear your thoughts."

He shrugged. "You're a businessman, though. So yeah, I can see where you'd want to keep everyone happy."

"That's true but not my point," Bobby said. "An emotional piece tinged with hate, even unspoken hate, fuels the fire. It shows them they can get to you, and once they've got an in, it's hard to get them to back down. If I were writing, and don't ask because creative writing and I are not friends, I'd write something positive about what people from all walks of life in Cedarwood are doing. There's a lot of good in this town that no one knows about. The Coalition can get mad about plenty of things but not people who are being nice and positive."

"They can and will, but you're right. You're the bigger man, too." Remy grinned. "I like it."

"It's always about size." Bobby kissed Remy again. He'd never get enough of the way the man tasted or how he made Bobby feel.

"Your size works fine for me," Remy murmured.

"You'll make me blush, and I don't do that often." He held on to Remy and swayed to the music playing in his head. "This is happening crazy fast, but I don't want this night to end."

"I know how you feel. It's the same for me, but I don't have kids." Remy kissed him once more, this time drawing Bobby's tongue into his mouth. He sucked on Bobby's tongue and swallowed Bobby's moan. When he broke the connection, he eased away from Bobby. "I'll call you tomorrow and see you Wednesday, if not before."

"Promise?" He hadn't asked that question about a date in forever. But Remy made him giddy for their next moments together.

"I do." He winked, then stepped off the porch. "See you."

"Yeah." Bobby watched Remy climb into his car, then back down the driveway. He waited until Remy disappeared down the street before he headed into the house. He closed and locked the door, then collapsed on the closest chair.

Bobby touched his lips. The tingling hadn't gone away. He sank back on the seat and closed his eyes. Remy wasn't the guy he'd expected. No, he was more complex and interesting. Hot, smart and a good fuck as well as a good conversationalist — when he got Remy to relax. So Remy wasn't a fan of the kids. At least he saw them as decent human beings, not an inconvenience. Maybe Bobby could get him to come around.

Remy didn't strike him the same way Neil had. Neil had voiced his dislike for the kids from the first moment he met them. He wasn't willing to come around when they were home or did so under duress. Remy hadn't jumped into the pool or anything, but when the kids talked to him, he treated them like equals. Neil never would've done that.

Bobby opened his eyes and grinned. For the first time since he'd met Neil, his heart was light. The dread he'd carried around since Terry had left wasn't there. He had hope for the future. Would he have a chance at long-term with Remy? He wasn't sure, but there was the possibility.

He turned off the lights downstairs, then made his way to the second floor. When he peeked in on Darcy, she'd already fallen asleep. He kissed her forehead, then closed her door most of the way.

Light was visible beneath Chris' door. He crossed the hallway and knocked first. The door opened. Chris had his tablet on his lap and one earbud in. He looked up when Bobby stood in the doorway.

"Hey." Chris yanked the single earbud free. "Did your boyfriend leave?"

"He did." He leaned against the doorframe. "Well? What'd you think?" Chris' opinion wouldn't make or break the relationship, but he wanted to know from the start if there were issues.

"He's nicer than Neil." Chris closed the tablet and tucked his legs under his body. He rested his elbows on his knees. "I didn't get squicked by him, if that's what you mean."

*Good to know.* "I asked him to come along with me to your 5k this week."

"Think he'll write something about me in the paper?"

"Maybe, if you do well enough, but that's not why I invited him."

Chris shrugged. "Whatever."

"If you don't like him, I want to know. You were dead on with Neil. I don't know how you do it, but you've got a sixth sense for this stuff. Be honest with me." He still wanted to see Remy, but if Chris had a problem, then he'd re-evaluate the situation.

"Dad, you're smiling. I haven't seen you do that since before Neil. Not the plastic smiles like you do in your business photos or for the website, but a real one. Darcy noticed too. I think she's got a crush on him."

He snorted. *Wonderful.* If things didn't work out, then she'd be crushed too.

"He was weird at the dinner, but maybe he hates crowds." Chris shrugged again and stretched out on his bed. "If he makes you happy, then you got my vote."

"Thanks, kid. Get some rest. You've got practice in the morning, don't you?"

"Every day but Sunday." Chris grinned and yanked the blankets over himself. "Good thing I like running."

"Yes, it is. Night, kid." He closed Chris' door most of the way and waited for the light to go off before he headed down the hall. He flipped the light on in his bedroom and sighed, then turned the light back off again. *What a week.* He collapsed on his bed and closed his eyes. He hadn't expected to meet the handsome man from the running trails, much less go home with him. He'd never have thought a friendship would've formed between him and Remy, if for no other reason than he hadn't worked up the courage to talk to him until Remy had made the first move. He rolled onto his back and stared at the ceiling. Streaks of moonlight filtered across the room. He had two kids, a mortgage and bills to worry about, and the only thing on his mind was Remy. Love wasn't possible after a week and one round of sex, but there was something about Remy. He shook his head. He'd been called an adoring fool once or twice. Never by Helene or Neil, but others had said it. Was he? He hadn't been starry-eyed with Remy, per se. More like hormonally charged. Still, he couldn't wait to hear Remy's voice on the line or feel Remy's body against his.

Maybe he was a romantic and just needed the right person to make him see the light.

# Chapter Six

Remy unlocked the little door to his mailbox and grabbed the letters before he headed to his apartment. Bone-deep weariness filled him, but the desire to create was strong too. He tucked the letters under his arm and opened his door. Once inside, he tossed the mail onto the couch and locked up. He kicked out of his running shoes and left the messenger bag on the table.

He poured a glass of red wine, then flipped through the various letters. Three bills, two credit card applications, political ads, a magazine featuring sports heroes, and two legal-size envelopes with his name and address on them, but nothing more. *Odd.* He tossed the credit card applications into the shredder and recycled the political ads. He organized the bills with the others, then focused on the plain envelopes.

His address had been handwritten on the front and there was no return address. He tapped the second envelope on the table. *Open or not?* The flap on the back came unglued. He toyed with the loose edge. Nothing spilled out, so that was a plus. He'd read stories about the Coalition being accused of sending powder-laced letters. This one didn't leak anything, so hopefully no one was trying to kill him. He shook the letter from the envelope, then unfolded the page.

*Are you out of a job? Are you having a hard time finding another? Do you believe you were let go on account of your sexuality — because you're straight and a gay person now holds your position? Then the Coalition wants you.*

He groaned and crumpled up the page. *Good God.* Did this group have no bottom? No limits to what they'd try to do? He remembered what Maureen had said. Not all of Cedarwood agreed with the Coalition. Was this their Hail Mary, last-ditch attempt to get rid of anyone they didn't like? Or a fishing expedition?

He opened the second letter. The rhetoric was the same, but the wording was a little different. He balled the paper up and tossed it into the trash with the first one.

What kind of message was this sending to anyone in the gay community who hadn't come out? He picked up his glass of wine and downed half of the Merlot. He had to do something. Maureen had encouraged him, and Bobby had mentioned a better route than going off. He sighed, then grabbed his tablet and the little keyboard from his bag.

He sat at the table, wine close by, and opened a blank document. He still had the interview to write up as well as a report on the swim meet, but those could wait. He needed to get these words out first.

He grinned as he typed. He'd considered writing an editorial piece about the town and its wealth of shops and restaurants. If one was willing to look, there was culture all over the place. Not everyone in town wanted to run the undesirables out past the city limits. He knew just how to write up his first anti-Coalition piece and show everyone Cedarwood was a great place to live.

Remy worked for the next five hours on the article, taking short breaks here and there to stretch or refill his glass. He downed the majority of the bottle before he finished the first page. He sat back in his seat and reread the article. He took pride in all his work, but this article had a certain sparkle to it. He wasn't doing this small act of disobedience for himself. This was for the kids who were starting to realize who they were, the people stuck in the closet and afraid to come out, and all of the people who didn't give a rip about another person's sexuality. They deserved a voice and to see the community was full of opportunity.

He saved the article and pounded through the interview as well as the write-up on the swim meet. When he'd finished those, he wrote an email to Maureen. She'd love to know what he'd done. He sent her a copy, hoping she'd have input for him.

When he finally shut down his tablet for the night, the weariness he'd felt all along hit him hard. He carried his glass to the sink and trudged into his bedroom. He should've brushed his teeth or at least stripped down to his underwear but didn't bother. He hadn't looked at the clock, but by his rough estimate, it had to be nearly three in the morning. He nestled in his bed and cuddled the other pillow to his chest. He hadn't done anything revolutionary in writing his article. Hell, some might consider it a fluff piece, but damn it, he'd made the town look good. There was a thriving art community in Cedarwood, and he was determined to let everyone see it. Remy drifted off to sleep, and the dreams started right away.

\* \* \* \*

He wasn't in his bed but rather in a field. He should've recognized the location, but none of the trees looked familiar. He dragged a deep breath into his lungs. The scent of pine and cologne wafted on the breeze. The smells were familiar but confusing. He shielded his eyes from the sun and drank in his surroundings. How was he the only one there?

"You're not alone." Bobby strolled up to him. He grinned and stuffed his hands into his jeans pockets. "What's wrong?"

"I—I don't know." Was there anything the matter? He didn't think so.

"You look like you're a million miles away." Bobby dropped to his knees in front of Remy. "Let me take your mind off your problems." He opened Remy's pants and shoved the denim around his ankles.

Remy shivered as the cool air wrapped around him. When he glanced down at Bobby, he realized Bobby was still fully clothed, but Remy had forgotten his underwear.

Bobby caressed Remy's shaft and rubbed the blunt head of Remy's cock over his lips.

"Oh damn." Remy wobbled. His entire being tingled. As Bobby engulfed Remy's dick in his mouth, Remy curled forward. He threaded his fingers into Bobby's short hair. His nerve endings were on fire.

"Like that?" Bobby asked around Remy's erection.

"Yes." He needed more. *Holy shit.* From his head to his toes, he tensed. The heat in his lower belly spiraled through his veins. He rocked his hips, shoving his cock in and out of Bobby's mouth. Dear God, he was so close. *Already.* He jammed his dick between Bobby's lips and gritted his teeth. He squeezed his eyes shut. He couldn't slow down. Not now. He pistoned his hips. Blood rushed through his veins.

"What?" Bobby asked.

Remy opened his eyes and glanced down at his lover. "Huh?"

Bobby stood and stepped away from Remy. "I need to go."

*When I'm on the verge of fucking coming? What the hell?* Remy widened his stance and focused on Bobby. "What do you mean?" He blinked and noticed the group of people milling around them. Some shouted and others held signs. None of the people appeared to be happy.

"We're in public." Bobby wiped his mouth with the back of his hand. "I don't know you out here. I can't. It's bad for business."

Remy stuffed his dick back into his pants and growled. Bobby had pricked his ego and pissed him off. He disliked when a guy stopped the blow job just before the big O and really hated Bobby's switch in attitude. Bad for business... *What the fuck?*

"What's going on?" Remy asked. He buttoned his pants, then grabbed Bobby's arm. "I thought you liked me."

"I can't. They're watching. They're always watching." Bobby shrugged away and disappeared into the crowd.

"Bobby. Wait. Stop." He couldn't see Bobby through the wandering people. Remy pushed through the crowd and tried to chase his lover. The more he moved forward, the more people showed up and blocked him. "Bobby?"

A woman with black hair tugged into a bun stepped in front of him. "Get out of Cedarwood."

"No," he snapped. "This is my home too." *Just try to run me out of this Goddamn town.*

"We don't want you here," a man in a business suit said. He held a sign proclaiming Cedarwood should be a moral town.

"So what if you don't want me here? I'm staying." He needed to find Bobby.

"You'll never work for another news organization." Another man, this one in a T-shirt and jeans, rested his hands on his hips. "This is a town for families. Not for people like you."

He stepped toe to toe with the man, but instead of responding, everything went black. Remy swatted at the air. Was he falling? He didn't know where the hell he was, and it freaked him out. A shiver ran the length of his spine and his blood chilled.

"Bobby." His lover's name ripped from his throat, and his chest ached. What had he done? Why was this happening? He wasn't a bad guy. He simply had fallen for another man and wasn't interested in fucking a woman. *What the fucking hell?*

\* \* \* \*

Remy sat up and opened his eyes. He gasped for breath. As he woke up fully, he realized where he was—in his room. Six-forty-five a.m. Rain splattered on the windows and clicked against the glass. *Holy shit.* He hadn't gone anywhere, and the whole mess had been a dream. He wiped his face with both hands, then reached for his phone. He scrolled through his emails. Each one he'd sent the night before had gone through. His work was in, and even Maureen had responded.

*This is great. Nothing offensive, and it makes the art community look fabulous. Great job. It's going to print.*

At least she was happy.

Remy collapsed on the bed. With all his work turned in and no appointments until after lunch, he could sleep a little while longer. *Good thing.* The dream had shaken him to his core. Between the wine and his blossoming feelings for Bobby, as well as his concerns over the Coalition, he'd worn his brain out.

He closed the apps on his phone, but the email icon blinked. Out of habit, he retrieved the message and frowned when he read the name. *Dale Emery.*

He'd worked with Dale at one of the news channels in Cleveland. Hell, now he couldn't remember which, because he'd made the rounds at each station. They'd dated while they'd worked together, and the moment Remy had been transferred to a different one, Dale's calls had stopped. It hadn't been a long relationship — four dates and a lot of sex — but still. He wondered what in the name of God Dale wanted now, after so much time had passed.

He read through the email and sighed.

*Hadn't talked in a while and someone mentioned your name at the station. Missed you. Still do. Have my number still? Call me so we can catch up.*
*D.*

Remy frowned. He'd wanted Dale so much when they'd worked together. It wasn't love between them — not after four dates — but God, he'd admired the guy. Dale read the news on television. Everyone knew him, even if he wasn't ready to come out of the closet.

Remy closed the email and the app, then tossed the phone onto the mattress. He had Bobby in his life. Why would he want an old flame who wasn't really interested? Especially if he had no real idea what Dale wanted? He didn't love Dale and wasn't interested in being with him, but he'd probably email Dale back — later.

He closed his eyes and settled into the blankets. He'd worry about his ex and Bobby later. He needed sleep, strong coffee and a run before he could deal with them. He yanked the comforter over his head and succumbed to sleep. Hopefully, this time, there wouldn't be any fucked-up dreams.

* * * *

Remy rolled over and sighed. He stared at the ceiling, then picked up his phone. According to the clock, he'd slept five hours. He stretched and tossed the device back onto the bedding. He probably could use another couple of hours, but he needed to get moving if he was going to make the hot stove league baseball game in time.

He showered, shaved and tried not to think about Bobby and Dale. He shook his head as he stared at his reflection in the mirror. He needed to stop being so hard on himself. He wasn't a bad-looking guy. Maybe a little odd — he wore his hair shaggy, but kempt — his eyes seemed too light for the shade of his hair and his lack of a tan, but he hadn't altered anything other than losing the hundred pounds back in college.

He flexed his arms and sucked in his stomach. The more he looked at himself, the more he didn't see the flaws. The years of running showed in his toned arms and legs. He still had a bit of a paunch in his belly, but nothing a few sit-ups wouldn't help fix.

The words of his former therapist came to mind. At some point Remy needed to move past the bad things in his life and embrace the good. If he wanted something, then the logical step was to do what needed to be done in order to attain it.

Then who did he want? He wanted closure with Dale and a few more dates with Bobby. He crinkled his nose, then squared his shoulders. He could do this. He could get what he wanted. The dream didn't matter, and neither did the Coalition. He wasn't doing anything wrong by living his life, and Bobby had been right — he should be an example to the next generation. No fear, no shame.

Remy dressed and tucked his phone into his back pocket. He grabbed his tablet, keyboard and notebook, then his keys, and made his way downstairs. He still had Dale's number in his phone. As long as the sequence hadn't changed, he should be able to get in touch with his former boyfriend. He settled behind the wheel of his car, plunked his bag on the passenger seat, then set his phone to speaker and called Dale.

The phone rang as he backed out of his parking spot. Three rings later, Remy got an answer. "Hello?"

*Hmm.* That didn't sound like Dale. The voice was lower. "May I speak to Dale Emery?" he asked.

"This is. Remy? Is that you?"

Remy gripped the steering wheel and turned onto the main road through Cedarwood. "You sent me an email. What's up?" He tried to sound casual, but easy conversation had never been his strong suit.

"I talked to Pepper Dennings. Remember her?" Dale asked.

"Sure." Who could forget Pepper? *Good Lord.* She was the only anchor on television with blood-red hair and the palest skin. Whichever channel she was on, she held everyone's attention. "How is she?"

Pepper only noticed him when she needed something or someone. She used people and only cared about herself. As soon as she stepped in front of the camera, she grabbed the spotlight. He didn't dislike her for her drive or her appeal in the media. He'd fallen under her spell too. He wished he could be as forthright and determined as Pepper.

"She's fine. She moved to Chicago and got married. I called her the other day because we had some of her files here at the station. She asked me how everyone was doing, and your name came up." Dale paused. "She wanted to know if you had ever gotten in front of the camera. She thought you had a brilliant presence at the news desk."

"I see." He hadn't expected her to say that—any of it—but then he wondered if it was really Dale asking the question and adding Pepper in to make it sound more important. Dale had a tendency to make things sound bigger than they were in order to get what he wanted. He bit back a groan. *So what does Dale want?*

"I told her you'd left the station."

"Fired was more like it. They downsized and I had the least seniority." Depending on how he looked at the situation, it was a blessing or a curse. Bad because he wanted a chance to be on one of the daily broadcasts and to get his name out there for possibly bigger opportunities. Good because if he hadn't come to Cedarwood, he wouldn't have met Maureen, his one friend Sully, or Bobby and the kids. He smiled and his spirits lifted a bit. Bobby. His cock strained against his pants and he had to shift in his seat. He couldn't wait to see Bobby on Wednesday.

"Right," Dale said, grabbing Remy's attention. "Anyway, are you seeing anyone?"

"Yes." He wasn't about to lie. He and Bobby had a thing. Bobby had introduced him to his kids. Maybe he wasn't wild about children, but he liked Bobby and wanted to be around him. He stopped at the traffic light closest to the newspaper building and adjusted his jeans to relieve the pressure on his dick.

"According to the gossip—I've got friends here in town—you and an accountant there in Cedarwood got together." Dale chuckled. "Really? You settled for an accountant? He does taxes too, for God's sake."

*What does Bobby's profession have to do with anything?* "What's your point? I'm late for work."

"Where? I thought you were out of the media biz."

Remy rolled his eyes and turned into the newspaper's parking lot. For a guy who knew all about Remy's love life, Dale knew nothing about Remy's job situation. *What a great news anchor...* "I'm doing print media. Sports and lifestyle features at *The Cedarwood Tribune.*"

"You're kidding? You hate sports and detested writing for newspapers," Dale replied. "You wouldn't know a baseball from a football."

"One ball's brown and one's white. Now what is your point? I need to get to work." He parked and turned off the car. He'd never said anything to Dale about his preferences for journalism. He liked having the flexibility to write for either medium if given the opportunity. Plus, he wanted to branch out into more electronic media. A podcast or maybe webisodes for the paper. He'd worry about those later, but they weren't far from his mind.

"You learned something out there in the sticks," Dale said with a snort.

"If you just wanted to catch up, then cool, but I have to get going." He didn't want to talk to Dale any longer was more like it.

"I wanted to know if you were coming to Cleveland anytime soon. I miss you and wanted to club. Maybe we could rekindle the fire you know is still there." Dale's voice dropped to a murmur. "We never really ended things properly. How about we take up where we left off? My bed or yours?"

"Dale." *Shit*. This wasn't what he'd expected would happen. What in the name of God was Dale's vested interest in starting over?

"I love it when you say my name. You were always my favorite fuck," Dale said. "Such a sexy bottom. I want to tunnel that ass. I could get lost in your eyes."

He wasn't turned on by Dale's dirty talk, and he'd never sleep with Dale again. "You didn't like me that much when we were together or whatever you called what we did. What are you doing? Slumming? Trying to get right with God, or maybe you're with a counselor?"

"Jesus. This is how you play everything. You don't trust anyone. What if I'm actually interested and wanted to see you again? For old time's sake? You liked what we had," Dale said, venom in his voice.

He rolled down his window and rested his arm on the doorframe. He needed some air and a whole lot less of Dale. "I'm not interested. I've got a great guy in my life, and I'm happy. I know that's not what you want to hear, but it's how it's going to be." He glanced at himself in the rearview mirror and grinned. Standing up for himself wasn't his strong suit, but he'd done it. *Halle-fucking-lujah.* Maybe he had a backbone after all.

"You'd really pass up another go-round with me for an accountant? One with kids? You hate kids," Dale snapped. "Does he know that? Have you come clean with him?"

"He knows how I feel." Not that his feelings toward the kids were any of Dale's business. "Look, I have to go. I'm late for work." He disconnected the call and set the phone to vibrate. If Dale wanted to call back, he'd have to talk to Remy's voicemail.

Remy gathered his stuff and left his car. He locked the vehicle before heading into the building. Normally, he loved to talk and liked company. Right now he wanted to hide at his desk with his earbuds in as he worked on his outline for the next article in what he'd dubbed his *Positively Cedarwood* series. He navigated his way across the newsroom and did his best to ignore the world around him.

He wouldn't have this problem if Dale hadn't called and emailed. *For what? A booty call. Jesus.* He gritted his teeth and plunked down at his desk. He set up his workstation and turned on his music. Screw the rest of the world. He'd tried to be positive and not let the crap around him bother him, but damn it. Between the nightmare and Dale's call, his great mood had gone down the tubes.

"Hey there." Maureen dragged a chair over to his desk. "Your article won't be on the front page. It's getting buried by the editorials."

"That's pretty much what it is — an op-ed piece." He shrugged. "Could be worse. Could be blocked completely." He'd forgotten her true position at the paper. She practically ran the whole thing and owned a forty percent share of the company. She might take on some of the odd jobs around the building, but she had her finger in everything and knew exactly what went on.

"It's not subversive, so they won't." She folded her arms. "So? How are things with Bobby?"

He shrugged again. "Good. I met his kids — they're good kids, by the way. We talked and went to dinner after the swim meet yesterday. I acted like a dick because I wasn't expecting so many people to be there."

"How did you not expect them? You knew he had kids." Maureen sat opposite of him. "Come on."

"Oh, the kids were fine. It was the group of parents." He slumped in his seat. "The parents were great, actually. Nice people who all have kids in the swim program or who run with Chris. I would've been fine if I hadn't had the run-in with the woman at the metro park."

"Coalition?" Maureen shook her head and clicked her tongue. "They're tricky."

"She never specifically said she was with the group, but it was pretty clear what side she was on. She didn't like me being there and made it her point to tell me. She was probably pissed because her kid didn't score well in the meet, but I can't be sure."

"Not everyone is part of the Coalition. Some people are just...dyed-in-the-wool. The rest of us have to work harder to keep everything level."

"You're right." He rested his arm on his desk. "The parents at the restaurant were really cool. According to Bobby, they've been tight since he moved here. I'm glad. I can't imagine having kids and having to deal with the crap from people with negative attitudes."

"Oh, honey, it's everywhere. If you're a woman, a minority, gay, whatever... We're all dealing with someone who doesn't like us, but it's up to us to show the rest of the world that those people can't keep us down." She toyed with the papers on his desk. "So?"

"So what?" He hated being clueless.

"You like him?"

"Yeah." Despite the pride in admitting what he wanted and how he felt, a tinge of irritation showed. He liked Maureen, but something hadn't sat right with him from the start. "Please tell me you're not trying to get us together in order to make us an example of a stable relationship. Try someone and somewhere else. A hookup and dinner with a group doesn't constitute much."

"Wow." She put both hands up. "You're negative today."

Her wide-eyed expression and the way she'd scooted her chair away from him spoke volumes. He'd been too harsh, and she hadn't done anything wrong.

"I'm sorry. I had a lot happen in the last twenty-four hours." He scrubbed the back of his hand across his forehead. "It's—I'm not used to dealing with this kind of thing. People who don't like gays are one thing, but people who don't like gays with kids? That's another level of hell."

"You're right. It's not cool." She stood.

"Maureen." He had to make this right. "Wait." Although she'd walked away from him, he caught up to her. "I'm scared. He's got kids, and with this Coalition crap, I don't want them to get hurt. Then there's me and relationships. I go way too fast and have always been the 'get in, get what I want, then get out' kind of guy. Now there are kids involved. I don't want to rush and fuck with their lives, but I also don't want to miss out on Bobby. Does that make sense? The odds are so against us. I'm not a kid person, for God's sake."

She faced him and met his gaze. "You're smart, despite being a prick sometimes. So what's the issue?"

He had to be honest with her. She deserved that much. "Well, there are a lot of reasons. One, I'm worried. Relationships and I don't tend to work out. I'm not a trusting soul, and that's what's needed in a stable relationship. Two, kids have always been a sticking point. Yes, I like Chris and Darcy, but I don't see myself as dad material. I'm not exactly the most grown-up man I know. Three, I'm worried the shit with the Coalition will affect them."

"Sounds like you're already dad material." She threaded her arms around his biceps and directed him to one of the vacant offices. She didn't close the door, but lowered the sound of her voice. "The Coalition is already affecting them. It's affecting everyone."

"I hate that."

"A lot of people do." She stayed beside him and continued to hang on to his arm. "Stop being so wishy-washy. You keep talking yourself out of the relationship. You like him, and I know because I see it in your eyes and the way you light up when you mention Bobby's name. You've got issues, but don't we all? Stop giving up so easily. You're coming around on the topic of kids—you might not believe it, but you are. You'll be surprised how fast it happens once you're willing to see it." She paused. "As for the Coalition, let them do their worst. If you and Bobby are meant to be, you'll find a way. If you're the man I think you are, you won't let a few overzealous people do something that'll harm Darcy or Chris."

He draped his arm around her shoulders. She'd given him so many pearls of wisdom. Good thing he had her in his life. Still, she'd figured him out way too fast. "How'd you come to that conclusion?"

She laughed and rested her head on his shoulder. "I never introduced you to my husband, Ivan." She slid her phone from wherever she kept it and swiped the screen. The image of a man in a white button-down shirt, black trousers and suspenders filled the screen. His silver hair stood in tight but wild curls around his head. "I might know a thing or two about being ostracized."

She'd married a black man. He wasn't shocked. Instead, his respect for her soared. "Maureen, I had no clue." He felt silly. If he'd have known about her husband, he would've confided in her a long time ago. "How'd you overcome it?"

"The insults? I ignored those. Being denied entry into places because we were a mixed-race couple? We went to better, more exciting ones. We didn't let society win and that's what you've got to do. Stand up or shut up." She swiped the screen to an image of her standing with Ivan. She barely came up to Ivan's shoulders, and she clung to his arm the same way she'd clung to Remy's. "We've been together for almost forty-two years. Married for forty-one."

"That's sweet." He wasn't sure what else to say.

"So, sweetness…what are you going to do?"

He bowed his head and took a moment to think about what she'd said. He'd been fired from the news channels because of downsizing and because he was gay. The Coalition didn't want him around kids because of his sexuality. He wasn't a bad man or out to do anyone harm. He simply wanted to live his life and have a relationship with Bobby.

"Well?" she asked.

He knew what he wanted to do. "I'm busting out the '80s power ballads on my phone, then outlining the next *Positively Cedarwood* article before I call Bobby when I'm done for the day."

"And?"

"I'm working on an apology to deliver to Bobby's friends the next time I see them." Yes, he needed to let them know in words and actions that he wasn't a dick.

"I knew you were a smart guy." She hugged him, then stepped back. "How about you talk to Bobby right now?"

He bobbed his head. "Sure. I could call him right now. Might be nice to hear his voice."

"No." She pointed to the foyer. "He's at the counter right now." She nudged him out of the office. "Get your man."

He swatted at Maureen but kept moving forward. "Bobby? Hey." He swished through the swinging half-doors and stepped behind the half-circle reception desk. "I wasn't expecting to see you here."

Bobby grinned. "I figured you'd be out chasing your next big lead."

"Or a softball game. Was there something you needed help with?" he murmured. "Or did you come to see me?"

"Both." Bobby grinned again and flattened his hands on the desk. "I wanted to take out an advertisement for my accounting firm."

"Oh. Maureen should've done that." He fumbled for the correct piece of paper in the top drawer. "Usually she handles ad sales." He turned the page around. "I can help with some. I don't know the pricing, but I do know you fill this out with the pertinent info."

"I've got the file in my email. I thought maybe I could forward it to you or whoever handles the ads." He placed his phone on the counter.

The digital version of the paper needed more hits and an upgrade, really. He'd been told that if he was willing to put in the hours on the website, he could place ads there for free—not that he had anything to advertise. But Bobby did. "Well, I'll still have you fill this out so we have that for the print paper. I can't guarantee the graphics you've got will work with the printer, but I know it will on the digital version." He pulled one of his business cards from the rack. "Send it here."

"Great." Bobby twiddled with his phone. "How much extra for the digital ad?"

"On the house." He folded his arms. "I believe the print ads run upward of two hundred a month, but because you're a new client and I'm the one putting the ad on the website, you'll only have to pay for the print ad."

"Nice. Email sent." Bobby met Remy's gaze. "Thanks."

"You're welcome. I'll work on getting that placed later this morning."

"It's already after one," Bobby replied.

"Well, shoot. I'll get to it after lunch." He paused. "Have you eaten?"

"Nope." Hunger in Bobby's eyes. "Can't say I have."

"Are you available for a lunch date?" He focused on Bobby. "Even a half an hour?"

"I've got nothing to do until four. Chris and his friends went to Kingsville to see a movie, and Darcy went shopping with my mother."

*Score!* "I'm due for a break. How about a walk to the food trucks?" Not exactly romantic, but he didn't have too many options.

"Better yet, how about I drive, and we go over to the diner?" Bobby stuck his phone in his back pocket. "I finished up at the office and could use adult time."

"Sure. Uh…" He needed his stuff. "Let me give this to Maureen and I'll meet you…" He stopped short. "Want a quick tour of the paper?" He opened the swinging doors leading to the back of the building. "I'll be your guide."

"Sounds kinky." Bobby rounded the desk and met him at the door. "I'd love to."

"Great." He hurried through the room to Maureen's space and stuck the paper in her filing tray. "So this is the main work room. It's not that exciting. A few desks and some reporters. We do our work pretty much everywhere, so yeah." He grasped Bobby's hand. "This is my desk."

Remy shoved his tablet, keyboard and phone into his messenger bag. He checked the pocket on the side for his keys, then tucked the papers behind the keyboard. "I'm ready when you are."

"This was the worst tour I've ever been on," Bobby muttered.

"It wasn't supposed to be great," he said and fiddled with his bag. "Sorry."

"No need. I'm amused, if nothing else."

"We can leave this way." Remy opened the door for Bobby. "It's a nice day out after the rain this morning. The ball fields will be muddy but playable." He adjusted his sunglasses. "I'm ready when you are."

Bobby headed across the lot to his car and opened the passenger door. "You're sexy when you're flustered."

Remy blushed and slid onto the seat. *Sexy. Wow.* He was not going to let Bobby go without a fight.

Once Bobby rounded the hood and settled beside him, Remy grabbed Bobby's hand. "Lunch dates rock," Remy said. "Oh, and you're not too bad yourself in that suit." He whistled. "I'll have to beat the others off with a stick."

"I'd rather you do that to me." Bobby kissed Remy's knuckles. "Or let me have my way with you."

"I suck at topping, so yeah, you can do whatever you want. I'm yours." He stole a glance over at Bobby, then grinned. Admitting what he wanted and being himself were so much better than being alone.

# Chapter Seven

"I haven't been to the diner in forever," Remy said. "I can't remember the last time." He watched the scenery and basked in the togetherness he shared with Bobby. As Bobby drove past the diner, Remy sat up a little straighter. "You passed the restaurant."

"I know." Bobby continued across town to his street and pulled into his driveway. "Why have lunch when we can have each other?"

"Nice." Remy shut down the tablet and tucked it into his bag. "I said I'm yours." *Like I'd actually turn Bobby down? Not today and probably not ever.*

"I know." Bobby parked, then clicked the button to put the garage door down. "I want you to prove it." He grasped the back of Remy's head and mashed his mouth down on Remy's. He stole Remy's breath and Remy didn't care. Remy scooted across the car until the console got in the way. He ran his hand along Bobby's torso and under his sport coat. God, the man was hot as hell in business attire. Remy shivered and sucked on Bobby's tongue. He'd never considered himself a fool for a guy in a suit, but the more he looked at Bobby... Yeah, guys in businesswear were awesome. Especially Bobby.

"Fuck." Bobby wrenched his mouth free. "Want you."

Remy nodded. He tried to reply, but the words weren't there. He smoothed his palm over the growing bulge in his jeans.

"Looks like you want me too," Bobby said between kisses. "We should go inside."

"Couldn't hurt." He grabbed his bag and left the car, only to have Bobby pressed up tight behind him. Bobby wound his arms around Remy's waist.

"I could take your ass right here in the garage." He directed Remy into the house. Instead of stopping in the kitchen, Bobby yanked Remy's bag free and chased him upstairs. "The bedroom is better."

"You bet it is." Remy threw his arms around Bobby's neck and plastered his body to Bobby's. He couldn't get close enough. He cupped the back of Bobby's head and bumped noses with him.

"Eager. I like it." Bobby grabbed the hem of Remy's shirt and yanked the garment over Remy's head. He raked his nails down Remy's chest, sending shivers through Remy's being.

"Jesus." Remy bowed his head and closed his eyes. How in the hell had he found someone as hot and sweet...and great as Bobby? He didn't deserve Bobby, but he wasn't about to let go either.

"Just Bobby," Bobby replied, forcing Remy to look at him. He pinned Remy to the wall and opened the front of Remy's pants. He shoved the denim and boxer shorts down Remy's thighs. "Want me here?"

"Yeah," he managed as Bobby dropped to the floor. He grasped Bobby's shoulders. Standing in front of his lover with his dick out and Bobby clothed wasn't a regular activity. Usually Remy was the one on his knees.

Bobby wrapped his fingers around Remy's cock. "You're beautiful."

"Sure." This wasn't the time for self-effacing humor. He pressed his lips together and planted his shoulders against the wall. He widened his stance. Each time Bobby stroked him or blew across the head of his cock, another ripple of desire crashed within him.

"I could stay here forever." Bobby traced the seam of his lips with Remy's cock head. He fixed his gaze on Remy's. "Hot cock, sexy man... I'm happy."

Happy was a good word for how Remy felt too. He cupped the back of Bobby's head. Although Bobby was in control, Remy needed to hold on to him.

Bobby engulfed Remy's dick in his mouth and sucked him to the back of his throat. He slid one hand between Remy's legs and rolled Remy's balls in his fingers.

"Oh fuck." Remy opened his eyes and gasped. With the onslaught of sensation—hands on his body, warm mouth around his dick, the scent of Bobby's cologne surrounding him—he couldn't think straight.

Bobby set the pace, sucking Remy to the root before he pulled out and plunged in again. He worked up to a steady pace and frazzled Remy's thoughts.

Every synapse in Remy's body misfired. His balls tingled. From head to toe, he tensed. He gritted his teeth. Too much more from Bobby and he'd come.

Bobby stroked Remy's shaft while he bobbed his head. He continued to caress Remy's balls too.

Remy's body buzzed. Nothing mattered except what Bobby did to him. He held on with both hands and hoped to God he wouldn't fall over when his knees gave out.

"Fuck," Remy bit out. "I need to come." He curled forward and widened his stance a bit more. "Jesus, Bobby." He slammed his dick into Bobby's mouth. No amount of restraint would help him now. He balled his hands on Bobby's head, and his seed spurted down Bobby's throat. His knees wobbled.

Bobby swallowed, adding a new sensation to the mix before he licked a few more times, then sat back on his heels. He wiped his mouth with the back of his hand.

Remy sank to the floor. With his pants and boxers tangled around his ankles and his shoes still on, he stared at Bobby. "Holy shit."

"I thought you might like that." Bobby stood. He grasped Remy's hand and helped him to the bed. "Stretch out and catch your breath, handsome."

"Yeah." Remy collapsed on the mattress. He kicked his shoes off and out of his wadded-up clothing while he stared at the ceiling. "You're good."

"I know," Bobby said.

Remy turned his attention to his lover and sighed. Damn, Bobby was hot.

Bobby shrugged out of the sport coat. He dangled the jacket on a hanger, then tossed both onto a recliner. Without taking his gaze from Remy's, he unbuttoned his shirt. The man knew how to strip, and he sent tingles down Remy's spine. Once Bobby unfastened each button, he allowed the shirt to slide down his arms. He hadn't worn an undershirt, and the delicious expanse of his chest was revealed.

Remy focused on Bobby's chest. "You shaved," he blurted.

"Can't be all furry for you." Bobby tossed the shirt onto the chair with the jacket. "Plus, I like being smooth." He opened the buckle on his belt, then the button on his trousers. He shoved his pants to the floor, revealing his navy silk boxers.

"Fancy too." Remy propped himself up on his elbow. "You're one sexy bitch, businessman."

"You have no idea." Bobby removed his boxer shorts. The pants, his socks and the underwear landed in a pile at his feet. He shoved the clothing out of the way, then stroked himself as he crossed the room. "I'm going to own that ass of yours."

"Please?" Remy rolled onto his belly and propped his butt in the air. He grasped his ass cheeks. "Fucking hell, I need you."

"You'll get me." Bobby opened a condom packet and retrieved the lube from his nightstand.

Although Remy couldn't see what Bobby was doing, he could tell from the noises. The snap of latex on skin and the click of the lube cap meant pleasure wasn't far off. He gasped as the chilly lube slid between his ass cheeks.

"Fuck," Remy bit out. "Yes."

"I thought about you last night." Bobby pressed the head of his dick against Remy's hole. "Fucking you, sleeping beside you and holding you."

"You're a romantic." He bore down on Bobby as his lover filled his ass. Remy gasped and flattened his hands on his butt. *Jesus*. He'd been fucked by Bobby already and knew what to expect, but the fullness pleased him every time. He smashed his face into the bedding and groaned.

Unlike the other time, Bobby didn't take the romantic, slow route. *Nope.* He filled Remy to the hilt, then launched right into a steady rhythm of thrusts.

Overdosing on lust, Remy grasped the sheets and fought to catch his breath. The smell of Bobby, pine and something spicy, curled around him. He loved the feel of Bobby's hands on his body and the memory of the taste of Bobby's kiss lingered in his mind. God, Bobby filled and overwhelmed him. The sound of Bobby's voice was like a beacon. He'd find pleasure with his new lover every time.

Bobby dug his fingers into Remy's hips. "You hold me tight in there and make me never want to leave this ass." He swatted Remy's butt. "Love the way your skin gets all rosy when we fuck." He peppered Remy's skin with spankings, adding pain to the pleasure and pushing Remy to another level of desire.

Remy wanted to answer, but once again, Bobby had him lost for words. He rode the wave of desire and held on as the orgasm built in his lower belly. The mattress squeaked beneath them in perfect rhythm with Bobby's thrust.

Even though he'd come before, he was already back on the edge. His ass burned from the swats. *Holy fucking balls.* His legs trembled and his restraint shattered. "I need to come," Remy begged. "Please?"

"Remy," Bobby growled. "Fuck." He slammed deep into Remy's hole. "Jesus Christ." His words echoed in the room. "Fuck."

"You said that," Remy said and basked in the glow of orgasm. Everything that had been coiled tight within him loosened. He sagged on the bed and closed his eyes. He should've seen this coming, this change. He hadn't. He'd never expected to fall for Bobby Gagnon, but the inevitable had happened. He sighed. Was being in love with Bobby a bad thing? Not really. Bobby respected him and seemed to care. Maybe he could even love Remy in return.

"Are you sleeping already?" Bobby asked. He eased his cock out of Remy's ass. The bed dipped as he left the mattress. "Rem?" He flattened his hand on the small of Remy's back. "You're in there, right?"

"Yeah, I am." He tried to open his eyes but lost the battle. "I can't move and it's fantastic." He loved the used feeling.

"Oh." The bed sagged again as Bobby snuggled up to Remy. "You had me worried. I thought I'd killed you."

"Nah." He opened his eyes and bumped noses with Bobby. He'd never thought of himself as romantic, but he wanted the whole ooey, gooey lot with Bobby. A thought occurred to him, and the words tumbled out before he could take them back. "You could've gone home with any man at the festival. All of them would love to be right here right now. Why me?"

*Well, shit.* He'd gone and ruined the good mood. *Fuck.* He'd told himself not to get consumed by the negative and to embrace what he shared with Bobby, but the old demons came back.

"Why not you?" Bobby brushed Remy's hair from his forehead and tangled their legs together. "Is there something wrong with you?"

"I'm a mess." He might as well be honest. "You're all put together and know what you're doing. Then there's me."

"We're all a mess in one way or another." Bobby pressed a light kiss to Remy's lips. "We've all got shit we're freaked out about. So?"

Bobby had a point and his remark took some of the sting out of Remy. "You barely know me. I could be an awful person." *Christ.* If there was a way to shoot himself in the foot, he'd find it.

"I doubt it." Bobby palmed Remy's ass and caressed his tender skin. "They won't let horrible people work for the paper...and I might have searched you on the Internet."

"I searched you too."

"Then we're even." Bobby smiled. "You're convinced you're horrible, but you're not."

"Bobby." He needed to talk and get some of his past out in the open. Maybe Bobby would run, or maybe it would be the therapy Remy needed. He wasn't sure. "Remember the kid at school who doesn't exist? Not like physically doesn't, but he's there and no one really sees him? Either the super chubby kid or the scary smart kid who blends in a little too well?"

"Sure." Bobby shrugged and held Remy tighter. "Was that you?" He smiled. "I can see you as a wicked smart kid."

He relaxed a little. "I got myself into trouble on a regular basis because of my intelligence. I got to the point where I could pretty much figure out how long it would take me to finish my classwork, and I'd read instead. I'd put off the work until I had to do it because I wanted to keep reading whatever book I had. That mentality earned me straight As and twenty-three detentions for not following directions and reading instead." He'd always prided himself on those stats. Most kids got into trouble for not reading. He'd been the opposite.

"Rebel."

"When I got detention was the only time anyone knew me." He closed his eyes again. He couldn't meet Bobby's gaze — not right now. Even nearly twenty years on, he still looked back on his high school days with disdain.

"I'm sorry." Bobby kissed him again and flattened his palm on Remy's chest. "I wish we'd known each other back then. You'd have to have gone to Cedarwood, though."

"Yeah, I was over in Haliwell." He sighed. "It sucked. I was tall, chunky and not athletic. I pretty much didn't exist to my classmates. I know, you can say I need to move on. I'm trying."

"People weren't looking hard enough," Bobby replied.

"To make things more complicated, I knew I was gay back in high school. I didn't come out then. I waited until I was in college because I couldn't see how anyone would be interested in me with a lot more to love." He winced. *Jesus.* He sounded so lame. "Even when I finally admitted I was gay, the guys I was attracted to weren't attracted to me. They wanted hotter ones like you."

"That's why you started running." Bobby feathered his lips over Remy's. "I bet you were still a catch. I like the man on the inside. The outside is great, but if you're not sexy on the inside, the packaging doesn't matter."

He wished he'd heard that a long time ago. He wished he could've met Bobby a lot earlier too. He forced himself to open his eyes and focused on the rest of his story. He had to get the words out. "I ran, but not just in the physical sense. I switched from the local community college because of a guy. I told him I was interested in him, and he wasn't gay. The embarrassment was too much. Then once I got to Kent, I switched majors." He sounded so fucking lame.

"You're beating yourself up too much," Bobby said. "Did you do that because of another guy?"

"That time it was a girl who couldn't take a hint."

"Julia?"

"No. We tried, though." He'd used her as a beard to get Cathy to leave him alone. "She was my only girlfriend. I tried to love her that way, and it never worked." He nodded. "Edward R. Morrow wouldn't cooperate."

"Edward R....I like it." Bobby grinned. "I never named mine."

"You should. It's fun." He relaxed a bit more. "Anyway, with Julia, I tried and it didn't happen, but we spent so much time together that everyone thought we were a couple."

"I'd rather people know for sure that you and I are a couple." Bobby curled his fingers under Remy's chin. "I'm going to be a territorial son of a bitch, but I like you, and I'm staking a claim. I like you, just you, very much."

He wanted to ask if Bobby was feeling all right, then if Bobby had lost his mind, but he kept his mouth shut. Belonging to Bobby sounded so good. He sighed. "Are you suggesting we be a couple and all monogamous-like?" He sounded like a dork, but he didn't care.

"Uh-huh." Bobby kissed him again and rubbed his thumb along Remy's chin. "And all that's involved therein."

He loved the way Bobby could sound so sexy and smart at the same time. "I accept." He didn't have to think it through. He knew what he wanted and where he belonged. "The kids won't mind?"

"They want me to be happy, and I'm better when I'm around you."

"Even after a little less than a week?"

"Yes." Bobby swatted Remy again. "I will spank your ass until you get the hint. I like you, and I don't want to let go."

The words comforted him more than Bobby probably understood. "I still don't know why you like me, but I'm glad you do."

"You still see the chubby kid when you look in the mirror."

He sighed. "I try not to look at myself in mirrors, but yeah, he's always there." He chuckled, but didn't feel any happiness. "I was fifteen and filled out. My grandmother would clip coupons for skin cream and diet pills in order to help me. Mom agreed with her and Dad didn't care." He could still see himself as that kid with pimples and chub in all the wrong places.

"Acne and a few extra pounds?"

"The dynamic duo. She and Mom would regulate my food to make sure I'd lose weight. No sweets, carbs. Only veggies and fruit. They put me in swimming lessons and one of those boys camping groups. I don't do the outdoors unless I'm running, and I sure as hell don't camp." He shook his head. "I snuck candy in my bag. I felt like such a bad kid, but nothing I did back then helped. When I got to college and was turned down by Daniel, I started running. I ran to lose the weight and to get the hell away from the kid I saw in the mirror. I ran from Carson and Derinda. Journalism and running, the actual sport, were my outlets. I still eat candy and drink soda, but I run most of it off. I'm a flawed, fucked-up man." He wasn't ready to go into the deeper stories concerning Daniel or Carson. Not right now.

"You're human." Bobby tucked Remy to his side and rolled onto his back. "My human. I don't care if you're flawed or messed up. Perfect is overrated, and besides, you've got a huge heart that I like knowing is in my hands."

He snuggled up to Bobby and rested his head on Bobby's chest. "I like the way that sounds."

"Good." Bobby stroked Remy's hair. "Darcy and Mom will be back in half an hour."

"You're saying we need to get dressed instead of cuddling?" He toyed with Bobby's nipple. "Like right now?"

"Sooner or later we'll have to." He kissed the top of Remy's head. "Stay for supper."

"I haven't had lunch yet." But he was pretty sure he'd go wherever Bobby wanted. "I need to get some writing done, but yeah, I'll stay."

"Writing? For the paper?" Bobby stroked Remy's hair. "I thought you were caught up."

"I'm working on a novel." He pressed his lips together. Bobby would either be intrigued or sickened once he found out what the book was about.

"That's cool. What about?"

"Well, it's a sci-fi romance. There's a space pirate and he pillages a planet. After he's out of range of anyone's cannons, he goes through his stuff and realizes he's got extra cargo in the form of a prince. Both guys are hyper-masculine, but they're drawn to each other. Kind of a gay-for-you story. Anyway, they give each other blow jobs and enjoy the private quiet of his ship in space. See, being gay in this solar system isn't approved of, but these two do what makes them happy." He'd rambled and fucked up his delivery. Wasn't the whole idea of selling a story to do it in a sweet, succinct fashion to grab the reader? He hadn't done that. "There are other pirates who want the prince dead because there's a huge reward for his head."

"Hot."

"Not stupid?" He frowned at Bobby. "You're not...turned off?"

"I'd read it. Sounds interesting."

"Because it's mine." He should've figured that.

"Because it sounds interesting." Bobby curled his fingers under Remy's chin again. "The lack of confidence is kind of cute, but babe, you're more than your past. Have some faith in yourself. Try to see the Remy I see — the one who writes wonderful articles, has a big heart and a sexy ass."

Part of him didn't want to believe Bobby, but the rest of him did. *What the hell...* He didn't have much to lose if he bought into what Bobby had said. "I'll work on it."

"Harder. Work harder." Bobby's eyes flashed. "I know you can."

Remy snuggled up to Bobby. He could've sworn he heard something. A clunk? He held still. The noise was back, but now he knew what it was. "I hear a rumble. I'm guessing it wasn't the wind."

Bobby sat up. "That's the bad thing about this house. You can hear everything outside." He climbed out of bed and crept up to the window. "Yep. Mom's back with Darcy."

"So stand in front of the glass where everyone can see you, nudist." He shoved the sheets away from his body. *Shit.* If Grandma and the kid were there, then naked time was over.

"The roof is in the way of anyone seeing in here, but I can see the trunk of her car. Besides, I peeked through the blinds." Bobby strode over to the dresser. "We're safe."

"Ah." He yanked his boxers free from his rumpled jeans, then stepped into the underwear. He slid the denim on next. "They won't care I'm here?" he asked. He didn't want to intrude on family time or put Bobby into an awkward position.

"Darcy asked me when you'd be back." Bobby pulled a pair of briefs on, then shook out his jeans. "She likes you."

"Ah." He'd said that already, but really he had no idea what else to say. He yanked his shirt down past his head. He located his socks.

"She hated my ex-boyfriend Neil."

"Ouch." He picked up his shoes. "Want me to wait to go downstairs?"

"You're fine." Bobby unfolded a T-shirt. "My ex was a dick, so her dislike was understandable."

"Oh."

"He really didn't like kids." Bobby shrugged into the shirt, then faced Remy. "Neil only came over when Chris and Darce were gone. Unfortunately for our relationship, that was difficult. Once they're both in school, I work those hours. I'm flexible with my schedule, but still."

"Is that why you split? Because of the kids?" He gripped his shoes and waited for Bobby to button his jeans.

"He found someone younger. A pretty boy." Bobby shrugged. "I'll never be the pretty boy type."

"He's nuts. You're gorgeous." He didn't understand how anyone could not be attracted to Bobby.

"Well, if he weren't crazy, as you put it, and was still here, then I wouldn't be with you." Bobby strode up to Remy and kissed him. "It's a good trade-off and better for my sanity."

"I agree." He snagged Bobby in his arms. "His bad decision is my good fortune." He kissed Bobby right back.

"You're staying for supper, then, right?" Bobby grasped Remy's hand. He made his way into the hall. "I have no idea what I'm making, but you're not allowed to leave."

"I should go back to work, but if you put it that way." He had no place he'd rather be. "Want me to go downstairs in a few minutes?" He'd asked the question before, but hadn't gotten much of an answer.

"The kids have already figured it out, and if Mom doesn't understand, she soon will." Bobby headed down the stairs first and waved to Remy. "My daughter's twelve, but she's not clueless."

"Oh." He had so much to learn about kids. He had no idea what to expect from Chris or Darcy.

Bobby stopped on the landing. "See? You thought you weren't a kid person. You're warming up to the idea."

"Because of you." And the few hours he'd spent around Darcy and Chris had been fun.

When he rounded the corner into the kitchen, Remy forced himself to keep going forward. Darcy and Bobby's mother were sitting at the table. A mound of bags blocked the view of the rest of the room.

"There you are." Mrs. Gagnon hugged Bobby. "I was wondering what happened to— Oh. Hi." She stared at Remy. "Are you the young man I've heard about?"

"Yes?" He vowed to be more confident, but he rarely met the parents of his current date.

"Mom." Bobby draped his arm around Remy's shoulders. "This is Remy. You should know him. He's a reporter for *The Tribune* and works with Maureen." He nodded to the table. "So, kid, what'd you con Grandma into buying?"

Darcy smiled and clasped her hands together. "School clothes. I'll show you later."

"Did you max out her credit cards? Your grandpa will arrest me." Bobby remained beside Remy with his arm around Remy.

"He won't say a word," Mrs. Gagnon replied. "If I'm buying for the kids, he's happy."

"Mom." Bobby sighed.

"I saw Chris at the mall. They're seeing the double feature, and he said he'd be home around seven. I got to meet all of his friends. Nice kids." She folded her hands on the table top. "That Nicki is very pretty."

"Mom." Bobby shrugged away from Remy. "Thanks for checking up on him."

Remy ducked out of the kitchen and escaped into the living room. He didn't mind family dynamics as long as the family wasn't his. He shuddered. Just thinking about going back to the Nicholas homestead churned his stomach. But then he'd probably never introduce Bobby to his parents.

He sighed and stared out of the front window. *Parents. Kids.* He had so much to figure out and most of it revolved around him and Bobby being a couple. They weren't even an exclusive couple. He'd warmed up to the kids because of Bobby. In any other situation, he couldn't guarantee he'd be so happy to find out his lover had offspring.

"Do you like my dad?" Darcy asked. She appeared beside Remy.

He slapped his hand over his mouth to muffle the shriek. He'd forgotten how stealthy kids could be, especially when he wasn't expecting them to show up.

"Sorry." She darted behind the armchair and leaned on the back cushion. Probably to keep him at a safe distance and for a good escape plan.

"I wasn't expecting you." He gulped air and willed his heart rate to slow to normal. "I'm sorry too. I startle easily." He'd thought he was over that phase of his life. He guessed not.

"I used to, too." She shrugged and remained behind the chair. "When Dad and Mom split, I thought everyone was going to take me. I was really good at hiding."

"Why?" He sat on the couch and patted the cushion beside him. "I won't bite if you want to come over. Promise."

She smiled and joined him on the sofa. "I was five when Mom left. She told me and Chris that she'd come back for us. She did and I said no. That made her mad." Darcy flopped her hands onto her lap.

"Aww, honey." He draped his arm around her. Out of instinct? He wasn't sure, but she seemed like she needed a hug.

"Chris didn't want to go either. Mom shouted a lot and was always mad. She said she wanted to take us because Dad was yucky. I never told him she said that."

*And you're telling me this stuff?* She must trust him more than he'd expected. "I bet she only said that because she was angry that they didn't get along. But their arguing wasn't your fault. Still isn't."

"She used to say it was my fault. Mom told me if she and Dad hadn't had me, then she wouldn't feel like she had to stay. She blamed Chris too." Darcy sagged against Remy and curled her legs to her chest. "I'm not a bad kid."

"No, you're not." He hugged her a little tighter and kissed the top of her head. "That's over, and your dad loves you very much. He loves Chris that much too."

"I know," she replied. "Dad needs a boyfriend. I liked Terry. He was nice."

*Terry?* He didn't know that name, and he doubted Bobby would have two guys at one time. It didn't feel like something Bobby would do. "Was he?"

"He's in California now. I think."

"Oh." He tried to sound nonchalant, but his heart broke a little. He didn't want there to be competition for Bobby.

"Terry said he and Dad weren't meant to be." She sat up and faced him. "I tell the boys that at school too."

For twelve, she not only switched topics at warp speed, but she handled situations with more maturity than some forty-two-year-olds he knew. "You're in middle school. Boys are already sniffing around?" He hadn't shown interest in boys or girls until he was fourteen, but still.

"Yeah. My friend Kevin is going with Maya." She shrugged. "I don't want to. Chris can't have a girlfriend. Dad said so."

"He's a smart guy. Get through school first, then worry about boys and girls. There's time for dating and all that after you graduate." Christ, he sounded like a public service announcement or an after-school special.

"You sound like Dad." She folded her arms and grinned.

"There's nothing wrong with that," he said. "Speaking of your dad…did the kitchen eat him alive?"

"Nah. Grandma's talking to him. Something about necking and dates. My birthday's coming up. Maybe she meant that. I have no idea what necking is." Her eyes lit up. "Maybe she and Dad are planning a party!"

"Maybe." He had a pretty good idea what was being discussed in the other room, and thanked God Darcy hadn't heard of necking yet. She didn't need to know. Innocence wasn't overrated.

"So." She stared at him. "You never answered my question. Do you like my dad? Neil didn't."

"I'm sorry about Neil, but yes, I like your dad." He could say that with complete confidence, and knowing that liberated him. "I hope you and your brother like me enough to keep me around."

Darcy rolled her eyes and laughed. "You haven't called us shits or threatened to put us up for adoption, so you're cool."

He pressed his lips together to process what he'd just heard. Besides her swearing, she'd shocked him with the information. "You shouldn't say shits."

"Sorry." She plunked herself down on the couch again. "That was Neil's word for us."

"He was wrong." He rested his arm on the back of the sofa. "Please tell me Neil didn't threaten you and Chris… He didn't say he'd put you up for adoption, did he?"

"Yeah." She waggled her head. "Mom and Neil always said it. I heard him yelling at Dad one time. They thought I was asleep, but they woke me up. Neil was mad because Dad didn't want to go to the Rainbow. I found out that's a dance club." She grinned again. "I want to go there someday and dance."

"When you're older." *Much older.*

"That's Dad's answer too." She knotted her eyebrows. "Anyway, Neil said he wanted us gone, and if we weren't here, then he'd get what he wanted." She paused and her eyes widened. "I never told Chris that. He'd be mad."

"Jesus," Remy muttered. *What a thing to say to a kid, much less to the parent.* No wonder no one liked Neil. He'd never met the guy, and he wanted to rearrange Neil's face.

"Yeah. It sucked." She folded her arms again. "I should go try on my new stuff and make sure it all fits right. When school starts, I'm ready."

"Sounds like you're excited." He'd have to add keeping up with her conversations onto his to-do list.

"Uh-huh. School means sports, and I can't wait for ninth grade. Then I can join the swim team." She waved her arms as though she was soaring across the pool.

"Sounds like you're good to go."

"Oh yeah." She left the couch and waved. "I'm going to set records. I know it. Bye."

Darcy strolled out of the living room, leaving Remy in silence. His mind whirled with all of the new information. She talked a lot and at a rapid pace. And he thought he could chatter someone's ears off... He sighed. She was a smart kid and seemed to have adjusted well, considering the circumstances. Raising kids was not easy. Did he have it in him to handle the complications?

"Oh my God." Bobby strode into the living room. "That lasted forever."

"What?" Remy focused on his lover. "Your mom?"

"Yes. She grilled me." He sat beside Remy. "Every freaking thing... She wanted to know it all."

"About me?"

"Who else?" Bobby settled against Remy and rested his head on Remy's outstretched arm. "I'm sorry. It's just, after Neil—".

"You're right. Darcy didn't like him," Remy said. "Not a bit."

"I know." Bobby met Remy's gaze. "How'd you know...other that what I said?" He stared at Remy, wide-eyed. "Don't tell me she told you? She's a talker, but she usually only opens up to Chris."

"We bonded." He grinned. "She must've thought I was okay enough to tell me. I didn't pry."

"I'm impressed, although you are easy to talk to." Bobby resumed cuddling up to Remy. "For a no-kid guy, you're a kid guy."

He wasn't convinced, but if Bobby was happy, then that was wonderful. He turned his attention back to his conversation with Darcy. "She's still messed up about Neil and the divorce. She mentioned Terry too."

"Fuck," Bobby muttered. "She was in elementary school. Seven years old."

"I don't know how you're going to bring it up, but you need to talk to her. According to Darcy, her mom said some really fucked-up stuff."

"Goddamn it, Helene," Bobby snapped. He sat up and scrubbed both hands over his face. "I should've known."

"Just show Darcy you love her and help her understand that you're not going to let someone come along and adopt her."

Bobby glared at Remy. For a split second, Remy wondered if he should run. He didn't like the way Bobby was looking at him.

"Helene said that? She'd let someone else adopt the kids?" Bobby shook his head. "Over my dead body."

"She said that along with some other things. Neil reiterated it, too." He hated being the messenger, but Bobby needed to know what had been said.

"Rem..." Bobby sagged in his seat.

"If I'm going to date you, I need to know all of that stuff. I need to hear the baggage and be prepared for what might happen." Remy grasped Bobby's hand. He shored up courage he didn't realize he had. "I want Chris and Darcy to like me. I want you to like me too."

"That's one of the sweetest things I've ever heard," Bobby replied.

"I don't want to be like Neil. I don't know what happened between you and Terry, but I don't want us to split and mess up the kids."

"Me neither." Bobby bridged the gap between them and massaged Remy's thigh. "You're here now, and we're at the beginning of something awesome. I feel it. We'll do this our way."

Remy nodded. "Our way sounds perfect." He had no idea what the future held or if the kids would keep warming up to him, but as long as he and Bobby were solid, he could handle the pressure. Bobby was worth the effort.

# Chapter Eight

Bobby sat on the back patio and watched Darcy in the pool. For the last three weeks, he'd spent his days and a few nights getting to know Remy much better. He crossed his ankles and adjusted his sunglasses. The life he'd carved out with the kids and now Remy was simple. They were all settled and seemed to get along great—no small feat, considering. He hadn't run into many men interested in being with a family man, let alone things working out.

He tossed the newspaper he'd been reading onto the picnic table and folded his hands on his belly. Remy's latest column focused on the school system and the band. With summer nearing an end and the start of the school year soon, he'd chosen to feature the good things happening in at the school. That article, as well as the one about the sports in town, were both positive, easy pieces. Mentions of intervention and the Coalition had been left out.

All in all, things were nice and quiet. *Too quiet.* Bobby shook his head. Life had a way of kicking him in the ass when he thought he had everything in order. Maybe it was his one shred of self-doubt, but he feared whatever storm was coming.

Still, he, Remy and the kids had a good schedule going. Every morning, Bobby took the kids to practice and met up with Remy to run the trails. When practices ended, he and Remy parted. The kids went home with his mother while Bobby worked. They shared suppers together — including Bobby's parents — and Remy accompanied him to most of Chris' races. Remy cheered on Darcy at her meets too.

Bobby cherished the occasional nights he spent with Remy and the blessed quiet existence they shared.

"Hey, Dad?" Chris strode out onto the deck. "There are signs all over our front lawn. It looks like when we decorated at the old house when you turned thirty, but these are flag-looking things. You're thirty-four, and your birthday isn't until November. What gives?"

Bobby sighed and left his chair. He hadn't noticed anything that morning, but that didn't mean much. He wasn't one for staring at the front lawn unless he had to mow it. "Are the kids from the team TPing you?"

"No one does that anymore," Chris said.

"They should," Bobby replied. "It's fun." He hadn't been out tossing toilet paper on someone else's trees in years, but the two times he'd joined in the festivities, he'd enjoyed himself.

"Did you? TP?" Chris asked.

"I did a couple of times. It was fun." He'd said 'fun' twice in the space of two minutes. *Boy, am I getting boring.* Bobby opened the sliding door. "Keep an eye on your sister while I check this out." He headed into the house and crossed through to the living room. He didn't need to look out of the picture window to see the damage to his lawn. "What the hell?" he muttered.

Rainbow flags with a black circle and slash had been jabbed into the grass. *Who would do such a thing?* Surely not the kids on the cross-country team.

"What's wrong, Dad?" Chris joined him at the window. "Darcy went upstairs. She's mad I told her to get out of the pool."

"You're a smart kid, Christopher." He whipped his phone out of his pocket. He dialed his father at the police station. The call went straight to voicemail. He gritted his teeth. The chief probably had too much going on already. He pressed the numbers to call Colin while he waited for his father's line to free up.

"Is it bad?" Chris asked. "I know those are pride flags, and whoever did that doesn't like you or us or whatever."

"Yeah, someone's really pissed off." He groaned. "Why don't you go upstairs with Darcy? Find a movie or something and watch it in my room."

"Sure." Chris nodded. "Sorry, Dad."

"It's not your fault." He dialed Colin's number and waited for Chris to exit before he muttered, "It's not anyone's fault." Not really. Being gay shouldn't have the stigma it still carried. Who gave a rat's ass who anyone else was doing as long as they were all of age and consenting?

After three rings, Colin answered. "Did they hit you too?"

*No hi. No how are you. Nice.* "I'm going to assume the flags aren't just at my house." *Fuck.* He'd hoped it was an isolated incident.

"They're on my front lawn. At the house Jordan owns. Colt's got them in front of the restaurant and his house, plus they're at Ashley's place as well as Niall's. Coincidence? I'm not buying it," Colin snapped. "I'm sorry. It's not your fault. That band of...ugh."

"What do we do?" Bobby asked. "I don't know if it's against any laws since it's not permanent, but I'm not sure how to proceed."

"Jordan has his friends on the police force on it. I'm sure your dad's being inundated. I'd report it as vandalism. It's not permanent, but it is on your lawn, and I doubt you normally decorate with that many defaced pride flags."

"That would be correct." He wasn't one to fly the rainbow colors on normal days. If someone asked, he'd tell, but he wasn't going to advertise.

"I'm sick of this. What do we have to do? It's not like we're cramming our lifestyle down the collective throat of Cedarwood. We're living our lives," Colin growled. "I thought this was a good town with decent people. I'm starting to wonder."

"I'd be interested in seeing how many yards were defaced. That's a lot of flags out there, and if there are the same number at the different places you listed, as well as ones you don't know about...then this was coordinated." He didn't know the law, but he knew his math. Someone wanted to send a pretty big message.

"We had a great turnout at the festival. Jordan and I thought we'd made strides toward getting this hate erased," Colin said.

"You did. People came out and had fun. You also didn't force everyone to accept that you're gay. That I'm gay. Whatever."

"Not to be a prick, but what's your point? So what about the flags being a coordinated effort? Someone —

probably on the Coalition — is pissed, and this was their way of showing it."

*What's his point?* "Are that many people really against us? Think about it. There were a few pride flags at the festival, and the bands were LGBTQ friendly. All kinds of people were there. They wanted a party and didn't seem to care who we partnered up with." He paused. "How do you know that many people are really pissed? What if this is a smaller group that's gotten more...enthusiastic?"

"I don't know." Colin sighed. "We've got kids. I don't want them in harm's way. I feel like I'm failing all of them." He paused and the line went silent for a minute. "If you don't like someone, you don't bully and insult them in order to get your way. At least that's not what I'm trying to teach Gage."

"That's the kind of message this flag shit is sending. You're right. It's telling kids, no matter what their orientation might be, that it's okay to use scare tactics and anger to get your point across." Bobby clenched his fist. He hated what was happening and wasn't sure how to stop it, but damn it, he'd try. His kids — all of the kids in Cedarwood — were too important for them to give up.

"I love living here, but not like this," Colin said.

Bobby paced the length of the living room and thought about the situation. There had to be a solution. But what? He pinched the bridge of his nose. "I'll call the police department, but I'm making more calls. Something has to change, and it'll have to start with us."

"I don't know what you're thinking of doing, but I'm game to help," Colin said. "We can't do much more than we're already doing. Keep me posted."

"Will do." He disconnected the call, then dialed his father. "Hey, Chris?"

Chris rounded the corner from the hallway into the living room. "Right here."

"You've been there the whole time, haven't you?" He shook his head. "Doesn't matter. You'll find out about all of this sooner or later. Okay, will you take pictures with your phone and email them to me and to your grandfather? I would, but I'm trying to call him." When the call didn't go through, he dialed again.

"You want pictures of the lawn?" Chris held up his phone. "Okay."

"It's for proof."

Chris rolled his eyes, then plopped onto the couch. "It's sending. Five photos and they've got the time stamp. I downloaded a sweet app that makes them look like they were taken by one of those old camcorder things."

*Old camcorder things... Jesus.* "Thanks." After two rings, the call connected. "Dad?"

"I'm going to assume you have new landscaping," Chief Gagnon said. "Something in the rainbow category?"

"How'd you guess? I'm not the only one who called, am I?" Bobby asked. He shooed Chris out of the room and held his hand over the receiver. "Keep an eye on your sister. Thanks."

"I've had over twenty complaints this fine morning alone. I've got two officers writing up the complaints and three more investigating each. I see Chris emailed me photos of yours. Wonderful."

"How big is Cedarwood, Dad? Six thousand people? Something like that." He thought that was what he'd remembered from the article in the paper.

"We hit sixty-five hundred last summer." Chief Gagnon groaned. "This is ridiculous."

"I'm guessing twenty homes being targeted isn't that much for a town this size, then, is it?"

"There's more, but it's unusual. I don't know if it's only gay people who were singled out. I didn't ask them for their sexual persuasion." Chief groaned again. "Sorry, son. This is getting out of hand. I know a lot of the people in these reports, and I can't say all of them are gay, but the lion's share are."

"Jesus," Bobby bit out. "Fuck."

"Jesus could probably do more than I can. Look, I have to go. Call the desk and make a formal report. Keep the kids inside and call your mother. I don't want her to be alone, although I haven't heard anything from her about our house having new lawn ornaments."

"Will do. Thanks." He hung up and settled on the couch. Something had to be done. This was more than crazy or out of hand. People were being targeted, only because of who they loved. He dialed the main line at the police department and filed the report. He'd have to go down to the station later, but according to the officer, they were swamped. He'd wait.

Bobby dialed his mother's cell number. Instead of the call going through, he got a text saying she was out driving. He returned to the window. Hopefully she was on her way to the house.

Speaking of the house, he needed to get in touch with Remy. *God.* What kind of shit storm had rained down on him? Remy was a good person too, but he had a public job and wore his sexuality on his sleeve. He'd already had incidents with people at the swim complex.

His phone vibrated in his hand. He glanced down at the screen. Remy. His heart hammered as he answered. "Hey."

"Tell me your day is better than mine," Remy said.

"I doubt it. I've got hate flags all over my lawn. You?" He nudged the curtain aside as his mother pulled into the driveway. Bobby left the window. He rushed across the house to the garage door. He opened the door to the second garage bay and motioned for his mother to park in there.

"I'm covering the story," Remy replied. "I'm supposed to report on the hate flags for the front page. My editor knows I'm gay. I didn't hide it at the paper, but goddamn it, they think I'm the perfect person to cover the story. I don't want to cover this crap."

"Babe, I'm sorry." Bobby held the door for his mother. "Hang on." He turned his attention to his mother. "The kids are upstairs. Dad wants you to stay here until things blow over, meaning probably when he gets off work later."

She nodded and patted his arm. "I'll find the kids. Thanks."

"Sorry." Bobby focused on Remy. "Mom's here. It's all gone to hell in a handbasket."

"I'm sure," Remy said. "This isn't your fault any more than it's mine or Colin's or whatever. I'm tired of lying about who I am in order to fit in, but I'm more tired of kids who want to come out being scared because of shit like this. No one wants to be the target of this stuff."

"What are you going to do?" Colin had just asked him that question too. *Does anyone really have the answers?*

"I'm going to cover the story. It's my job, and I'd like to keep that job." Remy paused. "But I have some counter-story ideas. There's an LGBTQ support group meeting coming up, right?"

"Later tonight, why? Colin will probably cancel it or have it somewhere other than the church." *Where's Remy going with this line of thinking?*

"This story has more than one side. I want to tell the story of those who were targeted. I want to show the public the people of Cedarwood are great people, regardless of their sexuality." Remy said. "Do you mind if I come over tonight?"

"I'd be pissed if you didn't." He massaged his temple. "Rem, you're important to me, and I want my people around me at a time like this. You're one of those people."

"I like you too." Remy chuckled. "You're not a bad person, and neither am I. This is a shitty scare tactic, and if I can, I'm going to help put an end to it."

"Be careful. Your crusading is sexy, but don't get hurt while you're out chasing ghosts." He wished he could've sounded more upbeat, but he was beginning to think the whole situation had gone too far.

"We're stronger than this. All of us. I might be doing this for what amounts to nothing, but I've got a good reason," Remy said.

"You've gained confidence. I like it."

"Being with a great guy tends to help." Remy laughed again. "You're pretty special to me too."

"Right back atcha." Bobby sighed. "I'll keep an eye out for you."

"Sounds good. I'm at the city building. Looks like the Coalition meets there. I'm supposed to talk to the head of the group in ten minutes. I'll call when I'm on my way. Love you." Remy hung up.

Bobby stared at the silent phone. *Love you? What the hell?* He and Remy hadn't ventured into using that word. Not yet anyway. He liked Remy—a lot. It could be love, but he wasn't ready to admit it out loud. His head swam. Remy loved him. It didn't feel wrong, but different.

He roamed the house and locked the doors. His family, save for Remy and his father, were safe and there with him. He ventured upstairs to his bedroom.

"I'm going to talk to your dad," Esther said. "I'll be right back."

Neither child answered. Apparently whatever movie they were watching was more interesting.

Esther stepped into the hallway with Bobby, then over to the stairs. She sat on the top step with him. "That's quite a sight out there."

"Are there any at your house?" he asked.

"No. The Coalition wouldn't dare. Your father still has a lot of clout in this town. People respect him, even if they don't like that his son is gay." She patted his thigh. "It's none of their damn business."

"He's supposed to set an example. I'm not helping that image." He wasn't ashamed, but more irritated. Who gave the Coalition the right to determine who could and couldn't live in the town? "Are you sure your friends are against the Coalition? It seems like the group has long arms."

"They don't like the division, no. Most of my friends either have a child or grandchild who is gay or they know a gay person. We want Cedarwood to be a place of acceptance," she said. "A place to raise a family no matter how it's made up."

Her words rang in his head. *A place to raise a family no matter how it's made up.* He could use that as a slogan, but for what? The festival hadn't worked as well as they'd thought. But those words could band people together. He clasped his hands. He had no real idea how to get people organized.

"Hey, Dad?" Chris called. "Practice is cancelled. Coach doesn't want us out running in this climate. He says there are community issues that are impeding our practice. We're supposed to get a run in, but whatever time and wherever is up to us."

"Okay," Bobby replied. He turned his attention to his mother. "Mom, I'm stuck. This is affecting the kids. No practice? I don't want him out there running while this is going on, either, but how do I know it's not because I'm gay and the coach doesn't want to deal with me? I'm not on best-friends terms with him, and I haven't talked to him in a few days, so I can't be sure it's not a team-wide decision."

"You're getting worked up over something you can't control." She grasped his hand. "It's probably for the entire team. No one really wants the kids out there if they can't be supervised while this is going on. Where's Remy?"

"Covering the story for the paper." He stood and started down the steps. "I'll be right back. I need to make another phone call."

He made his way to the first floor of the house and stopped in the kitchen. Anger bubbled within him. When he glanced over his shoulder, he noticed Chris in the doorway.

"Don't ream out the coach, Dad. I know you want to," Chris said. "He's trying to keep us safe."

"I know and I appreciate it, but this has gotten too big." Christ, he was on edge. With so much happening, he wasn't even sure what to tell his children. *We'll be okay?* He had no guarantee they would be. *This will blow over?* Eventually, but how much damage would be done in the meantime? *Don't worry about what's going on and live your life?* Yes, but he wanted to make sure they were protected. He preferred to be honest with his children, but he had no idea what to do.

"Dad? He's gay too." Chris shrugged. "He's got a boyfriend in Cleveland, but he won't bring the guy here because he's afraid he'll get fired from his job at the school."

Bobby paused. He'd had no idea about the coach. Then again, he hadn't exactly asked. "Who else knows?"

"He won't say." Chris leaned on the island in the kitchen. "Is Remy okay?"

"I need to call him again, but I hope so." Now he had that worry too. He knew the kids were safe. His father was the chief of police. He had the safety of the station surrounding him. Remy? He was walking into the fire. *Fuck.* He met Chris' gaze. "What do you think about this situation? Be honest. You're my pragmatic child."

Chris snorted and folded his arms. "I think people need to chill and get over themselves. The more they single people out, the more we're all divided. It's like my comic books. Once you start carving society up, then you're setting everyone up for failure. It'll all fall apart."

He had such a smart kid. Observant too. He'd figured out the situation better than most of the adults. The question was, how were they going to fix it? Bobby couldn't change the minds of the Coalition. If he could, he wasn't sure how.

Bobby checked his phone. No messages or skipped calls. He missed Remy. "Hey, Chris? What do you think about Remy?"

"What? Him and you?" Chris' eyes widened. "You want to know what I think? Are you going to marry him or something?"

"I want to know if you like him." *Marry Remy? Jesus. First Remy uses the word love and now Chris mentions marriage.* He wasn't ready to go to those points just yet.

Chris hesitated. He wobbled his head. "Yeah, Dad. I do. He makes you happy. You smile a lot more than before, and you're not all stressed like when Neil was around." He shrugged. "He's quiet and all, but he's chill. I guess he's handsome. I'm not into dudes, but Darcy thinks he's hot."

"Dudes...you're making fun of me." He needed the moment of levity to digest what Chris had said. His daughter thought his boyfriend was hot. His son wasn't interested in men but liked Remy. The rest of the world was fucked up—at least in Cedarwood, it was—but his family was stable.

"Uh, yeah...I'm making fun of you. You're ancient." Chris laughed. "In all seriousness, Remy's way better than Neil and Terry."

"Really? Terry too?" He hadn't expected to hear that. "I had no idea."

"Terry was all right, but he got too intense. It was like if we didn't want to do what he wanted to, he'd tell us you'd get pissed. We went along with most of those trips and went to those restaurants because he wanted to."

"Why didn't you tell me?" *Holy shit.* He'd thought Terry was so stable. "I had no idea."

"Dad, he said you knew. He said he'd tell you, and we trusted him."

"Chris." Now he wondered what else his former partner had done. "Was that all? He's history, so feel free to talk. I won't hold any of it against you."

Chris scratched his forehead. "He didn't do anything, like, illegal." He shrugged again. "I saw stuff on his computer, but when he found out, he told me he'd—ugh. He said he'd send me and Darcy off to boarding school. That it was what you wanted, and the only reason we were still around was because of him." His voice cracked. "Dad, I knew he was full of shit. You're honest with us. If you were thinking of that, you'd have brought it up and made sure we were okay with it."

"I had no idea." And now he second-guessed his choice in lovers. "Was there anything else?"

"Nothing. He didn't touch us or anything. I made sure he wasn't alone with Darcy after that." Chris' gaze didn't waver. "I think he had a boyfriend before you split up. A guy in Japan or something. Tai? Kai? I don't know. But it was right before he left for good."

"And you never said anything because of what he'd threatened?" Bobby asked.

"Yeah. You seemed happy," Chris said. "Not like now. After a while, I didn't trust Terry. That's why I didn't want him to go on runs with us. That's why I made sure he wasn't alone with Darcy in the pool."

"You took on a lot, kid." He rounded the island and hugged his son. Tears burned at the back of his eyes. "I wish I'd known."

"I don't get the skeevy vibe from Remy, Dad. He's cool." Chris nodded and pulled away from Bobby. He wiped his face with the back of his hand. "Call him. Make sure Remy's okay."

"Chris." *Fucking balls.* "I will." He'd been so clueless with his own kids. He'd failed at keeping them safe. He wasn't sure what Terry had done or told them, but still. His children deserved more.

"Remy's a decent guy. You should go out with him more. He'd be good dad material." Chris shrugged and strolled out of the room. "Call Remy," he shouted.

Considering what Chris had just told him and the decorations on his lawn...he wasn't a happy camper. He flipped through the pages on his phone until he got to the one with Terry's information. *The bastard.* No one fucked with his kids. He erased Terry as a contact and the photos he'd left on the phone. *Fuck that shit.* He'd keep his kids in a damn bubble if that was what it took to keep them safe.

He sank onto the closest chair. Bubbles, no matter how indestructible, weren't going to keep everyone out. Sooner rather than later, his kids would be adults and free to make their own decisions.

He wished he could trust his own judgment. He'd figured Neil out pretty fast, and once he'd gotten a bead on Helene, he'd realized the relationship wouldn't end well. But Terry... He'd thought Terry was a good man, but instead he'd been good at hiding his true self. *Bastard.*

Could he trust Remy the way he'd trusted Terry? He wasn't sure. Still, he liked the man and needed to know Remy was okay. He dialed Remy's number and waited. Fifteen rings before the call went to voicemail. Maybe he was still in the meeting. Bobby waited a few moments then called again. The least he could do was leave a message. Another fifteen rings and the call went to voicemail. He tried a third time and got the same result.

Bobby left his chair and strode into the living room. He stared at the flags waving in the early afternoon breeze. If they hadn't been painted on, the little rainbows would've looked kind of cool against the green grass. He gripped the phone and folded his arms. He had to do something. The town had to get involved. He snorted. If everyone in Cedarwood who wasn't connected with the Coalition put flags in their yard, then the whole town would be blanketed with rainbows. Sure, not everyone in Cedarwood was for the LGBT community, but still. No one would know the difference between the gay households and the straight ones. He chuckled. *Wouldn't that be a sight?* No way to be sure, so no way to label. Realization struck, and he snapped his fingers. That was what he needed to do — let the flags rain all over the city.

"Mom?" He made his way over to the steps. "Mom?"

She appeared at the top of the staircase. "Hold on." Once she reached the bottom, she sat on the third step. "What's wrong?"

"What if we got everyone in Cedarwood pride flags? Like everyone who is part of the LGBT community and those who support it, or even for those who just don't support the Coalition?"

"Pepper the town with the rainbow?" She rested her hands on her knees. "Could be good. I'm sure my friends would take part. Your father and I would."

Chris trotted down the steps. "I can help Grandma find flags on the Internet." He sat beside her. "I want to help. She probably needs the tech assistance, and besides, you taught us not to be afraid of who we are. I'm not afraid."

His respect for his son grew by leaps and bounds. Hell, his respect for his mother increased too. He hadn't expected either one to get involved.

"We'll go upstairs and look for the flags. If you can, call that single dad group. I'm sure they'd want to know about this." His mother winked, then stood. Chris ran up the stairs first and she followed.

*Oh boy.* Colin would definitely want to know. He'd call him next. First, he wanted to try Remy again. He hit the Redial button and waited. After three rings, he considered hanging up. Instead, he got through.

"Hi," Remy said. "Are you home?"

His voice sounded ragged and broken. Bobby stomped into the living room. "Where else would I be? What's wrong?"

"I'm at the hospital."

"What?" He gripped the phone tight. "What happened?" His heart hammered and his chest ached. He wiped his free hand on his pants leg. "How?"

"I got the interview. The Coalition was happy to talk to me. They took complete credit for the flags. Got some wonderful quotes too." Remy grunted. "I hadn't planned on talking to them, and I wasn't really prepped for the interview—I didn't have my contacts in or a button-down on. I wore my shirt that says ALL SHADES OF THE RAINBOW WELCOME. They were glad to talk to me, but when I left, no one followed me out. I should've been concerned, but I—I wasn't. When I got into my car, someone had stuffed something in the exhaust pipe. I noticed it and took the chunk of whatever—potato I think—out. I tossed it into the nearby trash, and when I turned to get into the car, a man from the Coalition sucker-punched me. I'm waiting for the X-rays, but the doctor doesn't think anything's broken. I've got a shiner, and my jaw is killing me."

"Babe." *Fucking hell. What in the name of God is the world coming to?* "Mom's here. Want me to come get you? Did you call the police?"

"Your dad's here. The Coalition headquarters aren't far from the police station, so I drove over there. They've got my car." Remy's voice cracked again. "Man, I'm sorry."

"Why are you sorry? Jesus. You were doing your job. So you wore the wrong shirt? That doesn't mean you should have the hell beat out of you." Bobby clenched his fist. "I'm glad you got to the police department."

"Me, too. Your dad and another officer took me to the hospital. I guess they'll keep my car in their impound lot, and Chief's driving me home. Can I come over instead?"

"I'd be pissed if you didn't." Bobby closed his eyes. "You're in good hands with Dad."

"I'll call you back or text you before I leave," Remy said. "The doctor's here."

"Of course." Bobby disconnected the call and opened his eyes. He needed to call Colin. Sure, his father was on the case, and if he knew his dad, the person responsible for hurting Remy would be brought to justice. But the whole situation had become bigger than him or Remy or even the LGBTQ support group. The whole town was in chaos because of a few devout people stuck fast in their hate.

Things needed to change — right now.

# Chapter Nine

Remy winced as he slid onto the back seat of the police cruiser. He preferred having room to stretch out, but being transported in the back of an official vehicle kind of sucked. For all anyone on the outside knew, he'd done something wrong. Was that the kind of image the LGBT community and *The Tribune* wanted to share? Not in the least.

Still, he wasn't in any shape to drive anywhere. His ribs ached from the punch, his face felt like someone had played the bongos on him and his head throbbed. *What a great way to spend my afternoon.*

His phone buzzed. He swiped his thumb across the screen to answer the call. Wearing his contacts might have been a good idea that morning, but he hadn't planned on doing an interview. God, he was in sad shape.

"Hello?" he asked. "This is Remy."

"Hi, Rem."

He settled against the seat back. Maureen. He could handle talking to her right now. "What's shakin', baby?" He didn't sound like his normal self and hated it. He wanted the whole damn situation to go away.

"I heard you went to the ER. Please tell me it's nothing important? You've got all your pieces, right?" she asked.

"They're all there. Some are a little bruised and tender, but I'll live." Thank God the X-rays proved he hadn't sustained any broken bones. "But this is the second direct attack on members of the LGBT community."

"Do you have your notes on the Coalition story?"

"Yeah, but what's that got to do with anything? They fucked me up." He hated to be blunt with her, but his restraint was gone.

"I know, honey. I'm sorry it happened. If I knew who it was, I'd go kung fu on their collective asses."

He snorted. "You don't know kung fu."

"No, but I'd learn. You're a good man, Remy Nicholas. Just because someone busted you up doesn't mean you can't get the story done." She dropped her voice to a whisper. "Mr. Novack wished he had cameras there to witness the attack. Said it would make a great spread for the front page."

*Wonderful.* He didn't want his broken face all over *The Tribune.* "Sorry."

"That said, he's behind you. Write the story. The interview. Their side. All of it. Then write about your attack. I'll polish for you, and we'll get it in *The Tribune.* This can't go unchecked."

"I'll see what I can do. I should have it in by now, and I don't have anything done." He rested his head against the back of the seat. "This is a mess."

"No, you were hurt. Rest and see if you can get the story done tomorrow. You need to get your head in the game before you can write that, and if that means TLC with that hot boyfriend of yours, then you do that." She laughed. "I'll call you later."

"Bye." He hung up and sighed. He hadn't expected that phone call. He figured he'd be looking for a new job. Mr. Novack and the other heads of the paper didn't talk to the staff much. Maybe he should've been thankful, but the lack of communication could royally suck. Still, Maureen said he had his job and an extension on the Coalition story. He should've asked her who was handling the flag story, but dropped his phone onto his lap. He wasn't in the mood to talk about the Coalition or their crap right now.

"We're here." Chief Gagnon climbed out of the car first, then opened the door for Remy. "I'm guessing Bobby's worried sick about you."

"Probably." His stomach soured. *Bobby.* He'd spoken to his boyfriend not long ago and explained his current situation. That didn't bother Remy. No, the memory of what he'd said before he left to do the interview came to mind. He'd told Bobby he loved him. They weren't that far into the relationship, and he'd jumped the gun. He doubted Bobby would cool things between them right now, seeing as he was fucked up, but once he got better he could probably count on Bobby ushering him out of the door and his life.

He winced as he headed into the house. Bobby waited in the kitchen. His mother came down the stairs and slapped both hands over her mouth.

"Mom." Bobby wrapped his arm around Remy's waist, then turned his attention to the chief. "You're on this, right?"

"I'm not, but I've got Delaney going over the scene. He found the hunk of potato that was in the exhaust.

Useless for fingerprints, but it's still evidence." Chief Gagnon pointed to the living room. "Why don't you take care of him? I'd like to see the kids." He hooked his arm around his wife's, then made his way to the second floor.

Remy sagged against Bobby. "Honey, I'm home."

"You are." Bobby walked Remy to the front room and helped him onto the couch. "What's hurt? Ribs? Your poor face? What else?"

"My face is normal," he said, trying to make a joke and smile. "Maybe they made it better."

"No." Bobby knelt between Remy's legs. "Hey." He curled his fingers under Remy's chin and tipped Remy's gaze. "Dad won't let them get away with this. Promise. He's highly respected and damn good at his job. If he has Delaney on the case, they'll get it figured out."

"I know." The truth was, he didn't know. The depression hit him hard. Not the wishy-washy, this-won't-end-well depression, but down-to-his-soul sickness. Nothing looked positive at the moment.

"I've got a huge bed and you're staying. The kids know we're together and gave us their blessing. Mom and Dad have a pretty good idea what's going on, and they don't care." Bobby brushed his thumb across Remy's bottom lip.

"I told you I love you," he blurted. *Well, shit.* He'd said it again.

"Do you?"

"Love you? I wouldn't have said it if I didn't." He grasped Bobby's hand. "I'm a mess at relationships."

"You're doing fine." Bobby rose up on his knees and feathered a light kiss to Remy's lips. "You're braver than I could ever be."

"How?"

"You admitted what you wanted and how you felt with abandon. You go for the things you want — like the interview and me. You probably see yourself as not good enough, but you're better than good enough. You're awesome." Bobby kissed him again. "I'm glad to be with you."

"Really?"

"Uh-huh." Bobby grinned. "Let's get you some soup. I've got news for you too. Stay there."

Remy blew out a long breath. News? "Like what?"

"Hang on." A few minutes later, Bobby returned with a bowl resting on a plate. "Okay. All I've got is canned chicken noodle, but it should help. It's warm and nourishing and makes the kids feel better when they're sick."

"Thanks." He accepted the food and rested the plate on his lap. "I'm not dying." He hated to sound ungrateful, but he'd been beaten up. He wasn't hanging on the edge of death.

"I know. Just— It's making me feel better...like I can control something." Bobby shoved his hands into his back pockets. "This isn't my forte. I help, but I know what's going on. Right now, I have no idea which side is up."

"I understand." He was more than a little mixed up too.

"Let me check on the kids." Bobby hurried out of the room again, leaving Remy in silence.

Remy held on to the bowl and sighed. His head ached, and the meds weren't kicking in. According to the doctor, he wasn't showing signs of concussion, so that was a plus. Still, he hurt all over. He forced himself to eat some of the soup. Bobby had gone to the trouble of making it, and at least he cared. The broth burned down his throat but was oddly comforting. He'd forgotten he hadn't eaten all day. No wonder his stomach growled. He devoured half the soup before Bobby returned.

"You're hungry." Bobby grinned. "That's a good sign." He sat beside Remy. "I'm not sure what to do. I've never had this kind of an incident with a boyfriend before."

"Neither have I." Remy finished the soup and placed the bowl and plate on the coffee table. "Once we get past the naked time, they don't hang around. I tend to deal with a lot of stuff on my own."

"Well, you're not alone." Bobby patted Remy's thigh. "Mom and Dad are leaving soon. Chris got the call that the 5k was postponed. No make-up date yet."

"Probably just as well for the run. The community is on edge." Remy folded his hands on his stomach. "You should've seen the people coming out of the police department when I was there. I couldn't tell if they were afraid of me or afraid for themselves."

"A little of both." Bobby rested his elbows on his knees. "What if everyone had a flag? Or a bunch of those little flags? No matter what our color, we're all represented and we're not differentiating?"

"Us or the supporters?" Remy shrugged. "It's a good idea, but will too many people be scared and unwilling to go along even if they agree? I can see the situation a couple of different ways. Some people would take part no matter what. Some would want to, but the outcry from the Coalition would be enough to keep them quiet. Then there were the ones who would have no part in any of it. Regardless of how they felt, they'd stay out. Lastly, there are the devotees of the Coalition.

They'd do whatever they felt was necessary to keep the town...clean. Are we willing to risk riling all those people up?"

"I don't think Cedarwood is as homophobic as the Coalition wants everyone to think."

Bobby could be right but Remy didn't believe so. "Okay, well, whatever the plan — I'm in."

"Yeah?" Bobby smiled again. "The LGBTQ support group meets tonight, but Colin probably won't want to get everyone together after..." He nodded to the picture window. "I've got a better idea. I want to have the meeting here. You can report on it and take part without having to go anywhere. Plus, it's safer here." He stood. "Where's my phone?"

"If Colin and company are fine with it, then sure." Remy sighed. He had the feeling that no matter what he said, Bobby's mind was made up. That was part of what he liked about Bobby.

Remy waved as Bobby darted out of the room. He should probably take the soup bowl to the sink. Should also be working on his story for the paper. *Fuck.* He hated to be late. He worked hard to ensure all of his stories made it without going over his deadlines. Then the Coalition happened. He managed to stand and carried the bowl to the kitchen. Bobby hardly noticed him as he passed.

Remy grabbed his messenger bag and hoped to God his tablet was intact. He returned to the couch and opened the front flap of his bag. The device and keyboard seemed to be in working order. He opened the folio case and turned on the Wi-Fi. Once the tablet recognized the keyboard, he pulled up a blank document.

## A CITY ON THE EDGE

He liked the title for the article. Bold and a little scary, but great for gaining the attention of his readers. He started working on the piece. The words came to him fast and furious. Within a few minutes, he had the first draft of the story nearly done. He read it over and twiddled with some of the lines until he liked what he'd written. The piece was informative and unbiased, just like he wanted. According to his notes, the Coalition had taken complete responsibility and weren't above doing so again.

*End of story?* He shook his head. The Coalition hadn't seen anything yet.

Remy opened another document and wrote about the incident he'd been through. The assault would be in the police blotter, so it wasn't like he was telling a secret. He zipped through the second piece and once he reached the end, read through what he'd written.

"Informative and unbiased," he mumbled. He saved both documents, then sent them off to the paper. He clenched his fist and grinned. He was beyond his deadline, but not by much.

He stretched and winced as his side ached. *Damn fools.* Beating someone because they didn't like his sexuality. *Whatever.* He opened a third document on the tablet. There were more words within him, and he needed to get them out.

*When will it end?* he typed. The town of Cedarwood is divided. Walk outside and look around. It's pretty clear. Surely you've noticed. From physical violence, name calling and public displays of hate to the quieter forms of intolerance — ignoring a local play because the playwright is gay or refusing to shop at the bookstore because the proprietor is a gay father — this needs to end.

Are we not a civilized community? Can we not accept the thoughts of others, especially if they don't mesh with our own? Are we unwilling to consider we might not have all of the answers?

To my knowledge, no one in the LGBTQ community is expecting to be given a free pass. They, me included, want to be treated with dignity. To be given the same freedoms as anyone else in the town of Cedarwood, that's all. How can this happen when there are bags of feces left on the porches of gay men? Or someone insulting another person at a public event because she happened to kiss her girlfriend?

I'm not sure how to answer those questions. Maybe there aren't answers. Maybe you don't see a problem with this. You should. What if you wanted to kiss your partner, but someone deemed it inappropriate simply because of your sexuality?

Now, you might be asking yourself, what about the opposition? If you're expected to accept the LGBTQ community, then why not accept those who have the opposing view? There are no laws stating everyone must get along. No person in charge demanding fair treatment for the masses. You're right — there aren't. But doesn't the Golden Rule come into play here? Do unto others as you'd have done to you. If you want to be treated with dignity, then do that for everyone else. You don't have to like the person in order to be fair. Live and let live. Right?

Then what is the grand solution here? What if you and I don't agree? That's the beauty of democracy. We don't have to. We can still treat each other fairly and not share the same beliefs. It's what makes Cedarwood great. You're welcome to your thoughts and feelings thanks to the Constitution. That's a pretty awesome thing.

But if you've got rights, then so does everyone else.

I ask again, then what's the solution?

You think for yourself. If you don't like the LGBTQ community or any other group, then that's your right. Understand, though, that there are those who don't share your opinion. They're just as vocal as you are. Don't shame someone else for being different. Simply move on. Don't insult someone because you don't agree with them. Move on and put your energy into something you're passionate about.

Live and let live. I've mentioned that already. Have your rainbow flag and your differences of opinion. This town is already great because we have choices. Cedarwood should be a place where kids feel free to be themselves and where families of all shapes and sizes can co-exist. A place where we can aspire to be greater than we ever imagined.

Love each other and accept your fellow Cedar-woodians. You never know what the future holds. Let's make right now the best it can be so we've got a future to look forward to.

Remy sat back in his seat and puffed out a long breath. *Holy fuck.* He'd written three articles in the space of forty-five minutes. He closed his eyes. His brain was fried. The first two stories would be fine and were probably being proofed already. If Maureen was working late, his work would be pushed through to the morning edition. He opened his eyes and saved the opinion piece. He wasn't sure if he wanted to turn it in yet or not.

Maybe he'd better let Bobby and the group read it first.

Bobby strode back into the room and sank onto the couch beside Remy. "Sorry about that. Once I got off the phone with one person, I had to field a call from someone else. My idea to have the group over went over well, and they want to discuss the alternative flags." He palmed Remy's thigh. "Looks like you got something accomplished. I'm sorry I left you in here so long."

"I had to get my work done." Remy detached the keyboard, then tucked it into his bag.

"I need to clean the house. It's a mess." Bobby hopped up from his seat. "I'm going to have a ton of people here. Shit."

"Slow down." Remy left the tablet on the couch and stood. "It'll be fine. The kids and I will help. Aren't your folks still here?"

"Yeah, they're upstairs." Bobby massaged his temples. "I suck under pressure." He met Remy's gaze. "And you should be resting."

"I feel better than I thought. I'll pay for it later, but I'll be okay." The safety in Bobby's house, plus the love in his eyes, more than made up for Remy's bad day. Sure, he hurt in plenty of places, but he had a purpose. More than that, he had someone who cared. For a guy who hadn't had anyone give a damn about him, Bobby's affection and worry made him feel pretty important.

"I don't have refreshments." Bobby shook his head. "I should've thought this idea through before I made calls."

He grasped Bobby's shoulders. "Chill. Call Colt. Maybe he can bring something from the bakery or has extra something made up."

"Yeah."

Remy glanced around the living room. "Other than picking up my stuff, this room is fine. How's the kitchen?"

"A mess." Bobby kissed Remy. "I forgot how good it is to have someone who can put up with...me. You ground me."

"I'm trying to do that, or something kind of like it." He squeezed Bobby's shoulders. "Call Colt. I'll help in the kitchen."

"If you keep doing stuff like this, I'll fall for you." Bobby held his phone to his ear.

"Oh, don't lie," Remy said. "You already have." He ducked into the kitchen before Bobby could speak. Part of him wanted to hear Bobby agree, but the rest of him didn't want to push.

Chris and Esther emptied the dishwasher. Esther shooed Remy from the stove. "We've got this," she said. "Sit. You've been through a lot today."

"I'm not an invalid." Instead of continuing to argue with her, he rounded the island to the barstools.

"That's true, you're not." She wiped off the granite on the island. "But I'm not taking no for an answer. My friend Maureen talks highly of you."

"Dad says he's hot." Chris waggled his eyebrows. "Dads."

"Hot, eh?" She grinned. "I haven't seen Bobby this happy in a long time."

The tips of Remy's ears burned. *Hot.* He assumed Bobby liked the way he looked, but to hear Chris say the words... *Are kids supposed to repeat that stuff?*

"You're cute in a you're-way-too-young-for-me sort of way." Esther placed a serving platter on the counter. "But you're Bobby's type, so it works."

"Thanks." *He has a type?* He hadn't gotten that vibe from Bobby at all. Then again, he hadn't seen pictures of Bobby's exes, so he wouldn't know. "Julia would agree that I've been pretty happy lately too." Speaking of his friend, he needed to call her. Not only would she be worried about him, but she'd insist on an update on the Bobby front.

"Julia? Is that your mom?" Esther asked. She balled the dishrag. Water dripped from between her fingers.

"She's my girlfriend." He knew the moment he'd said the words, he'd described Julia in the wrong way.

Esther's eyes widened. "I'm sorry?"

Chris shook his head. "Like Jenna's my girlfriend, but we're not going together. I wanted to be dating Nicki, but Dad axed that. Anyway, Jenna—a girl who is my friend. Girl friend. Dad would probably prefer I date Jenna. He knows her parents and her. He doesn't know Nicki."

"Oh." Esther didn't appear convinced. She folded her arms.

Remy hadn't ever felt the need to apologize for Julia or explain her to anyone else—until now. "I've known Julia for a long time. She's a great person, but we're not dating. I'm not interested in her that way." He pressed his lips together. He thought he'd sounded fine in his explanation, but Esther hadn't uncrossed her arms, and she continued to frown.

"Then you're not cheating on my Bobby with her?" she asked.

"No." He chuckled, not knowing what else to do. The tension was so thick. He laced his fingers together.

The idea of cheating on Bobby hadn't crossed his mind. Not with Julia or anyone.

"Good." She unfolded her arms and clapped her hands. "This place seems to be clean." She draped the dishrag over the divide in the sink. "I'll get the chief and we'll go. I'll be right back." She strode from the room, leaving Remy alone with Chris.

"Grandmas. She means well," Chris said. "If it makes any sense, she had issues with Dad being gay. They're chill now, but back then...whatever. She needs time to come around, but she will." He laughed. "People are so messed up."

"Humans are a messed-up bunch." He smiled and sighed. "Sometimes I wish they weren't."

Chris nodded. "I don't see why everyone is so mad about who's dating whom. You're not doing anything illegal. Right?" He grinned. "We talked about this at practice the other day."

"You discussed me and your dad at practice?" He gulped. "We're not doing anything illegal, by the way."

"I knew you were cool." Chris spread his hands on the other side of the island. "We didn't discuss you and Dad, but gay people and the Coalition thing. One kid, his mom is on that board for the Coalition, said the gay people are trying to rule the world and make everyone gay. You can't make someone gay."

"You're smarter than a lot of people." He still ran into individuals who swore up and down that touching a gay person would make them gay too.

"That's what I don't get. What's so bad about guys who like other guys and women who like other women? If you like the person, what's the big deal?" Chris asked.

"Without getting into a huge discussion about ideology, some—like the Coalition—believe the only relationships should be between a man and a woman. There are a ton of reasons why gay couples bother them. They can't produce children. It's not in the Bible. It's against God's law. It's gross. Gay people can't raise kids because the kids won't have a mom and a dad. Kids with one parent or another aren't raised in the same manner so they'll be screwed up. Those aren't true, but it's...one set of beliefs versus another. You're right, as long as we're not doing anything illegal, it shouldn't matter who you have for a partner. You can be bad and be heterosexual too." Remy unclenched his fists. He hadn't realized he'd tensed up. "Sorry. That was the novel answer to a short answer question."

"It's okay." Chris leaned on the counter. "I know you don't like kids—I heard you tell Dad that—but maybe you can learn to like us? Like maybe we can grow on you?"

"You already have." He wasn't lying. He'd grown quite fond of Chris and Darcy in the short time he'd known them. He'd lied to himself. He was a kid person—he just needed the right kids to come along.

"You're not shitting me?" Chris grinned and stood tall. "Nice."

"I'm not, but you shouldn't talk like that. Your dad would have a coronary." Remy exhaled. The tension was gone, and he felt like he was part of the family. He'd forged a bond with Darcy and now Chris.

"Sorry," Chris said. "Grandma's right. Dad needs to be happy. He doesn't act all tense and emo." He dropped his voice to a whisper. "He needs the help too. You know, someone to be there for him and stuff. To do parent-y stuff. Watch us at meets and runs. I kinda like knowing I've got a cheering section. We didn't have that when Dad dated Neil."

The kid was smarter than his years in so many ways. Remy respected Chris' honesty and wished Chris hadn't had to grow up so fast. "Well, unless your dad dumps me, I'm not planning on going anywhere. I'm more of a homebody than Terry, and I do like you two. I did from the start, but I didn't realize it."

"You're a trip." Chris' smile widened. "A good one."

"Thanks," he replied.

Bobby strode into the kitchen with Esther and Chief Gagnon right behind him. Darcy followed.

"Okay, so Colt's bringing sandwiches, plus dinner for any kids who tag along." He threw his arm around Darcy's shoulders. "Meaning you and Chris. Pick out a movie—I know. Too much television time usually gets you into trouble, but this is different."

"I'll help," Chris said. "We'll have fun. Come on, almost teen." He herded Darcy from the room. "Dad and Remy need privacy."

"For what?" she asked.

If Chris answered her, Remy couldn't hear him. *Good Lord. What is Chris telling her?* Remy scooted off the stool. "Are you leaving?" he asked. He extended his hand to Chief Gagnon. "Thanks for the ride and for saving my ass."

"You're welcome." The chief shook hands with Remy. "Now, Bob, Dr. Rhinehart said to watch for concussion symptoms. You know what to do." He turned his attention back to Remy. "And you. We used the photos from the paper to help locate the guy. My detective has him in custody. We'll get this sorted out, okay?"

"Good deal." Remy nodded. He wanted the whole ordeal to be over already.

"If Bob thinks you're good people, then so do I." The chief hugged Remy.

Remy met Bobby's gaze. Bobby's eyes widened and his lips parted. Was he as shocked as Remy?

"The same goes for me," Esther said. She caught the chief and Remy in a group hug. "Be good to my boy and I'll love you forever."

Approval from both parents. He couldn't believe his luck. He let go of Bobby's folks, then sank onto the stool. "Thank you," he said.

Bobby nudged his parents out to the garage, to his mother's car. He stepped out of the kitchen, and whatever he said to his parents, Remy couldn't hear. Remy rearranged the apples in the fruit bowl while he waited for Bobby. The synapses in his brain were at the point of misfiring. He had too much information and needed to talk.

Bobby stepped back into the kitchen. "I don't know what you did to get my dad to approve, but I'm impressed. He hates everyone."

"It's a cop thing. I've only ever dealt with one that didn't believe everyone was a jerk or out to do something irresponsible." Remy shrugged. He talked to cops on a regular basis for his job. Most of the time, the police were great people, but sometimes they weren't. Then again, the same could be applied to dealing with humans in general.

"Yeah, I guess." Bobby glanced over his shoulder. "I hate talking about the past with the kids, and I don't want them to think of their grandparents in a negative light."

"I heard your father had a problem with you being gay. Chris mentioned it." Remy put both hands up. "I had a heart-to-heart with him. It wasn't my plan. It just happened."

"If you can get him to talk like that, then consider it a win." Bobby leaned on the counter in the same manner as Chris had done earlier. "Look, I'm going to throw this out there. After what happened and everything, I need to say it." He bowed his head, but didn't continue.

Remy leaned over enough to scope out the stairs. "I don't see the kids," he whispered. "What's wrong?" *Is Bobby having second thoughts?* He wished he could read Bobby's mind.

"You weren't the only one Chris opened up to today. He told me something I didn't know, and it's got me on guard." Bobby met Remy's gaze. "I didn't realize it at the time, but looking back, I can see each maneuver."

"About me?" Remy asked. Goddamn it, he was confused.

"No. About Terry." Bobby waved his head from side to side, then stopped. "Terry had this way of expecting everyone to go along with whatever he wanted. I got used to it and didn't notice as much once he moved in. I thought he kept his pushiness to a minimum, but now I've found out he'd manipulate the kids. If he didn't want to do something, he'd plant the idea in Chris' or Darcy's head that they didn't want to, either. Why? Because he was selfish."

Remy nodded. "I see." Although he wasn't sure how this applied to him.

"If I ever catch you using my kids like that, I will tie your testicles together and hang them from the front porch," Bobby bit out.

Remy scooted back from the island. Besides Bobby's words coming from left field, his anger was unprovoked. "Bob, I can't imagine who would do that to a kid, let alone do it myself. I'm in awe of Chris and Darcy, and I appreciate how you've raised them. I even appreciate the warning." He lowered his voice to a growl. "But I haven't done anything wrong. Call Terry and bitch him out. He deserves this piece of your mind. I need a guy who sees me — not some version of his past that he's worried will come back again." He left the stool. "I'll be in the living room picking up my shit. Once the meeting is over, I'll leave."

Remy strode past Bobby and winced as he stopped in the front room. The pounding in his head had returned. He and Bobby weren't supposed to fight. Not over something like this. He wasn't ready to give up on his boyfriend, but he also wasn't sure Bobby still wanted the relationship. *Fucking balls.*

# Chapter Ten

Bobby scrubbed both hands over the top of his head and bit back a growl. He hated it when his partner was right. Remy hadn't deserved to be yelled at any more than Terry deserved not to have to deal with what had happened. He didn't want Remy to go, but he'd created one hell of a wound in the relationship. What a way to explain some of his issues — to threaten one of the few people who cared about him and the kids.

He was so fucked in the head.

Now he had to figure out how to keep Remy at the house. Telling Remy he couldn't leave because someone had to monitor him for signs of concussion was valid, but he doubted Remy would go along. He'd done so much damage.

"Rem." Bobby strode into the living room and stopped at the couch. He stepped between Remy's knees and grasped the back of the sofa. He tipped Remy's chin, forcing him to look Bobby in the eye. "Don't go. Okay? We need to talk, and that wasn't how I wanted any of it to go down. I messed up."

"You don't trust me," Remy snapped. "You think I'll mind-fuck your kids the way that asshole ex of yours did. I don't understand that situation, but that was him and I'm me. If you can't trust me, even a little, then this won't work."

Bobby wanted to fight Remy. He wanted to duke it out until they both saw reason and ended up fucking to make the negative go away. "This isn't over."

"Uh-huh." Remy tucked his tablet and keyboard into his bag. "Answer the door. You've got company."

"We've got company," Bobby corrected. He still wanted there to be a 'we'.

"I'm not a single father or parent."

"Honorary." Bobby swiped his thumb across Remy's bottom lip. "I want you here. Stay. Please?"

Remy shook his head, but didn't leave the couch.

Bobby sighed and pushed off the sofa. He glanced over his shoulder. Colin, Jordan, Farin and Steve waited on the porch. Gage and Genie were right behind them. He opened the front door. "Welcome to my home." He waited for them to enter the living room. "If you haven't met him already, this is my boyfriend, Remy Nicholas."

"The reporter." Farin crossed to Remy first. "The *Positively Cedarwood* columns are fantastic."

Bobby blew out a ragged breath. Remy hadn't objected to being called his boyfriend and he hadn't left. Not huge scores, but not awful, either.

"Colt and Ash will be here in a few," Colin said. "Michael's out on tour, so I called Niall. He gets lonely. Besides, this is more than a single father problem."

"You're right." Bobby nodded to the stairs. "Chris and Darcy are in the family room up there. They're supposed to be watching a movie."

Steve nodded. "Go. It'll be more exciting up there than down here."

"Told you," Colin said. He nudged Gage. "You know Darcy from being at the pool together. She won't bite. Go."

Genie tapped Gage on the shoulder. "Last one to the family room…" Instead of finishing her sentence, she bounded up the steps.

"Man," Gage groused, then followed her.

"Families are so much fun," Steve said. "I'm not even a dad. She's my sister."

Bobby leaned on the chair next to the front door. He'd forgotten how chaotic having people over could be. *So many bodies…*

Within a few minutes, Colt, Ashley and Wyatt were on the porch. Colt held three bags. "Knock, knock."

"Come in." Bobby held the door for them. "Wyatt, the kids are upstairs if you want to watch a movie with them." He met Ashley's gaze. "Sorry. If you don't mind." He'd overstepped his boundaries with another parent—something he'd sworn not to do.

"Go," Ashley said. He scooped one of the bags out of Colt's hands. "I was worried he'd get bored. I'm glad you thought of them."

"Oh." Bobby held out his hands. "Let me take those. I've got plenty of room in the kitchen."

"Nah. I'm good. Lead the way and we'll bust out the snacks," Colt said.

Bobby rushed around. He moved the fruit bowl off the island, then grabbed the stack of napkins. As Colt opened each of the boxes, Bobby set out paper plates. Now he remembered why he preferred not to host parties—he hated the stress involved.

"I'll get the kids and they can eat around the bar," Remy said. "That way they don't destroy the family room." He disappeared up the stairs before Bobby could argue.

Bobby backed out of the way. He had to admit it— Remy had a knack for dealing with kids. He was smart too. Fuck, he needed to fix things with Remy.

Half an hour later Niall arrived, and Colin called the meeting to order. Bobby sat on the arm of the sofa beside Remy. He wasn't going to let Remy out of his sight. Although Colin seemed to be in charge of the discussion, everyone spoke at the same time. The noise irritated Bobby. He preferred the quiet of his office versus so much chatter.

Steve nudged Bobby. "We keep it lively."

Bobby nodded. 'Lively' was one way to put it. They hadn't made this much noise at the last meeting, but maybe this was how the group normally acted. He'd only attended two, and those had been reserved.

Colin stood and stuffed his hands into his pockets. "Okay. We've eaten, argued and everyone's a little pissed. What's the next step? Bobby suggested we have flags for everyone who wants one. Like blanketing Cedarwood with positivity."

"I like it," Colt said. "Lord knows this town needs a few good things to happen to lessen the blow from the Coalition."

Bobby listened to the group talk but barely heard any of it. The issues with Remy still bothered him. He'd created the problem and wanted it fixed...like, yesterday. That wasn't going to happen. He couldn't say the words out loud, but he loved Remy. He couldn't stomach the possibility that they might be splitting up—if they hadn't already. He didn't want to lose Remy.

"I have a suggestion," Remy said. He grabbed Bobby's attention with his abrupt comment. Remy twiddled with his tablet. "I've been thinking about the flag idea."

*Oh great. He wants to put the kibosh on it.* Bobby bit the inside of his cheek to keep from groaning or saying something else to piss off Remy. *Hear him out, then ream him out. Christ.* What was wrong with him? It was like he wanted to destroy the good things in his life because he didn't trust people. Terry hadn't been trustworthy and neither had Neil, but Remy was a different situation.

"If we went the traditional route with the flags, we'd have to approach people in order to distribute them. Talking about fabric flags or even those tiny simple plastic ones will cost some serious money. A lot of people won't want to be bothered. So this is my suggestion. Keep the flag idea—it's a good one—but what if we have them printed in the paper?" Remy asked. "I've worked this out in my head and run the numbers too. We'd essentially take out a full-page ad in the paper, but instead of an advertisement, we'd have the flag placed in there. Then that way, anyone who wants to display it can without having to feel pressured."

"Do you mean like when *The Tribune* puts the American flag in around the Fourth of July?" Bobby asked. Remy wasn't totally shutting him down and had a better spin on the problem. His heart swelled with appreciation and love for his boyfriend. Damn it, they'd stay together. He wasn't giving up, and when the group left, he'd take Remy upstairs for some special TLC.

"Yeah, but we'd create our own flag," Remy said. "Not a pride flag, per se. A pride in Cedarwood kind of thing. Something with the rainbow incorporated into it, but a little of everything included too. Go with the stuff that makes Cedarwood great."

"How about the school mascot, the Cedarwood Ducks?" Bobby asked. He wanted to reach for Remy and congratulate him on the great idea, but held back.

Colt shook his head and rested his elbows on his knees. "Well, wait. It could get pretty involved if we used everything that makes Cedarwood great. Think about it. Whatever we left off could rankle people. Plus, wouldn't the flag be almost too busy?"

Farin nodded and widened his stance. He stood behind the chair Steve sat in. "The pride in Cedarwood is great, though. How about the duck, like Bobby said, and the school colors? Like, a row of the ducks in each color and a band each of yellow, white and green in the background? That says we're all in this together to me."

"With the label 'Pride in Cedarwood' and instructions for the flag along the bottom of the page so people know what to do with it." Ashley grinned. "We could sponsor it, but keep that kind of on the down-low."

"Nice," Colt said. He clasped his hand on Ashley's knee. "So smart."

Bobby sighed. He couldn't wait for the meeting to conclude. He'd agree to whatever they wanted to do if it meant he'd finally be alone with Remy.

"What if people complain? What if they feel duped?" Niall asked. "Like we're asking them to participate even if they don't agree with our message. I mean, what if they say they don't want to do this because they're afraid the Coalition will have a bitch fit? The Coalition have pride, but they won't put anything that smacks of LGBTQ pride anywhere on their houses. They've got pride. It's fucked up, in my opinion, but it's theirs."

"No matter what we do, someone will be pissed," Bobby said. "Our existence pisses them off. But we can't keep allowing them to dictate our lives. Let them keep punching. We don't have to give in."

"The punches fucking hurt," Remy muttered.

Bobby winced. He couldn't get the memory of Remy's bruises out of his mind. He needed to do something to help the cause. "That wasn't what I meant." *God.* Could he stop putting his foot in his mouth? "The point I'm trying to make is there isn't going to be an easy way out of this. I've thought about this a lot. If we move, then they win. If we stay, they stay pissed. If we shout, then they'll claim we're inciting...everything. Colin's right. We live our lives and show we're not going away. This flag idea is still valid. If people who aren't in the LGBTQ community display them, it'll prove to the rest of the town that we're not such a minority after all."

"I agree that everyone won't love it, but you're right. It'll prove we're not going anywhere and we have support too," Colin said. "We've all got pride, no matter what color it happens to be, and we're all living in the same town."

"Maybe this would help," Remy said. He handed his tablet to Colin. "I know it needs work, but that's the op-ed piece I want to put in Friday's paper. I'm all for input on how to polish it or whatever you think should be added. It's the working draft."

Bobby wanted to be the first to look at whatever Remy had written but didn't push. He'd get his turn.

"I already turned in my stories about the meeting I had with the Coalition leaders and the attack on me afterward. This I won't turn in until I've gone over it a few times." Remy sagged in his seat. "Colt, you weren't kidding. They're wicked with the punches."

"I'm sorry it happened," Colt said. He scratched his chin as he stared at the tablet.

"What exactly went down at the meeting?" Colin asked. The muscle in his jaw twitched. "Can you disclose it?"

"It's getting printed in tomorrow's paper, so it's not a huge secret." Remy folded his legs up under him and rested his hands on his lap. "There are seven members of the Coalition board. There's like thirty people who claim membership in the group. Of the top people, four are men and three are women. They believe in what their literature says—we're freaks and need to be stopped. We're brainwashing kids into thinking being gay is cool. We've turned being gay into an accessory, like a purse or belt. Why are we doing this? Because we can't make children, so we need to recruit. Oh and they think we're telling said kids that we can fuck whomever we want, whenever we want, and that makes it a turn-on."

"We're all parents," Colin snapped. "Okay, Niall isn't, but that's not the point. Being gay isn't a shirt we put on. Christ in a basket, we're trying to raise our kids to be accepting. This isn't accepting anything."

"Correct." Remy nodded and glanced over at Bobby. He half-smiled and grasped Bobby's hand. "The thing is, they're afraid of us. They think we're the 'young and in' thing, while their values are on the way out. What they're failing to see is we've all got the same core values — raising our children to be productive members of society, sticking with one partner and having a family. Our version of family happens to be a little more fluid than theirs."

Colin bowed his head. "What's the cost to run the flag ad, and who can create the artwork?"

"I'll double-check the prices, but around five hundred dollars to run it on one day." Remy let go of Bobby's fingers. "I've got some wiggle room with the boss and the advertising department, so that could go down, most likely."

"Nice." Colt handed the tablet to Steve. "Why don't one of you do the art? Ash? You could."

"I'd like to." Ashley stood, then waved to Colt. "Can we talk?" He left the room, followed by Colt.

Bobby knelt beside the couch. "How are you feeling?" he asked Remy. "That looked like it took a lot out of you."

"I'll be okay." Remy toyed with Bobby's watch. "I'm a low-drama kind of guy. This shit is way out of my comfort zone."

"It's extreme for all of us." He met Remy's gaze. "What I said was wrong. I'm sorry. I deserve for you to be angry with me, because I never should've opened my mouth. You're right — Terry and Neil aren't you. I can't measure you with their stick."

"You just don't want me to go home tonight." Remy lowered his voice to a whisper. "You want me in your bed. Horny toad."

"Damn right." He wanted Remy naked and beside him as he slept. He wanted him beneath him and begging to come too. Remy had become special to him. Part of the rush of feelings could be chalked up to what

Remy had just been through, but most of it boiled down to Bobby coming to terms with the situation. He'd found a great guy and wanted to keep Remy in his life.

"Everything hurts too much to argue. Besides, I can't go home. I don't have a car," Remy said.

"I'll take care of you." No hesitation or thought needed. "Love you too, Rem."

Remy's eyes widened, but he didn't get the chance to respond. Colin clapped his hands.

"Okay," Colin said. "We've ponied up a little under five hundred right now. Bobby, I'm putting you in charge of placing the ad once Ashley has the art done. Remy, thank you for the offer to put the flag in the paper. That was a stroke of genius. You and Bobby should collaborate more often. As for the op-ed piece, I've got some ideas to tweak it. No huge changes. I'll email them to you along with the input from the others."

Colt nodded to the leftover boxes of food. "Keep the extra food as my thanks for having the meeting."

"Thanks," Bobby said. "I appreciate it."

"We have to get moving. Wyatt is supposed to be at his grandmother's in forty-five minutes." Ashley said. "We'll see you." Ashley, Colt and Wyatt strode through the living room to the front door.

Niall shook hands with Bobby. "I've got to go too. I'm supposed to video chat with Michael tonight." He shrugged. "That's the fun of dating a musician. He travels, and I keep the house clean." Within moments, he'd left too.

Chris hurried down the stairs. "Dad? I need the steam cleaner. Someone spilled soda all over the carpet. I just found it."

"It's in the closet in the hallway." Bobby groaned. He hadn't wanted anyone eating in the family room but hadn't said anything to stop them.

"I'll give him a hand." Remy grabbed a roll of paper towels. He headed upstairs. Chris carried the smaller steam cleaner and went to the second floor.

"Sorry." Steve clapped Bobby on the shoulder. "Kids are slobs sometimes. I'll give them a hand too." He disappeared up the steps. Colin and Farin followed him to the family room, leaving Bobby and Jordan alone together.

"Thanks for having the meeting," Jordan said. He gathered up empty paper plates and tossed them into the trash bin. "We needed this."

"My pleasure. My carpeting might not survive, but that's life." Bobby closed the box on the uneaten pizza, then put the leftover portions of sub sandwiches into the foam box. "It's not the greatest carpet, but I wasn't looking to replace it for a while."

"If you put in hardwood and rugs, you can wipe the messes up easier, and the rugs can be machine washed." Jordan folded his arms and leaned against the counter. "So...you and Remy?"

"For now." He needed to talk with Remy more before he felt certain about their relationship. He'd admitted he loved Remy and hadn't given Remy a chance to answer.

"I didn't like him when he first moved to town. He seemed sleazy," Jordan said. "I guess it's that he's a reporter."

"Really?" Bobby put the boxes into the refrigerator. "Seems rather extreme."

"He's a reporter and seemed to be sniffing around everywhere."

Bobby rolled his eyes and wiped his hands on the dishtowel. "You're a cop. Does that automatically make you a dick?"

"Depends on who you talk to. Those who don't like cops would agree. Colin would say otherwise." Jordan shrugged. "You were so quiet in school. I thought maybe you and Colin might hook up. It was pretty obvious back then you were both gay and liked each other. You could've gotten a date with Daryl. He liked you and so did Lonie."

"Daryl? Lonie? I hadn't come out yet. How did you know and I didn't?" Bobby snapped. He hated that Jordan acted so smart about the situation.

"You could've hooked up with Lonie right now. He coaches the track team. I bet once you met, you'd hit it off." Jordan crossed his ankles. "He's nice and quiet."

"Well, the school year hasn't started, and track season is a while off. Chris will want to join the team, I'm sure, so I'll meet him sooner or later. Chris holds records back at Chagrin High."

"That's great." Jordan cocked his head. "He doesn't look like you. Darcy does, but Chris doesn't."

"He's adopted," Bobby replied. He opened a bottle of beer. Jordan hadn't completely changed—he was still an asshole.

"Oh. I— Sorry. Col says I've got to work on my tact." Jordan smiled, and red tinged his cheeks.

"He's right," Bobby replied.

Jordan sighed and bowed his head. "You're a good guy, Bobby. If Remy makes you happy, then that's cool. I'd keep my head on, though. Reporters can be bullshit artists."

He downed half of the beer in one swig, then swallowed. Maybe Jordan thought he was being a friend, but Bobby disagreed. The guy sounded like a jackass. "You're trying to protect me, I assume. I don't know why. We weren't best friends ever in our lives." He was on the edge of going off and gripped the bottle to keep his wits about him. "I'm good with Remy, but I appreciate the warning. I've got to say this, even though it'll make me sound like I'm seventeen, but you don't have to warn me about him. Everyone has their sleazy side. I bet you've got a few things you want to keep quiet because people would look at you a little differently."

"Like what?" Jordan met Bobby's gaze. "I'm not ashamed of my life."

"You're not ashamed of how you treated me and a few other people back in school? You used to close me in my locker on a weekly basis. Right before prom, you told me Jenna Newell wanted me to ask her out and to the dance. When she turned me down, you stood there and laughed."

"That was almost fifteen years ago." The muscle in Jordan's jaw tensed. "But I'd forgotten about it."

"I don't care how long ago it was. What if it were Gage going through that? All parents and kids have to deal with this kind of shit, and I seriously hope you've learned from it." Bobby wiped his mouth with the back of his hand. "It's crap. No kid should have to deal with bullies."

Jordan glared at him. "You're right, but still."

A thought occurred to Bobby. This was the root of what the group was dealing with in relation to the Coalition. Bullying. A few who weren't happy making others feel bad in order to make them feel better. "Is this what the Coalition wants? For us to argue? For us to fight among ourselves and come apart at the seams? If we can't get along with each other or them, then we're perpetuating their lies. We can place a hundred million flags around Cedarwood, but until we accept the Coalition will think differently from us and that we can accept ourselves, we're screwed." He'd lost his shit and his head ached. He needed his day to slow down and for less action to happen.

Colin strode down the stairs and into the kitchen. Remy hurried behind him. Colin sighed and stepped between Jordan and Bobby. "I figured this would happen," Colin said. He turned to Remy. "They hated each other in school. Like, down to their core hated each other."

Colin was talking about Bobby like he wasn't there, and it irritated Bobby.

"Bobby was sweet, quiet and so cute. I wasn't ready to come out back then or I would've made a move on him. He wasn't out yet, either, so it wasn't a big deal." Colin turned back to Jordan. "Stop acting like a hot shot. You don't have to play to the cop stereotype. He's still a sweet guy. Don't be a dick."

Bobby snapped his fingers. "That's what I meant. The Coalition expect us to play to our stereotype and act like flamboyant gay men. They want to bait us into reacting with anger."

"They expect us to rise up and march or picket," Remy said. "If we lose our shit, then they'll win and prove we're bad for the community." He stood beside Bobby. "It takes Bobby a while to get there with his explanations, but he's got a point." He sighed. "Maybe I shouldn't send in that op-ed piece."

Bobby draped his arm around Remy's shoulders. "You should still publish it, but put a positive spin on it." He bit back a snort. Who was he to tell anyone to be positive? He'd cornered the market on negativity lately. "Kill them with kindness."

"I like it," Colin said.

"I second it." Jordan offered his hand to Bobby. "Sorry about being a dick. I'll work on changing that. Back then, I was a mess. I'd probably have been in the Coalition if it had existed back then—all to prove to myself I wasn't gay."

"But you're comfortable with it now," Colin said. He hollered over his shoulder. "Gage. Come on."

Gage, Farin, Steve and Genie thundered down the steps.

"It's all clean," Steve said. "The carpet's a little damp from the steam cleaner, but nothing permanently stained." He dropped the takeout boxes into the trash bin. "Next time we put the kids outside."

"Or go to Colt's restaurant," Farin said. He laughed and squeezed Steve's shoulders. "We need to get going."

"Us too." Colin nudged Jordan. "You've got an early shift tomorrow, and I'm opening the store. Remy, keep us posted on the article. I think if you and Bobby work together on it, it'll be dynamite in a great way."

Bobby liked the sound of that. He showed the foursome out to the front porch and watched them drive away. When he turned to go back into the house, he bumped into Remy. "Sorry."

"Why?" Remy threaded his arms around Bobby's waist. "I like bumping into you."

"I figured you still weren't happy with me." He tugged Remy to the railing and leaned against the post. "I'll keep apologizing because that's who I am. Ask my ex-wife. She made my life miserable, and I kept telling her I was sorry for dicking her over."

"You're a good man, that's why. You don't like when crap happens." Remy bumped noses with Bobby, then kissed him. "It stung. I won't lie. I hate fighting with anyone, but you were looking out for your kids. I understand. I'd be just as vicious if it were my kids in that situation."

"The thing was, I didn't know what had happened. Chris never said. He and Darce suffered in silence." Bobby rested his forehead against Remy's. "I wish I would've known earlier. I would've kicked Terry's ass to the curb right then and there."

"That's why you didn't know. He knew he had someone wonderful and wasn't ready to give up on you." Remy kissed him. "I don't agree with what he did, but I understand. I don't want to lose you, either. I like the kids. They're great and you're right, I've always been a kid person who didn't realize he was a kid person."

"I'm glad." Bobby stuffed his hands into Remy's back pockets. He didn't care who saw them on the porch. Let the Coalition watch them. Let them get upset or put more flags in his yard. Fuck them. He was happy, just like his mom and the others had said.

A car driving by honked but didn't stop. No one shouted anything. Bobby held his lover tight. He wasn't sure how close he'd come to losing Remy — from his own anger or the assault — but he was damn happy he had Remy around. He could see Remy with him and the kids as a family unit. They could have a future together, and that was what he wanted.

"How about we allow the kids to swim a while? We can't hide in the house." Remy kissed him again. "Besides, I bet they'd like to get out."

"I'm sure." He eased his palm from Remy's pocket and swatted Remy's ass. "We should wear them out."

"Oh yeah, because Chris always goes right to bed when you tell him." Remy draped his arm around Bobby's waist and headed into the house.

"No, but it's worth a shot." He closed the front door and engaged the lock. "We should check out the damage in the family room too."

"It's not bad. The kids, the guys and I picked everything up. Like someone said, the carpet's damp from where we cleaned up soda and pizza sauce," Remy said. "Feel free to check, though."

"I trust you." Bobby grasped the banister. "Hey, guys? How about a swim?" He glanced over at Remy and blew out a long breath. Remy couldn't know just how big a step saying the words *I trust you* were for Bobby. He chuckled. For the first time since he'd split from his ex-boyfriend, Neil, he was ready to move on. Telling Remy he loved him had been a bit fast, and he wasn't sure if he could vocalize those feelings right away. But he did care for Remy. He loved and trusted him.

Darcy appeared at the top of the stairs. "Really?" she squeaked.

"Really, Peanut. Get your suit and tell your brother." Bobby clapped the railing. "Where is Chris?"

"On the phone with Nicki." Darcy shrugged. "He likes her. Sounds like she doesn't like him—in that way."

"I know." Bobby sighed. He wasn't ready to have a child in the dating arena. *Good God.* He was still trying to date. How awkward was that? He sure as hell wasn't going to go on double dates with his son.

"Sorry, Dad." Chris hurried down the stairs with his board shorts in hand. "We were just talking. She's got a boyfriend."

"Get changed and don't worry about it." He wasn't going to stop the march of time or keep his kid from growing up. He grasped Remy's hand. "Shall we go outside?"

Remy laughed. "We shall."

# Chapter Eleven

Remy strolled out onto the deck with Bobby. He marveled as the lights turned on around the pool. The slight wind rustled the leaves in the trees, and streaks of purple, orange and red stretched across the sky. All he needed was a beer and this would be a perfect night. He tugged a chair over to the edge of the deck. He faced the pool as he stretched out on the lounger.

Darcy darted past him and jumped straight into the pool. Chris ambled onto the deck. "She does love her water," he said. "The crazy fish."

"Just like you're a fool for running. It's great." He gripped the arms of the chair and sighed. He ached all over from the assault.

Bobby joined Remy on the deck. "You got the good chair." He yanked an Adirondack chair over to where Remy sat. "I like that one."

"I can see why. It's comfortable." Remy crossed his ankles. "I could sleep out here. The air's just right and the wind in the leaves is mesmerizing."

"Don't you dare go to sleep yet. How's your head?" Bobby asked.

"It's fine. If I feel off, I'll say something." From his head to his toes, he hurt. He felt wrung out. He did want to sleep, but he also wanted to not have to worry about anything. With Bobby, he could rest and let go.

Bobby handed Remy an open beer. Remy downed a swig of the tart brew, then rested the bottle on the armrest and slipped his hand into Bobby's. "So you're staying?" Bobby asked.

"Yeah. You wouldn't let me go." He laughed at his comment. He didn't want to leave anyway.

"You make me sound like an awful person." Bobby tipped his beer bottle. "I'm not." He drank the beer, then sighed. "I'd let you go."

"I bet you'd let me leave, but if you did you'd have a coronary and worry." He squeezed Bobby's fingers.

"I would." Bobby held up his bottle. "Every second you were gone I'd be a wreck."

Remy rested his head on the back of the chair. He loved the closeness he shared with Bobby. Bobby's admission of love had been rather spontaneous and Remy didn't put much stock in the feelings. He believed Bobby was fond of him and liked having him around, but love? Maybe. Besides, he wanted to move with caution. Remy could vocalize his love for Bobby, but Bobby had the kids to worry about. He massaged the bridge of his nose. He wanted to be part of the family unit. He was close to Bobby but yearned to be more.

He sat with Bobby and worked on his beer. He wasn't sure how much time had passed, but the longer they rested together and the kids splashed in the pool, the sky darkened and the lights around the pool and fencing brightened.

"Hey, guys?" Bobby sat up and tossed his beer bottle into the recycle bin. "Let's head inside for the night."

Darcy climbed out of the water first and threw her soggy arms around her father's neck. She dripped all over him. "Thanks, Dad."

"Welcome, Peanut. Get a shower, brush your teeth and head to bed," Bobby said.

She grinned at Remy, then draped a towel around her waist. She went into the house. Chris lingered a moment longer in the pool. Once Darcy was out of range, he strode up to Bobby.

"Thanks, Dad. I like my sister and the other kids, but I needed to get out of there." Chris toweled himself off. "I am not meant for babysitting."

"Good to know." Bobby stood. He gripped Chris' shoulder. "I appreciate the help. Things were out of hand today and you stepped up like a champ."

"Does this mean you'll add a little to my allowance? I've almost got enough for the better fitness tracker." Chris clutched his towel. "Yeah?"

"We'll see," Bobby said. "Same thing I told your sister. Get a shower and head to bed — after you brush your teeth. Night, bud."

"Night, Dad." Chris saluted. He nodded once to Remy, then strode past them.

He waited for Chris to disappear into the house. He faced the door and folded his arms. "I love my children, but they wear me out. This whole day has worn me out."

"Trust me. I understand." Remy recrossed his ankles. Ever since he'd shown the article to the group members, he'd been wondering if he'd done such a good thing. He didn't regret his words. They'd been written in a moment of emotional distress but were from the heart. He believed what he'd put on the tablet. But maybe he'd gone about getting his point across the wrong way. "I've been thinking about the article. You're right. I should've made the whole thing more positive. We're a happy community. We should show that rather than giving in and getting angry."

"Rem, you have been. The *Positively Cedarwood* articles have been great." He sat beside Remy again. "I've read them. If someone who doesn't know anything about Cedarwood doesn't think we're a wonderful community, then they're not reading the right stuff."

"But none of those have been about our community," Remy said. "I'll probably twiddle with the op-ed, but I've got a better idea for something more long-term. What about a weekly column that features different aspects of Cedarwood? Maybe a different business and business owner or a group around town. This way I can make sure some of the groups and businesses are from the LGBTQ community."

The more he talked about his newly hatched plan, the more he liked it.

"I'm convinced." Bobby nodded. "Sounds interesting."

"I like it." Remy held up his nearly empty beer bottle. "Cheers to a new article and me taking the weekend off. I need time to recuperate."

"I like the sound of that." Bobby opened a second beer. He clinked bottles with Remy. "We should celebrate tonight."

"Only if I get to be the bottom. I'm starting to run out of steam." He wanted Bobby in his ass, then to curl up beside the man he loved.

"So you want me to suck your dick while you lie there?" Bobby asked. "Licking your balls and making you come? Then you want my cock in your ass, making you come again?"

"Yeah, I want it all." Remy gripped the arm of the chair. He shivered. When he closed his eyes, the image of Bobby between his knees came to mind. He wanted to feel the softness of Bobby's hair under his hands and the silk of Bobby's tongue along his dick.

"Horny toad," Bobby said.

Remy snapped his attention to his lover. "You sound shocked."

"Nah. I'm just as ready to fuck as you are." Bobby left his chair and leaned over Remy's. He held on to the arms of the lounger. "We need to go inside. My bed is nice and big."

"I remember," Remy murmured.

Bobby kissed Remy and bit his bottom lip. "It's better with you in it."

"Is it?" Remy draped his arms around Bobby's neck. "I would think you'd like the space to move." He was stalling. He needed to gather the energy to go upstairs.

"Moving is overrated." Bobby kissed him again. "I'd rather hold you."

Remy grinned. "You're a closet romantic."

"I'm totally out," Bobby said. "I'm head over heels for you. I want you with me and the kids."

"I want to be here," Remy replied. He kissed Bobby again. "Let's go upstairs." He held on to Bobby's hand as he left the chair.

"Move in with me." Bobby held Remy to his side. He opened the door for Remy and switched off the pool lights. The security lights turned on, leaving the backyard illuminated. "At least stay over for the weekends."

Remy paused in the kitchen. "I haven't given you an answer yet, and you're already begging."

"I'm trying to work with you." He smoothed his hands up Remy's chest and pinched Remy's nipple through the fabric of his shirt. "I'm trying very hard not to let you go."

"I thought you wanted to slow down." Hell, he was ready to speed everything up. He wanted to move in with Bobby yesterday.

"I did, but not now. I had my life put into perspective today. I know you and trust you." He locked the sliding door, then ushered Remy to the steps. "I didn't trust my heart for the longest time. I can't not trust it now."

"So you love me?" Remy knew better than to expect to hear the crucial word again. Bobby could go to certain lengths, but no amount of perspective could push him out of his comfort zone when he wasn't ready. He needed to bide his time with Bobby.

"I'm very fond of you." Bobby helped Remy to the second floor. "Be right back." He ducked into Darcy's room.

Remy headed down the hallway to Bobby's bedroom. He stretched out on the mattress and groaned. Every muscle in his body screamed. The weight of the afternoon crashed down on him. *Fond of me. Jesus.* Bobby was just shy of saying the words...again. Although Bobby's hesitation irritated him, he wasn't ready to give up. He'd bide his time until Bobby felt strong enough to vocalize his feelings. There were more than just the two of them in the relationship.

He closed his eyes and listened to the soft conversation between Bobby and the kids. The sweetness between Bobby and his children wrapped around Remy's heart. If things went south between him and Bobby, there was more than their heartbreak involved. The kids would be affected. He couldn't hurt them. They were too important.

Wouldn't Remy's former lovers and friends back in Cleveland get a laugh out of this—the man who'd sworn he wasn't a kid person not only was but wanted to be part of this family. The funniest thing? He regretted nothing of his time with Bobby. Sure, they'd had some odd moments and an argument, but what couple didn't have a fight from time to time? Most of his prior relationships had involved lots of sex and twice as much arguing. Having a normal relationship soothed him.

The door creaked and the knob clicked. Bobby sat on the bed beside Remy. "Sleeping already?"

"No. I'm simply thinking." Remy laced his fingers together on his belly. "After everything that's happened today, I didn't expect to be right here." He opened his eyes and met Bobby's gaze. "This morning, I was on top of the world. I couldn't wait to get through the day so I could spend the evening with you. I looked forward to the race that should be taking place tomorrow. Then the flags happened and the interview. Things went to shit so fast. While I was in the hospital, I thought about you and us. I worried you'd tell me I was a liability. You wouldn't want me around the kids because of the Coalition."

"Because of them, I want you around. I can't see my life right now without you."

"You're crazy."

"More than a little, but who cares?" Bobby offered his hand. "Come shower with me. I'm sure you want the hospital stink and the funk of the day off you."

"You'd be shocked, but yeah, I do." He sat up and allowed Bobby to yank him into the bathroom. He shrugged out of his shirt and fumbled with his pants.

"I can help you." Bobby popped the button on Remy's jeans. "I play a wicked nurse." He eased the denim and Remy's boxer shorts down his legs. "I'm good at special care."

"I have no doubt." Remy grasped the edge of the shower stall for stability. He stepped out of the cumbersome clothing and swept his gaze over Bobby's body. The man was sexy. So caring and handsome, but sweet and had a huge heart. *How'd I manage to find such a great guy?*

"Here. Let me." Bobby reached into the stall and turned on the water. "I'm all for crazy-hot water."

"Me too."

When Bobby yanked his shirt up over his head, Remy gasped. He'd already seen Bobby naked, but looking at him never got old. Each muscle flexed as Bobby moved. The thin trail of hair down his belly dipped beneath the waistband of his pants. When Bobby stepped out of his jeans, Remy swayed on his feet.

"Get in there before you fall." Bobby eased into the shower behind Remy. He reached around Remy and plucked the washcloth and shower gel from the rack. "Babe, they really did get you." He kissed Remy's shoulder. "You're purple all over."

"I got a few return punches in." He sighed as the steaming hot water sluiced over his aching body. His nipples beaded and blood rushed to his cock. He slid his hand over his shaft. Just touching himself added to his pleasure.

"Turn around so I can wash you." Bobby didn't give Remy much of a chance to argue. Instead, he turned Remy around. Bobby feathered kisses over each bruise, then caressed the soap into Remy's skin.

Remy breathed in the scent of Bobby, the soap and whatever air freshener he had in the bathroom. Remy's head swam. Each stroke and kiss relaxed him and soothed his soul. Horniness overwhelmed him, along with the desire to give himself completely over to Bobby.

"Gonna sleep on me?" Bobby stood. He rinsed the washcloth, then added more soap. "Better not."

"Nah. You've relaxed me, though." The man was so tender, loving, and treating Remy like they were true partners.

"Good." Bobby eased under the spray and scrubbed himself down. He didn't take the time or the care like he had with Remy.

Remy tried to steal the cloth from Bobby's hands, but Bobby swatted him away. "I want to take care of you," Remy said. "You did for me."

"I wasn't assaulted today." Bobby switched off the water. "Shit. I forgot to wash your hair."

"You can do it later." Remy reached out of the stall for the towel, but Bobby beat him to the punch. "I'm not an invalid."

"I know." Bobby smoothed the terry cloth over Remy's body, taking care not to put too much pressure on the bruises. "But you've been through a lot."

"Okay."

Bobby grinned. "Stretch out on the bed. Stretch out while I get dried off."

Remy eyeballed Bobby, then did as he was told. Who was he to argue? He lay down again and closed his eyes. After the shower, stretching out did feel good. He could sleep for a week. The blood surged through his veins. He'd been hard since the shower, but now he tingled everywhere. He cupped his balls. No more sleeping now. He wanted to fuck or be fucked. He didn't care as long as he had an orgasm.

"Hey, you."

Remy opened his eyes and watched Bobby move around the room. Bobby dug through his dresser, then the drawer in the nightstand. He crawled onto the bed between Remy's legs and dropped three items onto the mattress. Remy recognized the lube and condom packet, but the second bottle had him flummoxed.

Bobby leaned over Remy and kissed his way down Remy's sternum. He scraped his teeth over Remy's nipple, then swirled his tongue around Remy's navel.

"Oh God," Remy groaned. He grabbed the sheets and rubbed his cock along Bobby's chest. He was so horny... He needed to climax.

"God, you're hot." Bobby kissed and licked along Remy's inner thigh.

Remy spread his legs even more and planted his feet on the mattress. "Need you," he whispered.

"You've got me," Bobby replied. He wrapped his fingers around Remy's shaft and flicked his tongue across the blunt head of Remy's cock.

Shivers raced down Remy's spine. "Feels so good."

"Knew you'd like it." Bobby dragged his lips across the underside of Remy's dick and continued to stroke him. "Love the way you moan," Bobby whispered. He engulfed Remy's cock in his mouth and bobbed his head.

Remy palmed the top of Bobby's head. He knew he and Bobby should be quiet. The kids were in the next room, and he doubted Bobby wanted anyone coming to check on them, but damn it...not making noise was hard. He bucked his hips.

"Bobby," Remy murmured. "Oh." He hadn't realized just how close he already was to orgasm until Bobby raked his teeth along the length of Remy's dick.

Bobby cupped Remy's balls and sucked Remy to the back of his throat.

A fresh wave of sizzles broke out in Remy's body. He grasped Bobby's head. "More," Remy bit out. "Oh God, more."

Bobby increased his speed and glanced up at Remy. He grinned as he sucked Remy's dick.

Remy shivered and bucked again. The muscles in his legs tensed and he arched his back. No matter how hard he tried, he couldn't hold the orgasm in check.

"I. Need. To. Come." Remy jammed his cock down Bobby's throat and embraced the climax. He panted. Everything within him that was wound tight loosened. He sagged against the bed and let go of Bobby. "You'll kill me."

He couldn't move. Couldn't think. The only thing that mattered was being in the moment with Bobby.

"You'll live." Bobby smacked his lips. "You taste good too." He picked up the extra bottle and dribbled the fluid onto his hand. "Now that you're loose, I'm going to rub you down."

Remy nodded. He'd allow Bobby to do pretty much whatever Bobby wanted. He belonged to Bobby, heart and soul.

Bobby grinned as he rubbed the oil into Remy's chest. His hands glided over Remy's skin and relaxed Remy even more. Each time Bobby met Remy's gaze, he smiled. When he worked his way back up Remy's belly to his chest, Remy whimpered. Nothing hurt. The weight of the moment overwhelmed him.

"You're okay?" Bobby asked. He nudged Remy's legs apart again and caressed Remy's semi-hard cock.

"I'm fine." Remy reached for Bobby. "Let me touch you."

"Touch away — while I fuck you." There was firelight in Bobby's eyes. He stroked Remy's dick. "You're mine."

Remy shivered again. He loved when Bobby took control. He eased his hands around the back of his knees and bared his ass to his lover. "Please, fuck me."

"You know I will." Bobby trailed his fingers up and down Remy's chest and plucked Remy's nipples.

Need and desire built within Remy. He flexed his asshole. "Bobby, please?" He barely recognized the begging in his voice, but he knew the ragged need very well. Bobby had him right on the edge.

"Mine," Bobby said. He nudged the bottle of massage oil aside, then picked up the lube. He dribbled it onto his fingers.

Remy couldn't look away from Bobby. The sight of Bobby between his legs turned him on. He'd used lube on his own body plenty of times, but Bobby made the act look so fucking hot. Sparks shot through Remy's veins.

Bobby traced the circle of Remy's asshole with his index finger, then breached the tight ring of muscle. Within seconds, he added a second digit. No warning. Instead, Bobby simply went for full throttle. Remy bore down on him and exhaled. There was never a dull moment with Bobby, and he liked it that way. Remy rocked his hips, moving Bobby's fingers within his ass. God, he was wanton and shameless, but he needed this.

"Feels so good," Remy said. He'd already come once, but the second orgasm built within his belly. "Jesus. Put your cock in me."

"Naughty." Bobby leaned in close to Remy and kissed him. "Love when you're raw."

"You made me this way." He refused to get stuck on Bobby using the word *love* again. Right then he was too far gone to let Bobby's words mess up his brain.

Bobby eased his fingers from Remy's hole, then opened the condom wrapper. "Put this on me."

Although his brain cells were misfiring, Remy moved on instinct and took the rubber from Bobby. He rolled the condom over Bobby's cock and stroked him. "So hard and sexy." He wanted to suck that dick between his lips. *Maybe tomorrow night? Or later after a shower?*

"Hard and sexy like you?" Bobby dumped more lube onto his fingers, then stroked himself. He caressed Remy's fingers on his cock. "I fantasize about you."

"Yeah?" He needed to hear this. "How? What am I doing?" As long as they were together and someone came, he'd be happy.

"You're on your hands and knees." Bobby folded Remy in half and eased his dick into Remy's hole. He sank in balls-deep, then groaned and paused. "You rock on me and beg me to fuck you."

"Like right now?" Remy met Bobby's gaze. He loved looking his lover in the eye during sex. "Except I'm not on my knees."

"Yeah." Bobby tipped his head back and his lips parted. He moaned, and the sound traveled around the room. He gripped Remy's knees.

"Move, please?" he whispered. He flexed his asshole. "Bobby."

"You keep begging like that." Bobby's Adam's apple moved along his throat. His nipples beaded and a fine sheen of sweat glistened on his chest.

Remy dug his fingers into his legs. "Bobby."

"Like that." Bobby bowed his head and closed his eyes. His brow knotted and little lines crinkled around his eyes. The muscle in his jaw tensed. He shifted his hips, finally moving within Remy.

The delicious game of waiting pleased Remy. He liked the act of lovemaking to be prolonged. He breathed in deep and the scent of Bobby's cologne wrapped around him. He forgot about the assault and pretty much everything else in his life except for Bobby.

"Jesus," Bobby bit out. He opened his eyes. His lips formed an *O*, as if he were about to say something, but no sound came out.

"You're blowing my mind." Remy couldn't move much and he wanted to. He needed to get Bobby going, but it was as though the man was stuck in slow motion. In to the hilt, then almost all the way out before he sank back again.

A slow smile curled on Bobby's lips. "I feel you in my soul." He focused on Remy. "Everything I want."

Remy tried to nod. Bobby made him happy in so many ways. "Fuck me."

"Aren't I doing that already?" Bobby's smile kicked up in wattage. He yanked Remy to the edge of the bed and plunged back into him.

Remy gasped. Despite the condom, he felt every ridge and nuance of Bobby's dick.

Bobby gritted his teeth and hissed. "Mine." He stopped the slow thrusts and built up speed. The sound of skin slapping skin echoed in the room. His fingernails bit into Remy's skin. Bobby shivered and leaned forward. He kept pushing in and out of Remy.

"Like that?" Bobby asked. "My cock in your ass?"

"Love it." Remy craned his neck and tried to kiss Bobby. "Need it."

"Do you?" Bobby grinned again. He slid his hand down to Remy's ass cheek and spanked. Hard.

Pain radiated through Remy. He gasped, but before he could protest, the pain morphed into a delicious pleasure. "Harder," Remy begged.

"Flip over." Bobby pulled out long enough for Remy to roll onto his belly. Once he gathered himself up on his hands and knees, Bobby plunged back into Remy.

"I can't hold out much longer." Bobby swatted Remy again. "Fuck. I'm there."

"Yeah." He wanted to say something else, but the words failed him. His knees weakened and he bowed his head. Tears formed at the corners of his eyes. Bobby knew how to sear him to his core. He opened his eyes.

"Fuck. Touch yourself. Come with me." Bobby spanked Remy again. "Do it."

Remy balanced on one hand and his knees. The muscles in his legs trembled and the breath ripped from his chest. He wrapped his fingers around his dick. He'd just come not long ago, but the climax was already there. He shook his head as Bobby growled again.

"Jesus, fuck." Bobby slammed into Remy. His cock throbbed, and Bobby's fingers jabbed into Remy's waist.

Remy stroked himself. How did Bobby manage to have him right on the edge so fast? Because they had a special kind of magic or some shit? *No.* Because he was in love with Bobby Gagnon. He wanted to give everything to Bobby. The man owned his heart.

Bobby kissed Remy's back and scraped his teeth along Remy's shoulder blade. "Come for me, Rem. Come apart again."

His restraint shattered and he squeezed his dick. Everything within him tingled and his nerve endings sizzled. He couldn't breathe or think, just feel. His vision blurred as he collapsed on the bed.

"Fucking balls. Rem? Are you all right? Shit. I forgot about..." Bobby eased out of Remy's ass and the bed jiggled.

Remy eased onto his side and blinked until the world righted on its axis. He'd stretched out in his own cum, but fuck it.

"Rem?" Bobby removed the condom then tossed it into the garbage. He leaned over the bed and brushed Remy's hair from his eyes. "You okay?"

"Never better." Remy dragged a sharp breath into his lungs and exhaled. From his head to his toes, he felt like a puddle. He stretched out his arm. "Come here."

"I should be ordering you around." Bobby cupped Remy's cheek. "Give me a second. I'll get you cleaned up." He left the room for a moment before returning with a washcloth. He wiped his cock down, then caressed Remy's backside with the warm cloth. Bobby held the cloth in one hand and yanked the sheet over Remy with the other. "Be right back."

"Sure," Remy whispered. He doubted he could leave, even if he'd wanted to. He nuzzled the pillow. The scent of Bobby surrounded him. God, the man was everything he'd ever wanted and more. He still wasn't sure how he'd gotten so lucky to have Bobby not only in his life, but in his bed, too.

The bed dipped, and Bobby stretched out beside Remy. He tucked Remy close to his body. "Happy?"

"Beyond words." Remy draped his arm across Bobby's chest and toyed with the few strands of hair between Bobby's pecs. "I may never leave."

"Then don't. I meant what I said. Move in with us." Bobby kissed the top of Remy's head. "I feel like myself when you're here."

Remy's thoughts cleared and his mind raced. *Move in...* He wanted to, but someone had to be logical. He had bills and his own place. He couldn't just abandon it. "The lease for my apartment runs through the end of the spring," Remy replied. He could probably get out of the lease. There were others wanting to move into that building, and he'd seen the waiting list. Still...what if things went south and he and Bobby split? He closed his eyes and tried not to succumb to the negative.

"You don't have to move everything in right away."

"Bobby." Remy opened his eyes. He placed his finger over Bobby's lips. "I'm being practical, not turning you down. You're a smart man. You do people's finances and tell people how not to dick around with their money. You should be careful with me and doing this." He propped himself up on his elbow to better look at Bobby. "What'd Neil do that fucked with your confidence? Or was it Terry? Someone got you believing you've got to practically beg in order to get love. You don't have to beg me. I already love you."

Bobby tensed and put some distance between them. "Between my folks not accepting me when I came out, the shit with Helene and how she treated my children like crap, then Terry manipulating them and Neil just not being honest—I don't trust many people and the truth is I want to. My gut tells me you're the one I've been looking for and I'm trying too hard. I'm all jacked up because I know my heart, but I'm terrified I'll screw up."

Remy understood the 'trying too hard' part. He did that all the time. Bobby needed reassurance. He could give him that too. "I'll move in with you—but only if the kids approve."

"Now who's the smart man?"

"I'm not trying to be someone I'm not, but the kids need stability, and I need to know they don't hate me. If we do this, it's not a one month and done kind of thing." Remy grasped Bobby's fingers. "We go all-in."

"The kids don't hate you," Bobby replied.

"But me being here on a permanent basis will affect them down to their core. It won't be easy and I accept that, but I want them to be okay with this."

"We'll talk to them tomorrow." Bobby eased up to Remy. "I'm the dad, but you're almost more concerned with Chris and Darcy than I am."

"I'm trying to see this from their point of view. This is new for all of us, and after what you told me Neil and Terry put them through, they're going to be leery." That was why he wanted to move in smaller steps. Yes, he wanted to be with Bobby and start their life together in the same house, but the kids were the biggest factor. He needed them to be on board with the idea. "When you tell them, don't do it like a special dinner or bribe them. Just bring it up. Be casual." The last time he'd been to a fancy dinner was the night he'd found out his parents were splitting. He wasn't about to put another kid through that kind of torture.

"You're too smart for your own good. We'll talk to them in the morning." Bobby tucked Remy to his chest and settled in the sheets. "This is what I needed. You beside me for always."

"Sounds good." Remy rolled onto his side and rested his back against Bobby's stomach. He grasped Bobby's arm and snuggled in to his lover. "Goodnight, babe." He closed his eyes. He was glad the day had happened but thrilled that it was over.

# Chapter Twelve

Bobby stretched and glanced over at the clock. Fingers of sunlight stretched across the room. *Is it already morning?* According to the bright green numbers, he'd slept past six a.m. He couldn't remember the last time he'd woken up after the sunrise. He sighed. Yes, he was up early, but Remy wasn't awake. Did he want to jostle the man? Not really. He'd rather let him sleep.

Bobby, though, was energized. Good sex, a great partner in his bed, and a full night's sleep... He was ready to do almost anything. He slipped out of the covers and tiptoed across the room to his dresser. A run in the early morning air sounded like heaven. He yanked a fresh T-shirt over his head and stepped into a pair of boxer briefs as well as his running shorts.

If Chris was awake, he'd ask him if he wanted to join him on the run. He unballed his socks and headed down the hallway.

Chris was sitting at his computer and looked up when Bobby ducked into the room. "You're up early."

"I am. Thought I'd see if you wanted to go for a run. Anything good happening on the Internet?" He eased the socks onto his feet. "Or just blah again?"

"I logged my times from my runs into the spreadsheet for Coach." Chris closed the lid of the computer. "I'll get my watch and we can go. Remy coming?"

"Nah. He's asleep." Bobby glanced into Darcy's room. Like Remy, she was still fast asleep. Bobby hustled down the stairs to the kitchen. He picked up his running shoes and retrieved his cooler of water from the fridge. He downed half of the icy water before Chris appeared.

"Sorry. I couldn't find my watch." Chris untied his shoes, then stepped into them. He followed Bobby to the front porch. "What are you going to do with the flags?"

Bobby stretched his calves, then rolled his shoulders. "I'll pick them up later. They aren't really hurting anything. So people know I'm gay? What's new?"

"No more freaking out like yesterday?" Chris asked as he ran through his battery of stretches.

"I'm not happy about them or that someone was on my lawn, but it could've been worse." He strode to the end of the driveway. "What's the type today?"

"I should be doing a long run. Fifty minutes. We don't have to race," Chris said. "Ready?"

"Go," Bobby said and started off. He fell into a cadence with Chris and made his way down the block.

"So Remy's sleeping. Is he okay? He really got beat up yesterday." Chris pumped his arms. "It looked bad anyway."

"It wasn't good, but there was nothing done to him that's permanent." He'd mentioned Remy sleeping over. He should probably have brought up the possible new living arrangement. "I wanted him to stay over in case there was any problem."

"Duh. He got his clock cleaned." Chris snorted. "He's already stayed over, Dad. It's not a big deal."

He'd forgotten about that. "What do you think about him maybe being at the house more?" He was fucking this up. *Jesus, man. Just say what you want to say.* "What if he moved in with us?"

"I think it's fine. Why? Are you going to marry him?" Chris asked. He turned from their street into the cross road.

*Wow.* He hadn't expected Chris to ask if he'd permanently hook up with Remy. The thought wasn't awful, but it knocked him for a loop. He needed a minute to sort himself out and decide how to answer. "Would you be upset if I did?" Not that he was thinking that far ahead, but he'd love to know what his son thought.

"You're nervous." Chris chuckled. "This is what you do when you're freaked out. You answer questions with questions."

"Okay, so I'm scared. This is a big leap for me. I never asked Neil to move in."

"True, but I would've moved out if you had." Chris nodded. "Turn left." He stopped at the traffic light. "Look, if I were you, I'd hold up."

"Chris?" When the traffic signal changed, he started across the street. He kept pace with his son, despite his shock at Chris' statement. "What do you mean? I don't disagree or agree with you necessarily, but I'd like to know what you're thinking."

"Promise you won't get pissed?" Chris asked between puffs.

"I promise." He needed a voice of reason—especially if his kids weren't thrilled about his decision.

Chris turned into a parking lot and stopped again. He leaned over and rested his hands on his knees. "I'm well short of the fifty-minute mark, but I can't say this and run at the same time."

Bobby slowed, then stopped. "I'm all ears."

Chris stood upright and met Bobby's gaze. "Remy's a great guy. Really. He seems interested in us and hasn't tried to buy us off."

"But?"

Chris laced his fingers together behind his head. His shirt stuck to his thin chest and darkened with sweat. "But you need to take the advice you're always giving me. Slow down and think about this before you go crazy."

Yeah, he'd told Chris those exact words many times. Besides, his son was making a lot of sense. Hadn't Remy warned him to slow down too? "I asked him to move in with us," Bobby blurted. "I didn't force it."

"Dad." Chris rested his hands on his hips. "Have you lost it?"

"No, I haven't. If it makes any sense, Remy told me to ask you and Darcy before he made his decision. If you and your sister agreed, then he'd move in, but if you didn't, then he'd leave things as is."

"Wow." Chris stared at him. "I didn't think he'd say that." He chuckled again. "He's more in tune with what you want than you are, if he said that."

"He did. I was the impulsive one."

"That's so not you, Dad."

Bobby glanced around at the buildings and the trees ringing the lot. "The more I think about what I said, the more I realize I'm very impulsive. Or I have too much faith in people. I never should've let Terry do what he did, but I believed things would get better or that they were better than I thought. I was trying to keep something that wasn't available. Neil... He was a mistake I wasn't willing to admit I'd made."

"And Mom?"

"That situation was me not being honest with everyone — including me about who I was and what I wanted."

"What about Remy?" Chris asked.

"The truth?" He couldn't believe he was about to say this to his son, but what the hell... "I'm in love with him. It's fast and I'm pretty sure I've lost my mind, but I do love him. I even told him, then sort of reneged on it. I mean, fuck. I'm impulsive. I want Remy, and I'm scared I'll lose him."

"Sounds to me like you need him." Chris tapped Bobby's arm. "Let's get the rest of the fifty minutes in." He started off and Bobby quickly caught up to him.

"I don't want you and your sister in the line of fire if things fall apart with Remy. You've already had to deal with your mom and I splitting, then Terry and Neil. I want Remy, but I don't know if I can put you through the wringer again."

"You're a dad," Chris said. "No matter what you do, it affects us. We'll always be in the way — well, until we move out."

"Jesus. I'm not ready to even think about you and Darcy leaving home. I'm not ready for either of you to date."

"Chill."

"I can't." Frustration built within him. He couldn't shake the helplessness or the confusion. He hated feeling so conflicted. "Chris, I know what I want, but I'm not sure I should have it, even though it's...ugh."

"If it helps, I don't get the skeevy feeling with Remy like I did with Neil or Terry. If you want my approval, then yeah. Let him move in. Do it."

"I—wow." He'd figured Chris would be completely against Remy moving in.

Chris held both hands up and continued to run. "I am the greatest," he shouted and pumped his fists. "I'm the bomb."

"You're a trip." He tapped Chris' shoulder. "You're also being left behind." He kicked his run up a notch. "Catch me."

"Dude." Within moments, Chris was right beside him and keeping pace. "Cold, man."

"I knew you'd catch me. Hell, I'm in shape, but I know you can lap my ass with ease."

"True."

Bobby remained in step with his son for the rest of the run. By the time he and Chris reached the house, his knees ached and he wanted to collapse. The fifty-minute runs would be the death of him—at least at such a fast pace.

Chris stopped in the driveway and flopped over on a patch of empty grass. "Go for it, Dad."

"Thanks, Chris." He rested his hands on his knees and gasped for air. He needed a nap and a bottle of water, but not in that order.

"So, what about me dating?" Chris asked. "Jenna wants to go to the movies next weekend. A bunch of other kids from the cross-country team are going, so it's not a date-date, and it'll be after the first meet. You and Remy can come—but sit far away...like in another theater."

"I'll think about it." Bobby jogged up the street and back for his cool-down run. He'd probably let Chris go to the movies. He and Remy would be there, most likely, so it wasn't like Chris could get into much trouble.

He helped Chris up from the grass, then headed into the house. Remy and Darcy were in the kitchen. Remy wore a shirt and shorts he must've dug out of Bobby's closet. Darcy wore an oversized T-shirt and had her hair pulled back into a messy ponytail.

Remy poured batter into the skillet. "Pancakes, anyone? Darcy begged me and showed me where the stuff was." He grinned. "Like I could tell her no."

"Remember that when you take her shopping." Bobby gripped the back of the closest barstool. "When your credit card is crying, you'll learn to say no way, baby."

Remy met Bobby's gaze and his eyes widened. "Well, okay then."

Bobby rounded the island and eased up beside Remy. He kissed him.

"Did you tell him?" Remy asked in a hushed tone.

"Yeah." He kissed Remy's temple and patted Remy's ass. "I did and he gave me the green light."

"Whoa," Remy murmured. He managed to flip the pancake. "Wasn't expecting that."

"Neither was I." He squeezed Remy's ass cheek, then turned his attention to Darcy. "So you got him to cook."

"I did." Darcy folded her arms and rested her chin on her hands. "So. Is he going to live here?"

"That's sort of out of the blue," Remy said. He flipped the pancake, then faced her. "Would you be okay with it if I did? I like you and your brother as well as your dad. Living here would be fun, but I want to know your opinion before I decide."

"What you think is important to us," Bobby added. He leaned against the counter and crossed his ankles. "What are you thinking, Peanut?"

Darcy waved to Chris then, when he stood beside her, she held her hand up in front of her mouth. "What'd you say?" she asked.

If she was going for a whisper, she'd failed. Bobby heard her with ease. He didn't stare at her and instead studied the seam of his sock. *She's not thrilled about Remy potentially moving in? Or is she being guarded?* He wasn't going to groan and show his hand. He wanted a candid response from his daughter without his intrusion.

Chris turned his back on Remy and Bobby, but didn't lower his voice enough for them not to hear. "Dad's happy and Remy's solid. This won't be like before."

"He's not like Terry or Neil?" she asked.

Bobby stole a glance at his children and met Chris' gaze. He hated to be caught eavesdropping, but the kids weren't exactly being stealthy in their conversation.

Chris nodded. "The past won't repeat." He faced Bobby and Remy. "Since you're cooking, I'd like two pancakes, please? I'm starving. Dad made me run my butt off."

Remy plated what had been in the skillet and offered the pancakes to Darcy. "Since Darcy asked first, these are hers, but I'll have yours done in a few minutes."

"Sweet." Chris rounded the island and washed his hands.

Darcy twiddled with her plate, then left her seat. She inched up to Remy. "Thanks," she whispered. "I hope you do move in. I like you, too."

Remy poured another pancake into the skillet, then put the spatula down. He gathered Darcy in a hug. "Thanks, kid."

Bobby sighed and closed his eyes. Things weren't perfect. Hell, they weren't even settled. For all he knew, the Coalition would come knocking on his door at any minute or they'd protest his accounting business. But at the moment, he had everything he wanted in his own kitchen—Darcy, Chris and now Remy. When he glanced around the room, he realized he had the family he'd always wanted. The missing piece was Remy. He'd blurted out his love for Remy once, then ignored the sentiment. Remy deserved more than that. Moving in was good, but he and Remy were solid together. Once he found the strength to be honest with himself and Remy, he'd be golden.

* * * *

Remy stared at his computer screen and sighed. His head ached. He probably should go to the eye doctor for an exam, but he'd worry about it later. He'd spent the last week moving his things from his apartment to Bobby's house. He still couldn't believe he and Bobby were living together. The kids had helped him lug his stuff across town and hadn't complained. Bobby had stowed Remy's bed in the finished portion of the basement and insisted Remy share his closet. Bobby had been the one to find someone to sublet Remy's apartment.

He massaged his temples. He loved Bobby with his whole heart and hadn't wrapped his mind around how well he and Bobby worked together. Life usually didn't work out for him. Although he thanked God for his good fortune, a tiny part of him wondered when things would go to shit. Yes, he had a positive attitude, but he couldn't shake his past.

Remy focused on the screen again and cracked his knuckles. He needed to finish the next *Positively Cedarwood* column. He'd reworked his initial op-ed into a happier piece of writing. He wanted to show the good things happening in and around Cedarwood, not give in to the negativity caused by the Coalition. He added the last few sentences to the story about the art fest that would be taking place that weekend, then saved and sent the piece off to Maureen at the paper.

He glanced over at his cell phone. He should call Julia. He hadn't heard from her or called her in over three weeks and had forgotten to phone her after the assault. Ignoring her in favor of Bobby wasn't cool. He had his commitments, but still. He swiped the screen and switched the device to speaker. After three rings, she answered.

"Wow. I thought you'd dropped off the face of the earth, except you've been in the paper," Julia said. "You asshole. You got beat up and never bothered to call me? What's wrong with you?"

He deserved her anger and let her vent. "Hon, I—I fell in love."

"Love got you beat up?" she asked. "With Bobby?"

"The Coalition sent a goon to beat me up because I bothered to go out in public with my boyfriend." He propped his feet on his desk and leaned back in his swivel chair. "Bobby makes me happy. He asked me to move in with him."

"Bobby?" Julia paused. "You're sure about this? I'm not saying you shouldn't be with him. Convince me this is a good thing. I already like him, so it won't be hard."

He loved Julia. She refused to be easy on him. "I jumped into this kind of fast, but I jump into everything fast. But he's sweet and hot as hell. He introduced me to his kids right away and let me know that the kids were very important in his life. We have fun together, and it's not all sex. He's got a good job and owns his own house. He knows how to take control in the bedroom and makes me feel special. It's not like with other guys. I look forward to being with him, and one of my favorite things is to sleep with him. Not just sex, but cuddling together. I'm a romantic, but Bobby makes being with him fun." He groaned. He'd rambled and probably sounded like a lovesick fool.

"I see." She didn't say anything for a long time, and her silence unnerved Remy.

"You think I'm making a mistake?" he asked.

"Rem." She went quiet again. His heart nearly stopped as he waited. Julia sighed. "I always thought you should've gone after him to begin with. He is a good man. I didn't know him personally, but I've seen him around. Just don't get stupid, okay? You've got a chance to do something awesome with him and two other lives you'll affect. Don't screw it up."

"Are you giving your blessing?" He bit back a chuckle. "Julia, babe, I love you."

"I'll always be the other woman," she replied. "I'm glad. You and Bobby will be great together."

"You're not upset? Really?"

"Nope, but I don't understand the part about the assault. Did the cops catch the guy?" Julia asked. "I haven't seen anything else about it in the paper."

"I heard from Chief Gagnon this morning. They've got the man who assaulted me in custody, and I guess he confessed. I met with the prosecutor at lunch and made a statement. I'll be available when this goes to court, but I'm hoping it's not a huge thing. I don't want to relive what happened." He shuddered just thinking about having to testify. He'd do whatever was needed, though.

"Don't blame you there," Julia said. "I've only seen court proceedings on television, and those don't look fun. I can't imagine having to go through it for real. If you need me, I'll be there. I bet Bobby will too. Speaking of Bobby, you'd better invite me over to the housewarming or whatever you're doing to celebrate," she said. "You owe me dinner or something."

"You've got it. I'll talk to Bobby when I get home, and we'll set it up. What are you doing this Friday or Saturday?"

"Going to your house. Hey, I've got to go. I need to get back to my job." She laughed. "Talk to you later, hon."

"Bye, Julia." He swiped his index finger over the screen and disconnected the call. Relief washed over him. He still had his best girlfriend around, and she approved of Bobby. Life was good.

Remy shut down the laptop and tucked his tablet into its sleeve. He put both devices away and gathered up the rest of his things. He'd been at the newspaper offices long enough. *Time to go home.*

He gripped his messenger bag and strolled across the building to the doors to the parking lot. He stepped outside and tipped his face to the sunshine. The warmth sank straight to his core. He paused a moment before heading to his car. Thank God he'd been able to get the vehicle back so fast. He wanted to enjoy the last vestiges of summer—in his own car. The kids were back in school and, despite the major upheaval, seemed to be taking it all in stride.

Remy didn't want to climb behind the wheel of his car. He hadn't bothered to fix the air conditioning and didn't look forward to having to air out the vehicle to cool it down. When he strode up to the car, he noticed a piece of paper stuck beneath the wiper. He rolled his eyes and opened the driver's-side door. He liked to think while he drove and usually, the free time allowed him to sort out his stories.

*Stop Causing Chaos*

He snorted. *What the hell does that mean? And who's upset with me? The Coalition?* He'd written optimistic articles and an op-ed that shone a positive light on the town. How could the Coalition or anyone else be upset with him? He opened his window and yanked the paper from beneath the wiper. He crumpled the page and tossed it into the back seat. *Fuck it.* He hadn't done anything wrong, and if someone was mad, then that was their problem.

Remy drove out of the lot and across town to Bobby's. He avoided the traffic around the school complex. He stuck to the side streets and navigated through the quiet neighborhoods on the way home. He'd forgotten how pretty Cedarwood could be. Most of the lawns had been mown and flowers bloomed in the various beds as well as from pots hanging on the street lamps. The town reminded him of a postcard. Hell, maybe the town council needed to have postcards and other merchandise made to celebrate Cedarwood. He couldn't be the only one who saw so many good things in the place he lived.

He pulled into the driveway and parked in front of the garage. Once he stopped, he switched off the engine. Remy picked up the newspaper and sat on the front porch. He wanted to see his articles. The excitement of seeing his words on the page never went away. He blazed through the piece on Colin and Farin's bookstore as well as his story on the library fall reading program.

"What are you doing out here?" Bobby asked. He opened the front door. "I didn't expect you home for another couple of hours."

"I wanted out of the cage." He patted the top step. "Got a minute to sit with me?"

"Always." Bobby strode onto the porch. "I've got a client coming over in half an hour, though."

Remy swept his gaze over his boyfriend. He loved the way Bobby filled out the suit and yearned to rip the clothes off him. "That's why you're dressed up."

"Sure. It's called making an impression." Bobby sat beside him and plunked his hand on Remy's thigh. "We're alone for a while. Chris has practice until five, and he's getting a ride home with Jenna. As much as I don't want to admit it, she's got a crush on him, and he's just as hot for her—already. I miss the days when he thought girls were gross."

"Your baby is growing up." Remy rested his head on Bobby's shoulder. "Nothing wrong with it. I know you're not ready for it, but it's a good thing that he's testing the waters."

"If you say so." Bobby sighed. "I'm not supposed to be that old."

"You're fine." More than fine. He made Remy's heart race and his cock hard with just a look.

"You're pretty good too. Speaking of good, I need an assist. I'm supposed to meet with John Thurgood in half an hour, and Darcy's swim team practice is done in forty-five minutes. Can you pick her up?"

"You know I will," Remy said. "We make a good pair." He liked being needed and playing the role of parent. He didn't have the pressure on him like Bobby, but he gladly wanted to help out. Besides, he craved schedules and stability. He gained both with Bobby and the kids. He'd fallen for Bobby, and the kids had his heart too.

"We are awesome." Bobby squeezed Remy's thigh. "Speaking of our kind of awesome, I was thinking about you and me later. We should pull out the blindfold. You'd have to guess where I'm going to touch next."

"With the prize of sucking your cock when I get it right?" The last time Bobby blindfolded him, he hadn't guessed where Bobby licked him—on purpose. The better prize was worshipping between Bobby's legs and the occasional spank he earned too.

"Uh-huh. My dick in your mouth. You're good at getting me nice and wet and hot. Then I'll fill your sexy ass. I'll go slow at first. Pull out, then go back in until you're full. You'll beg me to hurry, but you'll still have the blindfold on, so you'll still be guessing."

Remy pressed his knees together. *Shit.* He'd never be able to leave the porch at this rate. "You make me hard. Fuck." He gritted his teeth. "The worst part is we don't have time to go upstairs."

"I'm hard too."

"Your client will be here shortly." Remy bit back a groan. Bobby was so devious.

"Complaints, complaints," Bobby said. "We'll cool it for now, but just an FYI, I'm wearing my red silk boxers."

Before Remy could say anything, a car pulled to a stop in front of the house and parked on the street. Remy stretched his legs, partially to relieve the pressure on his dick and also to hide the growing erection.

"I should get going," Remy said. "You've got a job to do."

"I'd rather do you," Bobby murmured. He kissed Remy's temple. "Thank you."

"I love you." Remy stood, then leaned over and kissed Bobby. "See you at supper." He strode across the lawn and waved at the man getting out of the car. He didn't stick around to talk. He wanted to hide in his car and get himself under control before he made a fool of himself at the swim complex.

He slid behind the wheel of his vehicle and shook his head. His erection wasn't going down. Despite putting distance between himself and Bobby and thinking about everything except being with Bobby that night, he still couldn't get sex off his brain. *Christ.* He scrubbed his hand down his face and sighed. This was what Bobby had wanted—Remy on the edge and needing him. Bobby excelled at prolonging the pleasure in order to make the orgasm explosive. Remy just hoped he could get to naked time that night without combusting.

By the time Remy reached the metro park, Darcy wasn't waiting in the foyer. He headed into the building and glanced into the main pool room.

"Practice isn't over yet," Steve said. "I thought I'd see Bobby." He shook hands with Remy. "They'll be done soon."

"Cool, and yeah, Bobby had a meeting." He folded his arms. "I thought you were a coach."

"Not for the metro park swim team. I'll help with the high school one in the winter." Steve matched Remy's stance. "Gage and Genie wanted to join, so they're out there too."

"At least the kids know each other." He wished he'd had friends like that when he was back in school. He noticed a couple of adults striding beside the pool. "I thought parents weren't supposed to be in there during practice."

"They're not, but those guys look like they're coming from the back pool. There's the back hallway, but it's not as direct as barging through." Steve sighed. "People also don't follow rules."

Remy focused on the man in the tight red swim shorts. He knew the guy, or at least he looked familiar. Once the guy got closer, his heart lodged in his throat and he turned his back on the pool room. "Fuck."

"What?" Steve stared at him. "Did you see a ghost?"

"No, just my ex-boyfriend." He pinched the bridge of his nose. *Dear God*. Why in the hell was Dale at the metro park? He didn't even live in the county. "Be cool, and hopefully he won't see me."

"Too late." Steve swatted Remy's biceps. "Here he comes, and he's zeroed in."

"Fuck," Remy bit out. He faced his ex. "Dale."

"Look at you." Dale swept his gaze over Remy. "Funny seeing you here." He eyeballed Steve. "Is this your new boo?"

"What? No." Not that Steve wasn't handsome, but he was very much off-limits. "This is my friend, Steve. Our kids are part of the swim team."

"Kids?" Dale snorted and clutched his towel. "You hate kids. Like hate, hate, hate them. You never wanted kids and avoided any guy who had them. How did you get a kid? Let me guess. You slept with a woman and accidentally got her pregnant so now you're screwed?"

"The man I'm living with has children." Speaking of which, Darcy stood behind Dale. Her eyes were wide and the color had drained from her face. She held her swim bag tight.

"You've lowered your standards," Dale snapped.

"Dale." He needed to shut down his ex. God only knew what Darcy had heard.

"Let's face it. If this guy wasn't a good fuck, then you'd be gone. The kids have got to be in the way. What are you going to do?" Dale asked. "Send them to boarding school?"

He didn't have that kind of power and nor did he want it, but right now he wasn't going to tell Darcy otherwise. Because of Dale and his big mouth, all kinds of damage had been done.

"Who's this?" Darcy asked.

Dale snorted again and opened his mouth to speak, but Remy placed his hand over Dale's lips.

"He's my ex-boyfriend, Darce." Remy wanted to melt into the floor. "He's also needed in another room, and we've got to go."

Steve, Genie and Gage stood in the foyer. "Hey, Darcy?" Steve said. "Why don't you wait outside with us? Genie wanted to talk about next week's practice, and Remy will be done in a moment. We'll kill two birds with one stone." He shot Remy a dirty look then guided the children out to the sidewalk.

"Thanks." Remy waited until the kids were out of earshot, then faced Dale. "What in the name of hell are you doing?"

Dale swatted Remy's hand away. "Talking to you." He leaned on the wall and tucked his towel under his arm. He adjusted his swim shorts and emphasized the outline of his dick beneath the form-fitting material. "We used to be something."

"A fucking mess," Remy snapped. "That's all we were. You never wanted me when we tried to be together. What are you doing here? You live in Chagrin."

"Jesus. I came with a friend, but he's back talking to the lifeguard. When I saw you, I decided to make a move, so yeah. I'm trying to get into your pants. I'm doubting you're worth it now, though."

Remy pinched the bridge of his nose again. "So you make a pass in front of my friend and my partner's daughter."

"We were something fucking hot when we were a couple," Dale replied. He shrugged. "Partner."

"Stop." He held up both hands. "Couple? We fucked. That's it. You walked because I got fired, and now I've moved on. I don't want you."

"You're not a family man," Dale said and stepped into Remy's personal space. "You like sex too much to be with a guy with kids. You like to party. How do you honestly think you'll be able to settle down?"

"Because I love my partner, Bobby, and his kids. I'm more of a family man than I ever thought, but you've fucked it up because now his daughter thinks I'm a monster." He had to do so much damage control. He wasn't even sure how to win back her trust.

"You're a loser. You used to be fucking awesome." Dale snapped his towel out from under his arm. "Used to."

"Because I slept with you or because I was willing to deal with your shit?" Remy backed away from Dale. He'd once thought the man was hot. Not any longer.

"You're sweet. Hot. I love tunneling your ass," Dale said, not bothering to use his indoor voice. "You know how to bottom without looking like a wimp."

"Christ, you're a dick." He faced Dale one more time. "Leave me alone. Okay? Forget my number, my face and everything about being with me. I don't exist to you. Got it?" He turned on his heel and strode out of the swim complex.

"You okay?" Steve asked. He herded the children across the parking lot. "Remy?"

"Fine." He opened his car door. "Darcy? Ready to go home?"

She didn't reply and sank onto the seat. He shut the car door and pressed his lips together. He motioned to Steve and lowered his voice. "This is a mess."

"That guy?" Steve nodded back to the building. "He's a jerk."

"Agreed, but he's also just fucked a lot of stuff up. The line about kids...that used to be me." He hooked his fingers into his front pockets. "Not any longer. Not since I met Bobby."

"My best advice is to be as honest as you can with Bobby. Let him handle things with the kids. When Farin and I had issues, he let me deal with my sister first. That's what I wanted to do, but it was nice to be in tune with each other. You are with Bobby, but you don't realize it." Steve clapped Remy on the shoulder. "Trust me. It'll probably make things touchy between you and Bobby for a while, but if it's going to work out, it will. You and Bobby are good together, and you've never said anything about not wanting the kids around, right?"

"I want us to be a family. I can't even fathom sending them away." His heart sank. *Damn Dale and his big mouth.* "I love Bobby, but I'm worried this will be heavier than I could ever imagine."

"You'll get through it and it'll work out." Steve half smiled. "I have faith."

"I'm glad you do." Remy rounded the trunk of the car and eased onto the driver's seat. He gripped the steering wheel. "Your dad sent me to get you because he had a meeting, and your brother is getting a ride home with Jenna."

"They're going out," Darcy murmured.

"Your dad will love that." He pulled out of the lot. "I'm sorry you had to meet Dale."

"Me too."

Remy drove across town but didn't know what to say. His brain hurt. He had too many thoughts in his head and no idea how to fix the mess he'd helped to create. *Fucking balls.*

# Chapter Thirteen

Remy stopped at the traffic light and shifted in his seat. He had to say something. Despite the advice from Steve, he couldn't let the silence continue to grow. "I know what you heard Dale say. I don't want to send you and Chris away. Not a chance."

"Stop," Darcy shouted. She held her swim bag tight. "Just stop."

"I can't, sweetheart. We need to go home." He turned once the light changed and headed to their street. "Dale is a jerk. He wanted to say something mean to make you mad." He made the left into the driveway and parked alongside the house. Before he switched off the engine, Darcy opened her door. She jumped from the car, leaving her door wide open and ran into the house.

Remy couldn't get out of the vehicle fast enough to keep up with her. He stopped short on the porch. Chasing her into the house wouldn't help anything. He glanced through the window to Bobby's office and saw

Darcy with her arms around Bobby's neck. She sobbed and his heart sank.

Remy sighed. He'd give them a minute. Hell, he'd give them plenty. *Why?* He doubted he'd be at the house much longer. Once everything got out, Bobby probably wouldn't want much to do with him. Dale had brought out a dead issue, but still. The kids were worried about being mistreated and had been in the past. They'd see him as just another asshole trying to get rid of them, even if that wasn't his plan at all. Everything was so wrong.

He sat on the top step of the porch and rested his head in his hands. He hadn't even bothered to see if the client was still at the house. The roar of a car engine caught his attention. He forced himself to look. The car belonging to Bobby's client wasn't parked in front of the house, but a smaller gray car parked behind his vehicle.

"Hey, Rem," Chris called. He waved, then leaned across the car and kissed Jenna.

Remy fought the urge to shake his head. *Won't Bobby have a fit if he sees that? Probably.* Good thing for Chris, Bobby had bigger things to worry about.

Chris left the car and waved at his girlfriend, then headed up the walkway. She backed down the drive and sped away. Chris grinned. "Why are you outside? Too hot in the house?" He waggled his eyebrows. "Needed a break from Dad?"

"He's talking to Darcy." He wanted to say more but couldn't.

"Cool." Chris stopped beside Remy and dropped his bag. "Dad would shit himself if he saw me kiss her."

"Probably." He wasn't in the mood to argue what Bobby would be angry about.

"How about it's our secret for now?" Chris grinned again.

"For now," Remy replied. *Christ.* He felt like a petulant child. "He'll figure you out, you know. He's a dad. They don't let much get past them."

Chris sat beside Remy and laughed. "Wow. Just wow. You and Dad are happy. Trust me. He sees nothing." He continued to laugh. "But now I get why you're so crazy. Being in love is awesome."

"Sure." Love was great. The fighting sucked and the misunderstandings could ruin everything, but yes, love was wonderful.

Remy rested his head in his hands again as Chris disappeared into the house. He tried not to worry or linger over the fact that he'd made Darcy cry. His heart sank lower — if it was possible. Bobby wanted the best for his kids. Remy, as much as he loved all three of them, wasn't good for anyone. He scrubbed both hands over his face. He really needed to stop the emo pity party, but his worst fear had come to light. His past was haunting him and affecting the life he wanted.

He listened for the sounds of Chris, Darcy or Bobby in the house but heard nothing. The silence bothered him and made his skin crawl. A decision must've been made. He heard footsteps on the hardwood floor, then the creak of the screen door opening. Remy smelled Bobby's cologne before he saw his boyfriend. Although he wanted to pour his heart out, Remy forced himself to be quiet. He'd fucked up by trying to talk to Darcy in the car. He wasn't about to screw up again.

Bobby sat beside him on the porch and rested his elbows on his knees. Instead of the business suit, he wore frayed jeans. His bare feet stuck out from under the cuffs. "Weren't we just here?" Bobby asked.

"Uh-huh." A lump formed in Remy's throat and his eyes prickled with unshed tears. *Fuck.* He refused to let anyone see him cry.

"The view is nice, especially with the flags gone." Bobby crossed his ankles. "I should mow tomorrow. Have Chris run the trimmer along the sidewalks."

*God.* The guy was stalling. Why prolong the inevitable? "Bobby, just spit it out." His lack of patience in tough situations would be the death of him. "Please?"

"What is there to say?" Bobby replied.

*Fucking goddamn balls.* "Let's see. Darcy was probably in a good mood until she heard me talking to my ex-boyfriend. He said I was going to ship the kids off. I'm not like your exes. I don't want the kids to go anywhere. I love your kids and you. I don't care who knows." He'd blurted so much out. *Damn lack of composure and calm.* "I've got all I've ever wanted right here in this house, but despite my best efforts, the cosmos doesn't want me to be a family man. I want that more than anything. You changed my mind. You brought out a side of me I didn't think existed, and I'm happy. I don't want to go, but your kids don't trust me."

"I wouldn't say the kids don't trust you. Darcy's upset, sure. Chris thinks he's got a partner in crime." Bobby sighed and rested his hand on Remy's thigh. "Here's the thing. My kids are genuinely worried something bad will happen. They've been through it a few times, and I can't say I blame them. But they're kids. I'm the adult here."

*Ah, fuck. Here comes the kiss-off.* Remy nodded.

"My life affects theirs. The decisions I make impact them." Bobby squeezed Remy's thigh. "I guarantee what Darcy heard was fucked up. I don't know your ex, but if he's who Darcy said, then I'm not surprised."

"Dale Emery. He works for one of the news stations in Cleveland. I'm not sure which any longer. He was at eight for a while, then moved to four." Remy couldn't look Bobby in the eye. He kept his head down and studied the pattern of the stones on the first sidewalk square.

"That's what I thought." Bobby bumped shoulders with Remy. "Dale, huh? He's kind of a celebrity."

"He's an asshole."

"Just what I was going to say."

Remy snapped his attention to Bobby. "You've met him?"

"No. That's the impression I got from watching him on the television. He projects confidence but also a sense of entitlement." Bobby moved his hand from Remy's thigh and draped his arm around Remy's shoulders, drawing Remy close. "Be honest with me. Completely honest. How do you see your future?"

Remy wanted to wait to reply, but the words tumbled out anyway. "I'm working at the paper, covering all of the stuff I don't want to and the stories I think matter. I'm watching the kids compete in their respective sports and cheering them on while they win and place well. I'm watching Chris, then Darcy, grow up and graduate. I want to be doing all of that beside you, but I can't force on you what I want."

Bobby rested his forehead on Remy's. "Who said you're forcing?"

"Bobby, I love you. I want to spend the rest of my life with you." He paused. "But if that's not what you want, I'm willing to walk. What's best for you and the kids is what matters to me."

"Are you interested in showing the community what a stable, loving and committed relationship looks like? Despite what the Coalition think?" Bobby asked.

"They never crossed my mind." He stared deep into Bobby's eyes. He could get lost there. "I want to be with you and the kids and be happy. If we show everyone what a good relationship looks like, then even better."

Bobby kissed Remy. Not the full-on passionate kisses Remy was used to, but a soft, feathery one. He barely brushed Remy's lips. His breath warmed Remy's skin.

"I deserve for you to leave me—I do—but I don't want… I can't." Remy closed his eyes and his tenuous hold on his composure split. The tears slipped down his cheeks.

"Rem." Bobby cupped Remy's jaw and tilted his gaze. "Look at me."

He forced himself to do as Bobby said. A fresh wave of embarrassment hit hard. He wanted so much to be the man Bobby needed, yet he felt so…inadequate.

"Hey. We've all got stuff we've done that wasn't our best moment. I've got lots of them. I bet if you asked the kids, they'd tell you all of the things I've done that are embarrassing. Singing along to the radio. Talking to myself in the grocery store. Wearing the wrong shirt with the wrong shoes. Saying the word 'rad' when it's not popular. Then there's the heinous act of wearing neon purple shorts when I run." He kissed Remy again. "But meeting you, being with you and loving you aren't on that list. I barely trust Dale to read the news. Why would I believe him now? I kind of understand, though, what he tried to do. He knew what he'd given up and wanted you back. If you did leave, I'm not sure

I wouldn't try something underhanded to get you to come home."

"Bobby?" He didn't believe what he'd heard.

"It's the truth. I blurted the words out and promptly acted like I hadn't said 'I love you', but I did from pretty much the moment we met. You're not like anyone I've ever met and I'm honored to have you in my life. I love you so much."

"But—what about…?" Remy scooted closer to Bobby. "I don't understand."

"I'll talk to Darcy again, but I tried to explain to her that sometimes adults say shit because they can. Like when they taunt the swimmers during the meets. It's not nice, and they wouldn't want that kind of thing said to them, but some just don't think. She's not ready to forgive you, I can't force that, but she'll understand. She'll get past it. You're right. You're not my exes and Dale is an asshole. We'll figure this out and move forward."

"Bobby." He threw his arms around his lover's waist. "We're a mess."

"But we're a mess as a family." Bobby kissed the top of Remy's head and sighed. "As for Darcy, she'll come around."

Remy sure hoped so. He sat up and wiped his hand across his face. The door creaked, and when he glanced over his shoulder, Darcy stood behind them.

Bobby didn't turn around. "Come here, Peanut." He patted the wood planks on his other side. "I've got room."

She inched over to them and settled next to Bobby. "You're—you're not going to kick us out?" Her cheeks were red and her eyes were swollen from crying. She held on to a stuffed rabbit that appeared to be in dire need of a bath. What Remy assumed had been a brilliant blue was sort of a dingy brown.

Remy dragged a long breath into his lungs, then exhaled. He'd needed the moment to compose himself. "Not a chance."

She half-heartedly smiled and leaned on Bobby. "You're coming with us to the cross-country meet tomorrow, right?"

"I sure am." And not even to cover the event. He could be there as a spectator this time. He'd probably have notes and something for a write-up in case the story was needed, but still.

"We run around to cheer for Chris." She clutched the rabbit. "Is that okay?"

"Will you show me where we're going? I get lost easily." Remy rested his elbows on his knees and met her gaze. "I hear you're a great guide."

"I am." Her eyes lit up and her smile grew into a genuine one. "We'll root for Jenna too?"

"Sure." He winked at her. God, having a family was hard — but rewarding too. He hadn't expected to feel such pride in Chris and Darcy. They weren't his kids, not his flesh and blood, but the longer he spent around them, the more he grew attached.

"Okay." She hugged her dad, then stood. "I have homework. I'll bring out my math so you can check it."

"We'll be in after a bit," Bobby said. "Leave it on the table." He waited for her to disappear into the house, then draped his arm around Remy's waist. "For a guy who wasn't a kid man, you're a good dad."

"I'm not good, but I'm learning and trying." He rested his head on Bobby's shoulder. "So. What do we do now?"

"Good question." Bobby stretched his legs and crossed his ankles. "We get through supper without me blowing up at my son for having a girlfriend. We'll sort out the schedule for tomorrow so everyone gets to the bus or the track on time, then once the kids are in bed and settled for the night...we fuck like rabbits and start all over again in the morning."

"Sounds like my kind of schedule." Remy tipped his head to look up at Bobby. "I love you, Bobby Gagnon."

"Love you, Remy Nicholas, and one of these days I'm going to marry you." Bobby grinned. "By the way, I'm not taking that back. Any of it."

*Marry him one day.* Remy had never heard sweeter words. He stood, then dragged Bobby to his feet. He could see them together as old men, chasing the grandkids and rushing across the field to cheer on the next generation of runners, then standing poolside for the future swimmers. Being with Bobby was the smartest thing he'd ever done. He chuckled.

"What?" Bobby asked. He gripped the front door, but didn't open it.

"I was just thinking I know what the next *Positively Cedarwood* story should be. The Coalition spent all that time and energy trying to get rid of all those people they thought didn't belong here in town, but what they succeeded in doing was bringing couples together. We didn't need the Coalition to give us the green light, but once Colin and Jordan started the trend, the rest of us felt comfortable to live our lives and love the men we wanted to love. That's what I'll write about — how the Coalition unintentionally brought the greatest love to Cedarwood."

"I like it. You won't shut them down. They'll always want an argument, but you'll take the wind out of their sails for sure." Bobby opened the door for Remy and stepped out of the way. "So, do you want a silver or gold band?"

Remy laughed and paused in the doorway. He collided with the solid wall of Bobby's chest. He stared into Bobby's dark eyes and shivered. "I'll love whatever you give me."

"I love when you say that." Bobby swatted Remy's ass. "We're totally using the blindfold tonight."

Remy grinned and gripped the front of Bobby's shirt. "I can't wait."

\* \* \* \*

Getting up that morning hadn't been hard for Remy. He loved early wake-up calls. The trek across the gravel parking lot to the start of the race wasn't even bad. What he hadn't planned on was the number of people crammed into the viewing areas at the metro park. Per Bobby's instructions, he kept Darcy beside him and kept an eye on her in the glut of people.

"Oh, hi!" A woman crossed the path and waved. "Darcy, how are you? And Remy, right? Nice to see you again. Chris made the varsity team, didn't he?"

Darcy nodded. "Yes, he did. Jenna did too, didn't she?"

Remy smiled and kept his mouth shut. He hadn't checked the lineups for either team and had no idea who'd made the varsity squad besides Chris.

"She's trying to get back on it. She had a rough week last week in practice." The woman shook hands with Remy. "I'm Jenna's mom, Jayce. There are so many parents here, it's easy to forget who's who. Shay and

Bret went with my husband, Kell, to watch the middle school boys' race."

"I should get the stats on the winners for the paper." He nodded once. "Thanks for reminding me. It was good to see you. Bobby should be back at any moment. He said something about taking Chris a protein bar or something. Would you like to watch the middle school girls' race with us? Or at least stand with us until most of the girls pass?"

"That would be fantastic." She stood on the other side of Darcy. "There are so many people here. Usually the first meet is busy, but this one...wow."

"When Chris ran at Chagrin, the meets weren't this big," Darcy said. "Only, like, seven teams."

"Did you run in school?" Jayce asked. "Bobby said you were a runner."

"Oh, no. I didn't take up a sport until college."

"Well, good for you. Running is a great way to blow off steam." She grinned. "I'm glad you and Bobby hooked up. I haven't seen that man smile so much in the time I've met him." She patted his arm. "You're cute together too."

"I feel the same way. Hopefully we last like you and Kell." He clapped as the first few competitors surged past his position.

"Absolutely. Go you." She nodded once and applauded. *The runners or me?* He wasn't sure.

He hadn't expected to be welcomed by the other cross-country parents. Of course, Jayce was just one parent, but she wasn't put off by him or his relationship with Bobby. He should've known Bobby was right and that a lot of the Cedarwood community wasn't offended by the LGBTQ portion. The main bunch of girls ran past, then the crowd around Remy, Darcy, and Jayce thinned out.

"I'm going to head over to the starting line. Feel free to join us. Bring Bobby." She waved. "And if I don't see you over there, I'll see you at the end. Kell and I are in charge of water for the varsity boys' race."

"Sounds like a plan." Remy waved as she strolled away. "Jenna's mom is really nice."

"Yeah. Her dad's pretty awesome too." Darcy nudged Remy. "Dad's taking forever."

"I didn't think it'd take him half an hour to deliver protein bars." Remy glanced around at the people milling about. He didn't see Bobby anywhere. "I'm sure he'll be back."

Darcy nodded. "He sent a text. The girls are over by the parking lot and he's waiting on them to pass before he comes over."

"Well, there you go," Remy said. "I forgot how much standing and running is involved in cheering for the cross-country team."

"It's not even Jenna's or Chris' turn yet," Darcy replied and laughed. She tucked her phone into her back pocket. "Remy?"

"Right here." He met her gaze. He wasn't sure what she was going to say, and he had no plans to interrupt her. If she was ready to talk to him about yesterday, then he was all ears.

"I'm sorry I didn't believe you. I'm sorry I thought you'd be like Neil." She toyed with her ponytail and ran her fingers around the length of her hair. "I got scared."

"I understand." He dropped to one knee to look her in the eye. He brushed a few flyaway strands of her hair from her face and smiled. "I'm not Neil or Terry. I love your dad very much and I love you and your brother that much too. I'm sorry I didn't tell my jerk of an ex-boyfriend to shove off before he said that stuff."

"Really?" Her eyes widened.

"Uh-huh. He was out of line and he shocked me as much as what he said shocked you." He glanced around again then motioned her close. "I want to ask you something because your input is important."

She nodded and a smile lit up her face.

"Can I marry your dad? Not just live there, but marry him?" Remy asked. He guessed Chris would be fine with his decision, but he needed to know Darcy approved.

"Would you adopt me and Chris too?" She laced her fingers together. "So we'd have two dads?"

"If your dad will let me." He hadn't thought that far ahead, but now that she'd mentioned the idea, he liked it.

She pumped her fist and shrieked. "I get to have two dads all of the time!"

Remy stood and stumbled backward as she threw her arms around his waist. He held on to her tight. Compared to the day before, things were definitely looking up.

"Someone's happy." Bobby ducked under the caution tape and crossed over to where Remy and Darcy stood. "I take it you and Remy patched things up?"

"Yeah." Darcy shrugged. "We did." She tipped her head to the side. "Can Remy adopt us?"

Bobby's gaze switched between Remy and Darcy. He scratched his chin then chuckled. "I don't know where that came from, but it's an option."

He hadn't exactly said no, so that was a plus. Remy grinned. "I asked Darce if she was okay with you and me for the long-term."

"He's going to ask you to marry him," Darcy blurted. "You'd better say yes. I so want two dads."

Bobby's lips parted and his eyebrows rose. He didn't say anything for a moment.

Remy shrugged. "Well, it was going to be a surprise." Like once he had a ring and a speech prepared...and maybe a nice dinner ready on the deck, along with rope lighting and candles or something.

"You discussed it with Darcy." Bobby's expression didn't change and there was no inflection in his voice.

Remy paused. Had he overstepped his boundaries? *Shit.* He second-guessed himself and wished he hadn't been so quick to talk to Darcy about his plans for the future.

"Dad." Darcy grabbed Bobby's hand and swung his arm. "Yesterday you said to trust Remy. I do. You also said you weren't letting his hot ass go."

From his hairline to the neck of his T-shirt, Bobby blushed. "I don't think you were supposed to hear that."

"Well, talk quietly next time." She rested her hands on her hips. "You told Chris you wanted a guy who liked us and you. Remy does."

Remy nodded. "She's right. I do."

Bobby shook his head and some of the color bled from his face until he reached a normal shade. He met Remy's stare. "I can't fault her for repeating the truth. I wish she hadn't used the colorful language, but that's on me for using it while she was within earshot."

"She's right here," Darcy said.

"You are." Bobby turned his attention to his daughter. "What about your brother? Think he'll accept Remy as his other dad?"

She rolled her eyes. "Yeah. Remy didn't yell at him when he kissed Jenna yesterday."

"Oh?" Bobby pinched the bridge of his nose. "The kid's looking down the barrel of sixteen, has a girlfriend and is kissing her. What is this world coming to?"

"Dad, Bliss is here. See her?" Darcy pointed at a woman and a girl who appeared to be about Darcy's age. The girl waved. Darcy yanked her phone from her pocket. "I've got my phone and I can see you from there. Can I go talk to her?"

"Sure," Bobby said. "Five minutes, then we're going to the starting line."

"Five minutes," Darcy repeated as she jogged over to her friend.

"So." Bobby kept his attention on his daughter. "Chris kissed a girl."

"Yeah. I didn't say anything because it wasn't my place." Remy clasped his hands together behind his back. "I'll mention it from now on."

"How about we sort it out as we go along? We're partners, and although they're my kids, we'll do this together." Bobby draped his arm around Remy's shoulders. "I'm not sure I could get through the teen years with both kids without help."

"You'd be fine."

"I just wanted to make sure she was okay with another change," Remy said.

Darcy trotted back to where he stood with Bobby. "Wait. Chris doesn't like when we stand by the starting line."

"True." Bobby nodded to the group of parents along the fence. "We're starting here. If he's on pace, he'll pass there in no time."

"He doesn't like you to watch the start?" Remy asked. "Really?"

"Parents aren't allowed by the starting line and Chris tells me it messes with his Zen." Bobby shrugged and stopped at the fence. "I don't want to get in his way."

Darcy rolled her eyes. "His Zen headspace. My brother is weird."

"It's like you before a swim." Remy eased into the spot on the other side of Bobby. Darcy stared at him but didn't answer. He waited for her to flip out. For a moment, he worried he'd overstepped. He'd thought he'd asked an innocent question, but who knew?

"He's right, Darce," Bobby said. "You're just as focused as your brother."

"Wow." She gripped the railing. "I knew that — but I didn't." She grinned. "I am like Chris. Whoa." She slipped her earbuds into place and rested her arms on the fence.

"That's my girl." Bobby shook his head. "She's blunt."

A shot rang out and Remy flinched. He knew the noise — the starting gun signaling the beginning of the race. *Still.* He hated sounds like shots and bangs. The memory of the assault came back to mind. He'd thought he was past the moment, but sometimes...

"Chris should be coming up this way in a minute or two." Bobby leaned in close to Remy. "We're safe. Promise. No one will hurt you or them here. I won't let it happen."

"Thanks." He kissed Bobby's neck. He appreciated Bobby's reassurance. He loved his boyfriend so much.

An all-terrain vehicle rumbled by, followed by the first runners. A blond kid was two steps ahead of Chris.

"Chris! Go, Chris," Darcy shouted. She jumped up and down. "You got it. You got it!"

"That's my boy," Bobby said and clapped. "Keep your pace. Run this thing your way."

Remy applauded too. "Great job," he hollered. "Keep it up." He probably sounded lame, but he'd never cheered at one of the races. He wasn't sure what to say.

Before Remy could figure out what to say next, Chris and the forerunner disappeared into the woods.

"Now, we run." Bobby grabbed Remy's hand. "Darce? Come on." He broke into a jog. "If we go over by the playground, we'll catch them once more before the end." He waved his arm, nudging Darcy in front of them as he and Remy charged past the swings.

Remy hustled the short jaunt to the path. A line of caution tape prevented anyone from crossing the course. People crushed against the edges and strained the tape.

"Wow, there are a lot of people here," Remy said. He plastered himself to Bobby's side. "I thought it'd be packed, but man."

"It gets nuts." Bobby let go of Remy and clapped. "Here he comes."

Remy peered down the trail. Sure enough, the ATV led the way, followed by the blond kid and Chris.

"Wow! Great job," Remy shouted. "Awesome pace." *Holy hell.* He hadn't looked at his watch when the race started, but he knew he couldn't run nearly two miles in such a short period of time.

"Knees up," Bobby growled. "You got it."

Darcy jumped up and down again as Chris passed. Within seconds, more runners came down the path, but by then Chris and the kid in first were back into the woods.

"The pack will show up in a bit," Bobby said. "They string out the longer the race goes. Plus, the big hill around the one-mile mark tends to slow them down." He grasped Remy's hand. "Chris is doing great, but if he wants to win, he'll have to dig deep at the end. Bryson set a blistering pace."

Darcy strolled out ahead of Bobby and Remy. "Let's go. We'll miss the end." She jogged across the playground and down a grassy slope to the knot of people and the gigantic timing board. More caution tape blocked the parents' and fans' access. Remy blew out a long breath as he made his way to the finish line. He hadn't realized how much running was involved on the part of the parents. Then again, he'd never participated in a sport.

Along the final six hundred meters of the course, people waited. Some clapped and most of them shouted.

Remy glanced down at the timing board — 16:55. When Bobby had said 'blistering pace' for a 5k run, he hadn't been kidding. *Damn*.

"There they are," Darcy screamed. "Yay, Chris. Go, Chris!"

Remy clapped and focused on his lover's son. "You got this. Keep it up." His heart pounded as Chris matched strides with Bryson. He was so close. If he found just a tiny bit more speed, he could overtake Bryson. "Come on, buddy," Remy murmured.

"Yeah, Chris. Yeah. Dig. PR! PR!" Bobby pumped his fists. "PR." He kept his focus on the race, but spoke over his shoulder. "Personal best or personal record."

*So that's what PR means...* Remy balled his hands. Pride and excitement rushed through his veins. He wasn't a dad to Chris, but he wished he had been all along. He understood the thrill of watching the athlete — Bobby's son — excel.

Chris matched Bryson's pace and had him step for step, but at the finish line Bryson pulled inches ahead of him.

Bobby whooped and Darcy screamed. Remy clapped, but he wasn't sure how to feel. On one hand he was thrilled that Chris had finished a very respectable second, but then he wondered if Bobby expected Chris to win everything. Remy shook his head. He needed to learn more about the sport and Bobby's expectations for his kid.

"Hell, yes." Bobby hurried to the finish line and the roped-off area beyond the line where the runners were expected to remove the little tag attached to the laces of their shoes. Some of the boys were bent over and others had collapsed. Chris stretched out on the grass with his knees up and his arms over his face.

A man wearing a bright yellow and green Cedarwood Cross-Country shirt rushed around the tape. He grasped Bobby's hand. "That's a school record." He grinned. "You should be proud, Dad."

Bobby nodded and matched the man's — Remy assumed the guy was the coach — smile. Darcy grabbed a cup of water and offered it to Chris. He didn't take the cup right away.

"You've got to get up, son. Walk around and cool down." Bobby snagged another cup of water. "Keep moving."

Remy watched the scene but felt a little like an outsider. They had the family thing down, especially at the end of a race. He was in the way.

Chris sat up and dumped one of the water cups over his head. He turned to Bobby. "Dad?"

Darcy yanked Remy over to the fence. "Chris just earned his lifetime PR. How cool is that?"

Emotion overwhelmed Remy. Pride, thrill, love... Tears burned at the corners of his eyes. "That's awesome."

Chris re-laced his shoes and stood. He walked around the roped-off area with his hands on his lower back. "Let me get my cool-down run completed and we can talk," he said. "Thanks, Dad, Darcy, Remy. You're all awesome, too." He grimaced, then started away.

Bobby grabbed Remy in a bear hug. "We did it."

"Uh-huh." He wound his arms around Bobby and Darcy. "We did." He wasn't sure what he'd really contributed, but he wasn't going to argue.

Bobby kissed him. "You're a great support to me and the kids. Love you." He kissed the top of Darcy's head. "You too, Peanut."

"Dad." Darcy didn't pull away.

"Love you both." Remy held them tighter and glanced over Bobby's shoulder. He noticed a man behind Bobby. While the other fans and parents clapped, cheered and shouted, this guy stood quiet and stared at them. Remy looked away but noticed the man still watching them. His annoyance grew. *Who is this person and why is he staring?*

He focused on the man and snorted. He recognized the stare-er. Francis Loperman, the vice president of the Coalition. Was he pissed about Remy and Bobby kissing in public? If so, why did it matter? There wasn't anything illegal about two men showing affection. Would someone have a fit if they saw Francis kissing his wife, Ree? *Not a chance.* What made what he was doing with Bobby any different?

Remy remained close to Bobby. *Fuck Francis and his narrow-mindedness.*

"What's wrong?" Bobby asked. He must've followed Remy's gaze. "Jesus."

"What are you doing?" Francis asked. He folded his arms and stood as tall as he could. "This is a public place."

"So?" Remy growled. He wasn't about to be intimidated by the man or the Coalition any longer. "We're not doing anything wrong."

"No, we're not." Bobby draped one arm around Remy and the other around Darcy. "I'm cheering on my son. Is that a crime?"

"You're corrupting children," Francis snapped.

"Honey, please," Bobby replied.

Jayce and Kell, along with Bret and Shae, strolled up behind Francis. "What's going on?" Jayce asked. "What's this clown want now?"

Francis paled. "You're friends with him? Them?"

"They are good people, and yeah, we are. So?" Jayce matched Francis's stance. "What's your point?"

"He's part of the Coalition and we don't fit their requirements to be in public," Remy said. "It's crap."

"What would your wife say?" Bret asked. "Where's Ree?"

If it was possible to pale even more, Francis did. "Bret."

"So you can make judgments on gay people, but you can't handle it when someone realizes you're not here with your wife?" Jayce asked. She shook her head. "You're getting a divorce because you had an affair with your secretary. We don't care. A lot of people don't care."

Remy stepped in front of Bobby and Darcy. He was tired of being shamed too. "Don't you see? There's no point in embarrassing anyone or trying to run people out of town. Who cares what we do or who we're with? We've got to live with the decisions we've made. I have no regrets."

Francis' mouth opened and closed, but no sound came out.

"All we want is what everyone else wants. To be equal and to live our lives. The Coalition is entitled to their opinion, but so are we." Bobby draped his arm around Remy's shoulders. "'Live and let live' is what Remy wrote in his opinion piece. I'm all for that motto."

"You're crazy," Francis squeaked. "This isn't over." He started away, then stopped and glared at Remy and Bobby. "Don't any of you mention Ree or my secretary. Ever." He stomped across the lawn to the parking lot.

"Wow." Jayce shook her head again. "He doesn't give up."

"It's not over," Remy replied. "Never will be. We're not going to change anyone's mind if they don't want it. Maybe that's the thing."

"Probably." Bobby hugged Remy tighter and kissed his temple. "The argument will never end, but as long as we're true to ourselves, we're fine."

"Cheers." Bret applauded. "Speaking of cheers, your boy took second overall. We should be congratulating him, not dicking around with Francis and friends."

"Very true," Bobby said.

"Lead the way." Remy slipped his hand into Bobby's back pocket. His lover was right. The difference of opinion would never go away, but it was healthy. Not everyone had to agree. As long as no one else was assaulted, then let the Coalition have their point of view. He had his.

"Proud of you," Bobby murmured. "You're hot as hell when you're riled."

"So are you." Remy squeezed Bobby's ass. "Then again, you're sexy all of the time."

"Tonight, your ass is mine." Bobby kissed him again.

"Isn't it always?" Remy grinned. He'd offer himself up to Bobby whenever Bobby wanted. "Love you."

"I love you too."

Remy sighed and sagged into Bobby's side. He never would've guessed he'd come so far in such a short period of time. His thoughts had evolved and his life was better because he'd opened his heart, not only to Bobby but to the kids too. Being together in Cedarwood as a family rocked.

# Epilogue

Bobby stretched out on the deck chair and stared at the ripples in the pool. He'd have to close it down soon. Despite having the heated feature in place, he refused to keep the pool open and available through the winter. But first, he'd enjoy the last warm weekend in October. He gripped the arms of the chair and listened to the gentle slap of the water against the side of the pool.

He missed the noise, though. A chaotic house meant a happy one. He had what he wanted—Chris, Darcy and Remy.

"This is strange," Remy said and sat beside Bobby. "No kids. I'm not sure what to do with myself."

"True." Normally, he'd be packing the kids off to bed and hitting the hay soon after in order to get up in time for the various cross-country events. But since Chris had only made it to districts and regionals, but had barely missed going to state, the season was over.

"I'm surprised you let him go on that date." Remy offered Bobby a glass, then sipped his own wine. "Darcy was thrilled to sleep over at Bliss', wasn't she?"

"She loves that kind of thing." Not that a sleepover was bad, but he worried. Call him an overprotective dad, but he liked knowing his kids were safe and happy. "As for Chris, he earned it—and her parents went along." He grasped Remy's hand. "It's quiet. The water splashing and crickets are a good lullaby. Plus, it gives me time alone with you."

"It's the first kid-free weekend we've had since the middle of August. That's what? Almost three months?" Remy replied. He placed his glass on the arm of his chair and settled on the decking between Bobby's knees. "We should celebrate." He smoothed his palms along Bobby's belly and up to his chest. "The last I checked, the gate's locked, the alarm is on and the fence is high enough to keep what's going on in your yard private." He leaned forward and kissed Bobby. "You should be inside me."

"I should." Bobby bit back a groan as Remy feasted on his mouth. Passion and desire spiraled through him.

Remy kept the connection but smoothed Bobby's shirt up. He broke the kiss and moved to Bobby's nipples. He scraped his teeth over the sensitive skin then sucked on one of the tight bundles of nerves.

Bobby threaded his fingers into Remy's hair and groaned. He tugged lightly on the silky strands. "Remy."

"Uh-huh?" Remy pinched one nipple and resumed sucking on the other.

"God. I'm on fire." Prickles assaulted him from within. Every nerve ending sizzled. He spread his legs and rubbed his groin against Remy's abs. The pressure from the cotton of his shorts added to his pleasure. Bobby let go of Remy's hair long enough to remove his shirt. He needed the temperature change, but that was what Remy did to him — made him hot all over.

Warm night air surrounded Bobby. He never had to think about what he needed from Remy. The man knew how to please him, and he always wanted to be with Remy. Now that they had the opportunity to make love on the deck, he was taking it.

Bobby nudged Remy away from his nipples. He'd let Remy have his fun later. His nipples beaded as the slight breeze kissed his skin. He blew out a long breath. He wanted to make Remy come apart. He knew what his lover needed, too.

Remy licked his lips. His mouth was swollen and his eyes wide. "What's wrong?"

"Nothing." Bobby curled his fingers under Remy's chin. "You're right. We're alone and I'm taking advantage." He helped Remy to his feet, then stood. Raw desire took over. He pinned Remy to the fencing around the deck and kissed him hard. Their teeth clashed, and he bit Remy's bottom lip. Remy battled him and won by sucking on Bobby's tongue. Bobby threaded his fingers back into Remy's hair. He loved the softness of the strands and how Remy kept it shaggy enough to pull but always looked sexy.

He breathed in the scent of Remy — pine and spice. The memory of the taste of Remy's kiss lingered in his mind. Bobby slid his tongue along the velvet of Remy's and groaned. He ran his fingers over Remy's abs, loving how his hard body felt under Bobby's.

Remy ripped his mouth free and groaned. Bobby snatched the opportunity to shove Remy's T-shirt up over his head.

"You are so sexy," Bobby said. "Fucking adorable."

"I've got a great running partner to keep me in shape." He raked his fingers down Bobby's chest.

"It shows." Bobby dropped to his knees and opened Remy's shorts. Remy's dick stretched out before him and he licked his lips. "No underwear? Since when?" He chuckled and brushed the tip of Remy's shaft over his mouth. Seeing his lover commando kicked his desire up a notch. Remy prided himself on his modesty, but Bobby liked the secret wild side. "I love this."

"I took 'em off once the kids left. I wanted to surprise you." Remy sucked in a ragged breath. "Like it?"

"I'm surprised." He trailed his tongue along Remy's shaft. He loved when Remy groaned and arched his back during a blowjob.

Remy palmed Bobby's head and massaged his scalp. "You could let me suck you off for a change."

"You will—in the morning." He plunged his mouth onto Remy's cock. The taste of Remy exploded on his tongue. The man tasted so good and soothed Bobby's soul.

"Bobby," Remy bit out.

Bobby pulled out, then sucked Remy all of the way back in again. He bobbed his head. Being in control of Remy and his pleasure thrilled Bobby. The saucy reporter made him happy and completed his family. Besides, Remy flourished when Bobby directed him. He shoved Remy's pants down his thighs until the garment plopped softly at Remy's feet. Bobby abandoned Remy's cock only to suck on one of Remy's balls. At the same time, he stroked Remy's shaft.

"Jesus," Remy said. "You're dangerous."

"How?" he asked between licks. The hairs on Remy's sac tickled Bobby's nose.

"I'm going to fall over the railing. My knees are weak." He gripped Bobby's head. "You know it and keep pushing me."

He didn't want his lover to get hurt. That wasn't his point. He wanted to nudge Remy closer to coming apart instead.

"Bobby. I'm close." Remy tipped his head back. "Do you know what you do to me?"

"I do." He bobbed his head again and flicked his tongue around Remy's shaft. He'd been saying the words 'I do' an awful lot lately. That and the word 'love'. He hadn't gotten around to buying a ring just yet. He probably should and make Remy an honest man already. He buried his nose in Remy's pubic hair and hummed. The man was a teddy bear, but hard as steel and so addictive.

Remy tensed. "Bobby. Fuck. You get me right to the edge, then change it up."

That was the point. He slid his fingers around the back of Remy's balls to his asshole. Remy's sharp intake of breath signaled to Bobby that he was close to climax. Remy tensed and dug his fingernails into Bobby's scalp.

"Relax, babe," Bobby reminded. "You'll blow a gasket."

"So close." Remy trembled. "Like right there."

He tapped Remy's hole and toyed with the puckered skin. Remy rolled his hips, jamming his dick into Bobby's mouth.

Bobby didn't pull back. He wanted Remy raw. He swallowed Remy's cock to the back of his throat and hummed again. He eased his index finger into Remy's hole. *Come for me. Come apart.*

Remy trembled. His knees shook and he curled forward. He rammed Bobby's mouth. "Oh Jesus," Remy shouted.

Cum spurted down Bobby's throat and he swallowed everything greedily. He continued to bob his head as Remy climaxed. Once Remy had sagged against the railing again, Bobby cleaned him up.

Remy let go of Bobby's head and wobbled. He widened his stance. "Damn. You know how to wring me out. I was supposed to be sucking you off," he puffed.

"I know." Bobby sat back on his heels. "Lean over the picnic table." He wanted way too much from Remy right now — including his cock deep in Remy's ass.

"Bobby." Remy kicked out of his shorts and managed to cross the deck. He stretched out on the table and wriggled his ass. He exhaled and spread his legs. His dick pointed toward the floor of the deck. He grabbed his ass cheeks. "Fuck me."

"Uh-huh." Good thing he'd stashed lube just inside the door. Bobby retrieved the bottle. He thanked God they weren't using rubbers any longer. He wouldn't have been able to put the damn thing on. He dribbled lube on his fingers. Excitement and giddiness filled his brain. Every time he fucked Remy was intoxicating. He stepped up behind Remy and eased his first and middle fingers into Remy's hole.

Remy rewarded him with a grunt then a moan. He relaxed beneath Bobby. "More," Remy begged. He rocked backward and pushed Bobby's digits deep into his ass.

"You do want me." He twisted his fingers, then pumped. "Who do you belong to?"

"You, Bobby." Remy grasped the edge of the table. "Harder."

"You're demanding." Bobby eased his digits from Remy, then lined his dick up with Remy's ass. He added more lube before he pushed inside. He filled Remy to the brim and paused. Being in his lover was so good and perfect. Power radiated in his veins. He started to move and punctuated each thrust into Remy with a swat.

"Jesus, yes." Remy arched his back again. Red blossomed on his pale skin. He met Bobby thrust for thrust. He writhed and clawed beneath Bobby. Sweat slicked down his back.

Each whimper turned Bobby's senses inside out. He sizzled from within. The orgasm was so close. He spanked Remy harder.

"Fuck, that feels so good," Remy murmured. "More."

He loved giving Remy the painful pleasure he demanded. "Remy." Bobby stopped spanking him and focused on thrusting. His thoughts blurred and he embraced the heat swirling within him. He moved with abandon. "Come with me," Bobby said. "Come for me."

"Already there." Remy tensed under him and held the edge of the table in his white-knuckled grip.

Bobby slammed deep into Remy's ass and emptied his load. He shivered and slumped over Remy while adding a few more thrusts as the orgasm washed through him.

"Oh my God." Remy groaned again. "Wow."

"You say that every time." Bobby kissed Remy's shoulder and held onto his lover. "I can't be that good."

"Yeah, you are and you know it." Remy sighed. "Every time."

"It's you. I want to please you." He kissed Remy's back, then stood tall. The salty taste of Remy's perspiration lingered on his lips. He eased out of Remy's ass and winced. Remy's skin was so red.

"I'm not going to be able to sit later." Remy stood and stretched. His nipples were still hard, and cum slid down his thigh.

Bobby marveled at the way his lover looked. Disheveled worked for Remy. He'd already fucked Remy, but the urge returned. He could make love to the man forever and not get tired of him.

"What?" Remy grasped his shirt and wiped the cum from his leg. "You look like you're a hundred miles away."

"I'm drinking in the image of my hot boyfriend." He wound his arms around Remy. "Love you."

"Good thing." Remy snatched a towel from the bin and offered it to Bobby. "You should probably cover up. I saw headlights. If Chris is home, he'll come out here looking for you."

Bobby draped the towel around his hips. "You mean us?" He grasped the pile of clothes from the deck floor. "They consider you their father too."

"I'm still getting used to that." Remy covered himself and nudged Bobby toward the door. "I wouldn't change a thing, but it's hard to get used to."

"You belong here with us." He couldn't imagine a future without Remy.

"I hear voices. We need to get dressed." Remy hurried up the back staircase to their bedroom.

Bobby followed, and once in the bedroom, he tossed the soiled towels and clothes into the hamper. He stepped into a fresh pair of boxers and sleep pants as well as a T-shirt. Remy yanked on boxer briefs and jogging pants. He unfolded a shirt emblazoned with the words CEDARWOOD TRIBUNE across the chest.

Bobby grinned. His boyfriend looked hot nude, but he wore the outfit well.

"Dad? Rem?" Chris called. "I know you're home. I saw the wine out."

"Wonderful," Bobby muttered. "We have one bottle of wine…"

"We left lights on too," Remy replied. "We'll be there in a moment."

"At least you didn't say coming." Bobby kissed Remy once more, then headed down the main staircase first. When he rounded the corner, Chris, Jenna, Jayce and Kell stood in the living room.

"Hi. Wow. Everyone." He was glad Remy had convinced him to get dressed. "What's up? Bad date?"

"We didn't believe you were home," Kell said. "Had to make sure." He shook hands with Bobby then Remy.

"We were upstairs." Bobby nodded. "I appreciate that you checked."

"Can't be too careful." Jayce winked. "The kids were fine, and Chris is home safe. The movie wasn't that great, but what do you expect? We all had fun, so it was worth it."

*Home safe?* Bobby hooked his fingers into the waistband of his sleep pants. "Was there a problem?" He'd thought the crap with the Coalition had more or less died down.

"Nope." Jayce strolled up to Bobby. "We came inside just because. That and it drives our children crazy."

"Definitely." He eased his arm around Remy's waist. "Lord knows they put us through enough."

"Exactly." She held hands with Kell. "We've embarrassed our children enough." She hugged Jenna. "Did you have fun?"

"Yeah, Mom." Jenna blushed. She smiled. "I'll text you," she said to Chris then ducked out of the room.

"Just a minute." Chris hurried after her.

"Teens." Jayce shook her head. "Once they're done kissing, we'll be out of here. I'm glad things are working out."

"We are too." Bobby let go of Remy and opened the door. "Thanks. Next time we'll go along."

"Deal." Kell shook hands with both Remy and Bobby. "Have a great night."

Chris waited on the porch. "Thank you, sir. Goodnight."

"You've raised a very sweet boy," Jayce said. She escorted Jenna down the stairs.

"Be safe," Bobby called. He waved and waited with Chris and Remy until Jenna and her parents had backed down the driveway.

"Dad." Chris groaned. "You're such a parent."

"Are you embarrassed?" Bobby held the door for his son and Remy. "I could've been worse."

Chris rolled his eyes. "I'm used to it."

"You know the drill." Bobby hugged Chris. "I'm glad you had fun. See you in the morning."

"Thanks. Night, Dad." Chris grinned at Remy. "Night." He leaned in close to Remy and whispered something. Both looked at Bobby then blushed.

Bobby hooked his fingers in the waistband of his sleep pants again and considered the pair. *They're already conspiring?* Bad because he wasn't in on the dealings, but good because Chris trusted Remy.

Remy nodded and clapped Chris on the shoulder. "Night, kid."

Bobby waited until Chris disappeared up the steps before he spoke. He locked the front door and switched off the main living room light. "Keeping secrets with my kids?"

"The good kind." Remy paused. "I'll do this again tomorrow when the kids and Julia are here, but I'd like to know the answer in case it's not...so I don't embarrass myself." He disengaged from him and dropped to one knee. "I don't have a ring, but you've got my heart. I'm not a kid person — I'm this family's person. I love you and Chris and Darcy so much. I can't see my life without the three of you. Will you marry me so we can be a complete family?"

*Like I can tell Remy no?* Bobby nodded. Tears pricked behind his eyes. "I'd be honored." He helped Remy to his feet and captured him in a kiss. He gathered Remy in his arms. "I can't imagine being without you either. I love you, Remy Nicholas."

"I was so worried and scared you'd say no." Remy kissed him again. "Well, tomorrow during dinner, act surprised."

"I will." He curled his fingers under Remy's chin. "Why'd you think I'd say no?"

"Moving in together was a big step, just like going bare, but we can take those back. You know? But you can't go back from marriage. Or at least I can't. I'm a one-and-done kind of guy."

"I'm glad. I'm the same way." Bobby brushed his lips across Remy's. "I don't want to marry anyone else."

"You're my man." Remy slipped his hands under the band of Bobby's sleep pants.

"My soon-to-be husband," Bobby corrected. He held Remy and swayed with him. He'd thought coming back to Cedarwood would be the worst decision, but it had turned out to be the best. The kids were happy and flourishing. His business had stabilized and grown. Remy was vital at the paper and in their lives. The Coalition were still around but not as vicious. Besides, he, Remy and a lot of other people had found the gumption to stand their ground against the naysayers.

He breathed in the scent of Remy's cologne. He'd found more than his heart when he'd met Remy. He'd found his soul mate, and now he'd never let Remy go.

# Want to see more from this author? Here's a taster for you to enjoy!

## Cedarwood Pride: Doc Cedarwood
### Megan Slayer

*Excerpt*

"My name is Aiden and I'm not a parent." Aiden stood in front of the support group and laced his fingers together. "I'm the not-so-rare breed called the child of gay parents. I grew up well-adjusted and happy. If my father, Keye, hadn't died, we'd still be a happy family. My other father, Len, decided not to seek out another partner after Keye's passing five years ago. Last year, he decided to try again with a man named Ross. Anyway, I knew I was loved, cared for, I had boundaries, and if I screwed up, my dads and Keye loved me enough to punish me." He swept his gaze around the room. Meeting at the hospital wasn't the norm for the group, but he couldn't complain. They'd been able to come to him and he appreciated the gesture.

Colin Baker stepped up beside Aiden. "He's leaving out the best part." He grinned. "Aiden grew up big, strong and to become a doctor."

"Well, there is that." The tips of his ears burned. He wasn't embarrassed to admit his profession. Being a doctor was in his blood. Sure, he had a good job, but he wasn't much different from anyone else. "I'm here at the hospital and I've put my work number on the business cards in case you or your children have questions. I've been in their shoes and know a lot of how they feel."

He flexed his fingers and waited for questions, but none came. Some of the group members left their chairs and others turned to chat with those around them. He eased away from the people and made his way to the door. His phone hadn't buzzed — good thing. According to the schedule, he was off for the next twenty-four hours, but that didn't mean much. If the emergency room staff numbers weren't up to regulations, he'd be called in until he maxed out his allowed hours. He'd racked up so much overtime that if he were hourly, not salary, the hospital would go broke.

"Good turnout tonight, especially since we scheduled it for a Thursday." Colin straightened the pamphlets on the table, then arranged the various cards. "It's not one of our usual chatty meetings, but the others will be happy to have another resource in you. The kids need to know they aren't alone and can succeed."

"Gage is doing just fine and I guarantee he knows he's not alone," Aiden said. "I've seen his artwork in the children's ward. I'm glad the school teamed up with the hospital to do that for the pediatrics. It's awesome and boosts our morale, too."

"He'll be thrilled." Colin stuffed his hands into his pockets. "You're going to be at the wedding, right?"

"I am." How could he forget the wedding of Farin Baker and Steve Moore? He'd only known Farin since the seventh grade. Everyone in the gay community seemed to be invited to the ceremony. He wished he had a date. Going alone would suck and he despised hook-ups at such events.

"I'm ready to rip out my hair. I never realized how picky my baby brother can be," Colin said. "If it's not the flowers or lack thereof, it's the music or the events at the reception. He's got the whole damn thing organized. There's a time for dancing and one for sitting and being quiet. Who's quiet at a wedding reception?"

"The brother of the groom. It's Farin's day — well, his and Steve's. Let them do it how they want." Not that he knew anything about weddings. He'd never been married and his last relationship had lasted a whole three years. Other guys loved being with a doctor and the paycheck he received, but hated his hours and how much time he was expected to spend away from them. *Maybe I'm dating the wrong men.*

"I keep telling myself that. Jordan tells me the same thing, but I still want to clobber Farin when he goes Groomzilla on us. I wasn't this bad when I married Jordan — at least I don't think so. We walked, we stood, we said I do, then had one hell of a party at the house." Colin shook his head. "I just wouldn't have thought he'd be…like this."

"It'll be over in two days. You'll live." Aiden clapped Colin on the shoulder. "Speaking of days, I have exactly one day off before I'm expected back at the hospital. I'm on for an eight-hour shift on Saturday, so if I'm running late, that's why."

"We'll keep an eye out. Thanks for the heads-up and thanks for talking to the group. Have a good night." Colin winked, then strode away.

Aiden grabbed his jacket from the coat rack. The weight of a twenty-four-hour shift had gotten to him. He wanted to go home but wondered if he'd make it.

As he navigated through the halls of the hospital, he waved at a couple of the nurses and, in the foyer, nodded to the elderly woman behind the main counter. The moment he stepped into the chilly October air, he blinked and dragged a long breath into his lungs. Nothing worked to wake him up like crisp fall evenings. Well, nothing like those and a good blow job in the morning, but he wasn't likely to get one. He'd need a boyfriend first. He'd worry about his lack of a partner later. Right now, he wanted to go home, slip into a warm bath or hot shower and collapse for twelve hours straight. Maybe he would meet someone at the wedding or reception.

*Maybe hell will freeze over first.*

\* \* \* \*

Thirty-two hours later, Aiden strode out of the hospital again. Just as he'd guessed, the ER had been short-staffed and had called him in four hours before his eight-hour shift should've started. He rolled his shoulders. His joints cracked and popped. A long groan escaped his lips. *Why can't I meet a good massage therapist right about now?*

He made his way across the staff lot to his car. At least he'd had time to change into his suit before his shift had ended or he'd be beyond late. He checked his reflection in the driver's-side glass. The lines around his eyes were deeper than normal and the crinkles across his forehead were more visible. Christ, he resembled an ogre, not a thirty-five-year-old doctor. *Fuck it.* He had to get going.

Aiden slipped behind the wheel of the car, then sped out of the lot. According to the clock, he had exactly twenty minutes to drive across town to the church before the ceremony started. *Easy. Right?* He turned onto the main road leading away from the hospital. Unlike most hours of the day, few cars were on the thoroughfare. He increased his speed and headed north. A set of headlights blinded him.

"What the hell?" he groused. "Turn the brights down." He swerved to the right, but the vehicle with the LED lights kept coming at him. The closest street lamp illuminated the vehicle. A truck. Aiden yanked the wheel to the right again and was rewarded with a clunk. "Shit," he murmured. The lights went away and, when he checked the rearview mirror, the truck disappeared around the corner.

Aiden's hands shook as he limped his car into the closest lot. He parked in the gravel and left the car to check the damage. He rounded the hood. The scent of burned rubber curled in his nose. He choked back a cough and examined the passenger side of his car. "Fucking hell." He squatted beside the front wheel. "I'm not even sure how to fix this." He touched the deflated tire and bent rim. Getting to the wedding was now going to be even harder. He stood and whipped his cell phone from his pocket. Who was he supposed to call? Most mechanics would be closed by now. He'd have to phone Whit. He groaned. Whit Sherman was a nice man and a decent enough friend, though not dating material. But he was also invited to the wedding, so if he hadn't left yet, maybe Aiden could beg a ride.

Aiden stood on the side of the road. He could've sworn he'd seen the advertisements for an auto mechanic near the hospital. He spotted the neon over the garage and hope blossomed in his chest. If he wasn't mistaken, the sign read OPEN. He retrieved the keys from the ignition and locked the vehicle, then sprinted down the road. "Just don't close before I get there." He pushed himself, pumping his legs and praying. "Please stay open."

Part of him wished he'd seen the license plate number or markings on the truck that had run him off the road. But what would he be able to do? Turn the guy in? How was he going to prove the incident other than his bent rim and blown tire?

Aiden bounded across the asphalt to the front of the garage. At the door, he stopped to catch his breath.

A man strode out of the first garage bay and wiped his hands on a soiled rag. "Can I help you?"

"Hi." Aiden stood upright and puffed. Shit, he was out of shape. "Do you have a tow truck?"

"We do. What happened? Usually people come here in a vehicle. You seem to be without one." The man smiled. The five o'clock shadow darkened his cheeks and his blue eyes sparkled. He'd combed his hair into a short mohawk and the inch-long spikes glimmered in the pink light of the neon sign.

Aiden read the man's name tag. *Matt.* Funny, the guy didn't strike him as a Matt. More like a Roscoe or a Boss. He smoothed his palms over his thighs. Blood rushed through his body and his nerve endings tingled. Each time he swept his gaze over Matt, his pulse reacted. Either he needed a date and sex, or he'd lost his mind from sleep deprivation. He straightened his shoulders. He wasn't there for a date. "I ran over the curb down the road. I ruined my tire and probably more."

"If you hit the curb on Walker Road, then you jacked up more than a tire. If the rim isn't a mess, I'd be shocked." Matt disappeared into the garage bay, then stepped back out again without the rag. He snorted. "Most rims are a mess and if you did one hell of a job on it…" He whistled, then grinned. "Nice."

Aiden swayed on his feet. Go figure, he'd found the one mechanic in town to make a lewd joke about rim jobs. "Can you fix it?"

"I'll get the truck. I doubt I'll be able to get to it today because I need to find the right rim to fit your car. That'll take me at least a couple of hours tomorrow to locate. The tire will be easy—unless you did more damage. I won't know that until I get a look at the car." Matt tugged a set of keys from his overalls. "Where did you leave it?"

"Where I collided with the curb." He pointed down the road. "You're sure it'll take that long?"

Matt narrowed his eyes. "Guessing from your outfit, you're late. For a date or your wedding?" He knocked on the frame of the garage bay. "Aaron? I'll be right back. I'm retrieving a job."

"What?" Another man strode into the middle of the door opening. "We're backed up, man."

"Enough. It's right down there," Matt said. "I'm taking the job, so it's not your headache."

"I'll pay extra to get it rushed," Aiden added. "I'd say I'm desperate, but you've probably guessed that."

The man Aiden guessed was Aaron rolled his eyes and ducked back into the garage.

"The truck is over here." Matt pointed to the massive vehicle. "You're the black car about a quarter of a mile away?"

"It's dark blue, but yes, the sports car." Aiden toyed with the hem of his suit coat. "It was a splurge. A hiring bonus I bought myself." *Shit.* He sounded like an ass. "I'll shut up."

"Right now, I just need the keys. I'm going to assume you've locked it." Matt held out his hand. A tattoo showed from beneath the cuff of his overalls.

"Even if you didn't, I need the keys to unlock the steering column."

"Sure." He yanked the ring from his pocket. "Sorry."

"You're fine, but like I said, I can't get it fixed tonight. You might want to call someone to give you a ride. I'm out of loaners. Is it a wedding? Or a date?" Matt asked.

"What?" Aiden tripped in the gravel. He caught himself and appraised Matt's body again. He liked the way the overalls clung to Matt's muscular frame. Sweat glistened on the back of his neck. Aiden shivered. The vibrant blue of Matt's eyes and his facial hair appealed to him. He wasn't a fan of men with earrings, but the thick silver hoops worked for the mechanic. "I — it's not my wedding. I'm not getting married." He was babbling. *Fuck.*

"Oh, sorry." Matt opened the door of the tow truck and grinned. "I'll get your car. Feel free to wait in the lobby. We've got free Wi-Fi if you want. Aaron will set you up with the paperwork so we can expedite the process." He climbed into the truck and closed the door.

Aiden stood in the parking lot for another moment as Matt drove away. He should move. If he wanted to get to the reception on time, he needed to call Whit. His mind wandered. What would Matt look like without the overalls? Was he a T-shirt and jeans type or did he prefer cargo shorts and polo shirts? *How about naked?* Aiden shivered again. Yeah, he wanted to see Matt in the buff. *Like that's gonna happen.*

He shook his head and crunched across the gravel to the building. Once in the lobby, he tugged his phone from his breast pocket. The wedding should've started by now. Instead of calling, he texted Whit.

*Need your help. Car trouble. Can you pick me up after the wedding?*

He sighed. Fuck. He'd made a mess of the night and it was only eight o'clock.

"Here. Fill this out." Aaron offered over a clipboard. "Nothing exciting. I'll be out helping Matt."

"Sure. Thanks." He scrawled the information onto the form, then put the clipboard onto the counter. His phone buzzed in his hand. Not a text, but a call from Whit. He groaned, then answered. "Why aren't you in the church?"

"I ducked out," Whit grumbled. "You're late. Where are you?"

"I had car trouble. Didn't you look at the text?" He massaged his forehead. "It's a long story."

"Seriously? You? Nothing is ever easy with you."

"It's not by design." He had to think fast. "If you're not in the church, then the ceremony is running late? Or is it over?"

"Farin's a little behind. Do you need me to get you?" Whit asked. "I'm available."

He swallowed past the groan rising in his throat. "Are you able?"

"Wait. You're asking me to come and get you? Uh...yeah. I'll be there in five minutes. Where are you?"

"Um..." He turned the stack of magnets around on the counter. He'd never read the name on the garage when he'd passed it over the last two years. He'd seen the sign, but hadn't retained the information. "The Alpha Auto Shop." *Alpha? Is Matt the so-called alpha? Is he gay too?* Aiden could only wish.

"The one on Walker Road? Okay, I'll be there. Just...don't touch anything."

"Why?" Aiden asked. *What's wrong with the garage?*

"It's dirty," Whit said. "Grease, dirt, grime. You don't know what you'll pick up there."

"I don't know. It's pretty clean." Compared to the hospital, yes, the lobby wasn't sterile, but it could've been worse.

"Right. It's a repair shop. Those places are always filthy. Just hold on and I'll be there." Without another word, Whit hung up.

Aiden groaned again. He'd done that too much in the last half an hour. If he'd had his way, he would've called anyone but Whit. Walking would've been preferable. Whit tended to get the wrong idea about his level of interest. Aiden wasn't in the market to date, didn't want a quickie fuck in the hallway or a suck-off in the bathroom—and not from Whitman Sherman.

When Aiden looked up from his phone, Matt pulled into the lot with his car attached to the back of the truck. He drove through to the gated area to the left of the building and disappeared. Aiden crept over to the window and watched Aaron and Matt unload the car. He wasn't sure of the conversation between the two men, but from Aaron's body language—shaking his head and frowning—he guessed Aaron wasn't thrilled. Matt didn't say anything, or if he did, Aiden didn't notice his lips moving. His expression stayed still. Aaron waved his arms, then stormed back to the building.

Aiden forced his attention from Matt and the truck in favor of staring out of the window at the few cars on Walker Road. He hated weddings and relationships too. Men expected too much from him. They wanted things like for him to change his hours at the hospital to suit those relationships. *Not possible.* He didn't set his schedule. Dating another doctor made no sense. He knew the other ER doctors too well and considered them his brothers, and he spent almost no time outside the emergency room. If he hooked up with a doctor from another ward, they'd probably never see each other, either.

He bowed his head. The last guy he'd dated had admitted after four months that he'd only stuck with Aiden for that long to cash in on the doctor paycheck. He'd wanted a sugar daddy. Too bad Aiden wasn't bringing in huge bucks. The car—the damn thing—had been a splurge but a very second-hand item. The sports coupe looked good on the road and made a statement in the parking lot. But appearances meant nothing when the vehicle was attached to a tow truck.

Aiden rubbed his forehead and looked up when bright lights infiltrated the lobby. A sigh stuck in his throat. He'd know that expensive car anywhere—Whit. Instead of parking in the lot or the gravel, Whit stopped right beside the door and honked the horn.

Aiden bit back a growl. He left the lobby and opened the passenger door, but didn't get into the car. "Hello, fire violation? Move."

Whit shrugged as Aiden closed the door. Whit zipped forward into the closest parking spot. His brakes screeched.

Aaron hustled to the doorway and stopped beside Aiden.

"Sorry," Aiden muttered. He couldn't meet Aaron's gaze. "He's a little pushy."

"I'd say entitled." Aaron sighed. "Whatever. About your car. Matt'll hunt down the part and we'll see. If I know him, he'll call around until the junk yards close or his contacts stop answering the phone. He's relentless like that. Anyway, it should take about twenty-four hours to get the car back to being drivable. No guarantees."

"Thanks. I appreciate his relentlessness and your honesty. Have a good night." He went out to the lot and found Matt beside the tow truck. "Hi," he said. "Thank you." Aiden offered his hand to Matt. When they shook hands, Aiden's tingled. His breath caught in his throat and power surged within him. He'd never felt quite like this before. His thoughts muddled and he forgot what he'd come out to talk to Matt about. "Uh...I filled out the paperwork Aaron gave me. Call me when the car is done." He'd never heard himself sound so mechanical. *Yuck.*

"Will do." Matt smiled. "I'll see what I can do to get it back to you faster. I know what it's like to not have a car."

"No worries, but thank you." He lingered beside the truck longer than he should, but he couldn't make himself leave the spot. Something between him and Matt had started. Was he falling in lust with the mechanic? Or was his radar locating interested guys broken?

Matt leaned against the door of the truck but didn't say anything.

*Shit.* He'd been standing there for too long. Aiden nodded once. "I should be going." He'd said the words more for himself than anything. "Thanks."

"Aiden," Whit snapped. "Let's go. We're late and Farin will kill us."

"Right." He smiled but wished Whit had kept his mouth shut. He wanted to keep talking to Matt — or at least sharing the moment with him. Aiden forced himself across the lot to Whit's car and climbed into the passenger seat. He waved at Matt. Fate was a fickle bitch, but if this was the start of something, then he didn't mind.

"Why did you wave? He's the help." Whit sped out of the lot, spewing gravel from the back of his sports car. "You pay them, respect them, but don't get cushy."

"He's nice."

"For a mechanic." Whit's voice dripped with disdain. "Seriously. You can and will do better."

"Stop." He massaged his temples. Listening to Whit caused a dull ache behind his eyes. "I don't want to hear it."

"Are you okay? Is your head hurting? From the crash?" Whit zipped down the road past the hospital and blew through a yellow light. "I'll just take you home. If you've got a concussion, then you need supervision."

"I don't have a concussion. Christ, I'm getting sick of you. I appreciate that you came all the way out here to get me, but you're acting like an ass. He's a nice guy and while he's a mechanic, he's got feelings too." The throbbing increased. He closed his eyes. "How about we be quiet and maybe it'll go away." *Fat chance, but worth a shot.*

"You know…I'm tired of this." Whit smacked his hand on the steering wheel. "You wanted me to rescue you. I did. I've seen the way you eyeball me. Don't try to deny it."

"I've never looked at you that way." He didn't open his eyes. Since when had he been appraising Whit as date potential?

"I've noticed. I also told you we'd end up at the wedding together. Maybe I come on too strong, but that sizzle between us is real. You should really listen to me more." Whit brought the car to a stop. "We're here. The wedding should be over by now. It wasn't supposed to be a long ceremony."

Aiden opened his eyes. He'd rather have aspirin and time to crash in his armchair, but he had to see his friends. He'd power through the headache for them. Soft white lights twinkled in the trees and jazz music played. White flowers had been strung on and from poles surrounding the guests. Aiden left the car but paused before he entered the party. His breath lodged in his throat again. This was what he'd asked for. Not to marry Farin or Steve, but the desire. The passion the two men had and the opportunity to share it with their friends. He wanted someone to join him on life's journey. Whit eased up beside him and grasped Aiden's hand, but he swatted his friend away. He had to get himself together.

"People aren't looking," Whit growled. "You can touch me."

"I need some air." Aiden strode away from Whit. He didn't care where he went as long as it was far from his colleague. He spotted Farin and Steve under a floral arch. No one seemed to be bothering them. *Great.* He'd speak to them quickly, then find a ride home. He rounded the gathering of tables and guests. Farin spotted him first.

"You're here. I thought you'd skipped out on us." Farin grasped Aiden's hand. "You really need to be less important at the hospital."

"I had car trouble." He hugged Farin, then Steve. "Congratulations. I can't think of two better people to be married."

Steve winked. "Thank you." He rolled his eyes. "I need to take care of something. Looks like my great-aunt found the wine. Excuse me. Thanks for coming,

Aiden. Hopefully we can talk later." He darted away, leaving Aiden alone with Farin.

"I'm glad you made it and I'm sorry to hear about the car." Farin dipped his head. "Saw you arrived with Whit. You're playing with fire."

"Don't remind me." He turned his back on the party. "It wasn't my best idea."

"He's not your type," Farin said.

"Not at all." He wasn't about to argue. He and Whit would never work as a couple.

"Um...then why? Because he had a car? Come on. You could've taken a taxi." Farin leveled his gaze at Aiden. "Or are you having a lapse in judgment?"

"I just needed a ride and wasn't doing so hot under pressure."

Farin said nothing, but frowned.

"I wrecked my car on the way." He held up both hands. "My fault. I swerved to miss a truck that had gone left of center. The truck came right at me and I jumped the curb to not collide with it. That huge-ass curb by the hospital is dangerous. Anyway, I bent the rim and ruined the tire."

"Where'd you take it, Doc?" Farin asked. "Tell me you stayed away from Coby's. That bastard overcharges for everything."

"No. I know it wasn't there." He hooked his fingers in his pants pockets. "Alpha Auto Shop...that's the name. A guy named Matt is working on it. Seemed like a nice guy."

"Matt Phillips?"

"Maybe? I didn't ask for his last name."

"You just handed over the keys to someone you don't know?" Farin shook his head. "I'm kidding. How else will he fix your car? Doc, we really need to talk about getting you out of the hospital more and into the fresh air."

"Yes, we do, and yes, I did. But he was working at the shop and I think he owns it." Although now he was having second thoughts about his decision. "Was that a bad thing? Taking it there? I didn't have a whole lot of choice."

"Not at all." Farin rocked on his heels. "Matt is a good man. He looks like he'd kill someone — people see his tats and piercings and I've heard plenty of people claim he looks rough, but he's nice. He'll work hard for you."

"Good." If Farin liked Matt, then that was a plus.

"His turnaround time is awesome," Farin said. "Once he's on a case — or a car, whatever — he doesn't rest until it's fixed."

"That's good to hear. I can't handle Whit for much longer. He drives me crazy and he'll want to be my personal taxi." He sneaked a glance over his shoulder. Whit stood with a couple of muscle-bound men and two women at one of the round tables. At least he'd found someone to talk to instead of dogging Aiden all night.

"I can see why." Farin scrubbed his hand across his mouth. "He's hitting on the busboy."

Embarrassment washed over him. He should've gone with a taxi. *Fuck*. "Oh well, he's given me a reason to escape. My townhome isn't far away. I'll just walk home."

"The hell you will." Farin snapped his fingers. A waiter strode up to him. Farin nodded once. "Let Gareth know he's got a fare."

Without a word, the server disappeared.

"The taxis are still running this late? I guess they would still be running until midnight or two." Aiden watched people on the dance-floor area. "Or were you planning ahead?"

"Steve and I met this fellow, Gareth. He's nice and offered to ferry people who've had too much to drink. He's got a '57 Chevy with a red-and-yellow checkerboard design on it. He feels important and no one is driving home blitzed." Farin shrugged. "I hoped maybe he'd meet someone. He's sweet and cute, but shy."

"You're not trying to pair me up, are you?" He wasn't into shy men. He needed someone who could hold their own.

"Nah. You're not his type. He likes guys who are shorter than he is and he's only five-eight. Come on. He's parked out front." Farin waved. "I hate seeing you miserable."

"What's that supposed to mean?" Aiden asked. "I'm not that awful."

"No, but you're here with the wrong guy. Someone will let Whit know—if he doesn't run off with the busboy first."

"Thanks." He followed Farin to the driveway and the yellow Chevy. "Farin?"

"That's me." Farin faced him. "You don't want to go back and chase Whit, do you?"

"No." He shook his head. Not a chance. But he had a question. "How...how'd you know Steve was the one? That he was interested and it could work?"

Farin paused. "Wow. You know how to knock a man down." He folded his arms. "Well...at first, I didn't. He was so young. Still is, but I didn't think it'd work. We were so different too. But we started talking and those differences weren't so big after all. It's hard to explain. We just clicked. I swim more because of him and he's more open about his love of comic books."

"So it could be out of the blue?" He doubted that would happen. Life liked to throw him curveballs rather than make anything easy.

"Sure." Farin knocked on the window of the taxi. "Heya, Gareth. Would you take my friend Aiden home?"

"Sure," Gareth said.

Farin opened the back door. "I'll see you in a week. We're heading off to Fire Island for five days of just us. I love Genie, but I can't wait."

"Sounds fun." Aiden sighed. He hated to go home so early, but he couldn't be there any longer. "Well, congrats. I'm ecstatic for you."

"Thanks. Have a good night. I know we will." Farin wriggled his eyebrows.

"I'm sure." Aiden bit back a snort.

"You're jealous as hell. You should be." Farin clapped him on the shoulder. "Doc, it'll happen. I know. Cedarwood is for gay lovers. Trust me."

"Okay." He ducked into the car and settled on the seat. He wasn't sure what to think about Farin's comment. *Cedarwood is for gay lovers. What does that mean?*

"Where are we going, Doc?" Gareth smiled via his reflection in the rearview mirror.

"It's Aiden," Aiden said. "But you can call me Doc, I don't mind, and you can take me to Honeysuckle Avenue. I'm in the Briarwood Estates."

"You've got it."

Aiden rode in the back seat in silence. He'd missed the wedding and ducked out of the reception. Hopefully, the night had been magical. He rested his head on the back of the seat and closed his eyes. Was he wrong to want what Farin and Steve had? Maybe. But he did. Jealousy and longing filtered into his brain.

His dates never turned out right. The guy was either too greedy or needy. They were jealous of his job or wanted an open relationship. They didn't give a shit about his desires or needs. He craved a companion. Someone he could share a great love with, but was that man out there? He wasn't sure. Mr. Wonderful had to exist. Had to.

Sign up for our newsletter and find out about all our romance book releases, eBook sales and promotions, sneak peeks and FREE romance books!

# About the Author

Megan Slayer, aka Wendi Zwaduk, is a multi-published, award-winning author of more than one-hundred short stories and novels. She's been writing since 2008 and published since 2009. Her stories range from the contemporary and paranormal to LGBTQ and BDSM themes. No matter what the length, her works are always hot, but with a lot of heart. She enjoys giving her characters a second chance at love, no matter what the form. She's been the runner up in the Kink Category at Love Romances Café as well as nominated at the LRC for best author, best contemporary, best ménage and best anthology. Her books have made it to the bestseller lists on Amazon.com.

When she's not writing, Megan spends time with her husband and son as well as three dogs and three cats. She enjoys art, music and racing, but football is her sport of choice.

Megan loves to hear from readers. You can find her contact information, website details and author profile page at https://www.pride-publishing.com